waiting, Igarashi."

contribution
points we
earned, and
now everyone's
super happy."

# The WORLD'S STRONGEST REARGUARD | Labyrinth Country's Novice Seeker

★Forbidden Scythe's special effect was activated
★Merciless Guillotine was hit with auto-kill effect

"I'll bring you down!!"

Time seemed to stop.
I just barely caught
sight of Melissa circling
behind the giant crab
in midair and raising the
sinister-looking
Forbidden Scythe.

"I'll support all of you... Complete Mutual Support!"

Without a moment's hesitation, I activated my Morale Discharge, then immediately loaded my magic gun with a dark bullet stone and fired!

NewYork

# The WORLD'S STRONGEST REARGUARD | Labyrinth Country's Novice Seeker  4

**Tôwa**

Illustration by
**Huuka Kazabana**

# The WORLD'S STRONGEST REARGUARD | Labyrinth Country's Novice Seeker

**4**

**Tôwa**

Illustration by **Huuka Kazabana**

Translation by Jordan Taylor
Cover art by Huuka Kazabana

This book is a work of fiction. Names, characters, places, and incidents are the product of the author's imagination or are used fictitiously. Any resemblance to actual events, locales, or persons, living or dead, is coincidental.

SEKAI SAIKYO NO KOEI -MEIKYUKOKU NO SHINJIN TANSAKUSHA- Volume 4
©Tôwa, Huuka Kazabana 2019
First published in Japan in 2019 by KADOKAWA CORPORATION, Tokyo.
English translation rights arranged with KADOKAWA CORPORATION, Tokyo through
TUTTLE-MORI AGENCY, INC., Tokyo.

English translation © 2020 by Yen Press, LLC

Yen On
150 West 30th Street, 19th Floor
New York, NY 10001

Visit us at yenpress.com
facebook.com/yenpress
twitter.com/yenpress
yenpress.tumblr.com
instagram.com/yenpress

First Yen On Edition: November 2020

Yen On is an imprint of Yen Press, LLC.
The Yen On name and logo are trademarks of Yen Press, LLC.

The publisher is not responsible for websites (or their content) that are not owned by the publisher.

Library of Congress Cataloging-in-Publication Data
Names: Tôwa, author. | Kazabana, Huuka, illustrator. | Taylor, Jordan (Translator), translator.
Title: The world's strongest rearguard: labyrinth country's novice seeker / Tôwa ; illustration by
    Huuka Kazabana ; translation by Jordan Taylor.
Other titles: Sekai saikyo no koei: meikyukoku no shinjin tansakusha. English
Description: First Yen On edition. | New York, NY : Yen ON, 2019– |
Identifiers: LCCN 2019030466 | ISBN 9781975331542 (v. 1 ; trade paperback) |
ISBN 9781975331566 (v. 2 ; trade paperback) | ISBN 9781975331580 (v. 3 ; trade paperback) |
    ISBN 9781975315719 (v. 4 ; trade paperback)
Subjects: CYAC: Fantasy. | Future life—Fiction.
Classification: LCC PZ7.1.T676 Wo 2019 | DDC [Fic]—dc23
LC record available at https://lccn.loc.gov/2019030466

ISBNs: 978-1-9753-1571-9 (paperback)
        978-1-9753-1572-6 (ebook)

10 9 8 7 6 5 4 3 2 1

LSC-C

Printed in the United States of America

# CONTENTS

# The New Star and the Observer

A woman wearing a military uniform strode down the hall toward her section officer's work quarters in the Guild Saviors' District Six branch. Following right behind was a man who asked her:

"I wonder why you got called in all of a sudden? Maybe they're going to recognize you for your excellent conduct."

"I doubt it. The Administrative Department probably contacted us."

"Hmm, that doesn't happen often. We've had boring jobs here in District Six for so long and haven't had any orders to mobilize elsewhere, so we can't even get a change of pace that way... Oh, there I go running my mouth." The man had white hair but hadn't even reached thirty years of age. He was significantly larger than the woman and had the strength to go with his size. The eyepatch over his left eye made him look rather tough. Regardless, he treated the delicate military uniform–wearing woman with the utmost respect.

The woman smoothed her silver hair back in place and came to a stop, then glanced at the man who'd stopped with her and told him, "Khosrow, please wait with everyone else. You're not my adjutant."

"They are sort of letting me act as lieutenant commander, but you're right—I'm not your adjutant."

"…If you're trying to make me less nervous, there's no need."

"Ha-ha-ha, you're as tough as always, Commander Kozelka. Understood; I'll wait for you and play a game of poker or something with the others."

Kozelka silently watched the man leave, choosing not to reprimand him for his foolish jokes. She let out a deep breath and started walking toward the office again.

Third-Class Dragon Captain Kozelka Orfis. That was her full name and rank as given by the Guild Saviors. The man named Khosrow was almost ten years her senior. Many of Kozelka's subordinates were significantly older than her, but she still knew she had enough of their respect that the age difference didn't affect their duties.

No matter what duty she was about to be given, she would execute it. She double-checked that she actually wasn't nervous and decided that Khosrow's concerns were unfounded.

"Third-Class Dragon Captain Kozelka Orfis reporting for duty."

"Come iiiin."

Kozelka knocked on the door to her section officer's room and received a response far lighter than she was expecting. Unfazed, she opened the door and entered. Inside, there was no sign of her section officer, but seated on the sofa was a purple-haired woman wearing the Administrative Department uniform. She was waving her hand at Kozelka.

"Please have a seat. I came because I have a little favor to ask you. Your section officer said you were the one for the job, so I waited here."

"The one for the job... Is it a special mission, then?"

"Yeah, a really important one. We've got some 'new stars' for the first time in a while, and I want some information on them. I thought I could send someone from the Guild Saviors to take care of it." The lady's tone started off a little respectful, but it quickly slipped into something more casual. Kozelka had spoken directly with people from the Administrative Department before, but this young-looking girl addressed Kozelka with the least restraint.

The Administrative Department was, as the name suggests, the group overseeing everything in the Labyrinth Country. They were the ultimate authority, meaning even a first-class dragon captain would have to do exactly as ordered to.

"...By 'new stars,' do you mean promising novice Seekers?" asked Kozelka.

"Yep. They managed to make their way to District Seven without getting tripped up at all. Now they're trying to move up to District Six. No novice Seekers have ever managed to accomplish that in less than a month."

A Seeker's goal was to use the experience and equipment gained from seeking to grow stronger, move higher in the ranks, and eventually explore even tougher labyrinths. In other words, the speed with which a Seeker climbed the ranks was a direct indication of their potential. If someone were to make it to District Six within one month, you couldn't describe them with a word as simple as *excellent*. The word that popped up in Kozelka's mind was *extraordinary*.

"Regardless, it is against the Guild's...and the Guild Saviors' duties to show preferential treatment toward any given Seeker...," said Kozelka.

"I want to observe them to make sure such special individuals can keep doing special things. And if possible, I want to have them on *our side*... You understand what I mean?"

The purple-haired girl was here as requested by the Administrative Department, which meant that the department felt this party of "new stars" could become a threat to them if they became hostile. There were other promising parties in the upper districts that the department monitored, but for a group to show such promise in District Seven was just too quick. The seventh district existed to weed out any Seekers not cut out for progressing to the rest of the Labyrinth Country.

"You mean...that the Administrative Department sees this party as important, correct?" Kozelka didn't try to delve any deeper; she simply stated what she saw on the surface.

The purple-haired girl smiled and stood, then walked behind Kozelka, who was still seated on the sofa, and put her arms around her like a hug.

"I love children who catch on quickly. So you'll do it? Keep a close eye on Arihito and his party for me? You don't need to constantly meddle in his affairs—you just need to tell me what he's doing when it's necessary," whispered the girl as she stroked Kozelka's pale face, then turned to leave the room.

"…I haven't asked your name," Kozelka finally managed to say. She'd been completely unable to move since the girl had come up behind her. Kozelka was said to be stronger than any other soldier of her experience, but she'd been unable to lift a single finger. It took a significant amount of willpower just to speak.

"I…told them they could call me Yukari. You can call me that, too," replied the girl.

"…Understood, ma'am. Thank you for the assignment."

"Your section officer recommended you, but I didn't expect that I'd get someone this good. It makes me happy. Thanks for your help, Kozelka." Yukari's last words sounded like she was talking to a friend, then she quietly disappeared.

Once she was gone, Kozelka realized she was shaking. She needed a bit more time before she was able to stand again.

# CHAPTER 1

# Enhancement and Rest

## Part I: The Alliance's Leader

By the time we made it from the second floor of Silvanus's Bedchamber back to the first floor, dawn had broken within the labyrinth, and a pleasant blue sky stretched out above us. Having won our last battle without serious injury, we all walked with more of a spring in our steps.

My party had a total of nine members, which was beyond the limit of eight, so I had Cion join Four Seasons' party. Igarashi and Elitia were in the front line, followed by Theresia and Melissa in the midguard position, then me, Misaki, Suzuna, and Madoka in the rearguard position. I was at the tail end of our formation as we proceeded across the first floor. However, as long as we were still inside the labyrinth, we couldn't afford to celebrate just because we'd defeated Silvanus the Enchanter's Messenger.

"Grrrooooaar!"

Three Aero Wolves suddenly appeared out of nowhere and attacked from behind. Before I could use my Rearguard General skill, however, everyone promptly reversed the battle formation. Suzuna and Four Seasons' Anna and Ryouko used long-range attacks to control the enemy's movements, giving our close-range attackers time to follow up and finish off the monsters.

"Now how many Aero Wolves have we defeated...? We're going to get quite a lot of materials, aren't we?" Igarashi asked Madoka, who checked her license.

"Between the two parties, we've defeated a total of twelve."

Melissa put the monsters' materials away using her Repository skill. Madoka told us how many we had in total; twelve seemed enough to be useful for something.

"Igarashi, you have a change of armor in the storage unit; do you want to change to that?" I offered. "Or we can consider fixing or modifying your current armor and using it again."

"My spare armor doesn't have the lightweight attribute, so I wouldn't be able to move as quickly... Looks like it has good defense, though."

"If you want to keep your speed, then you're better off repairing or modifying your current armor," advised Elitia. "We got a lot of materials in this expedition that could probably be used to alter armor, plus we still have some magic stones and runes. I think it's a good idea for us to take some time after this to get our equipment in order." We couldn't afford to lose a single day as we progressed to our goal, but Elitia's advice likely took the impending situation into consideration.

"You're right... It's a waste of our treasure if we don't use our magic stones and runes effectively. No point in holding on to things without using them," I said.

"Since I'm a Gambler, I'm gonna get waaay stronger, and then we'll find tons of awesome magic stones, don'cha think? I just don't feel like I helped that much on this expedition. Even my Fortune Roll was off."

"That's not true, Misaki. Even though we set the traps, there was no guarantee Silvanus's Messenger was going to appear... If there were, anyone who hunted the Thunder Head before would've run into it."

"You thiiink? Well, if you say so, Arihito, then I guess I'll believe it. Hee-hee, thanks!"

I had another theory why Silvanus's Messenger appeared. Its Horn of Pleasure skill inflicted women with the Charm status, meaning the Messenger appeared when a party had more than a certain number of women in it. That's what I thought anyway.

"Arihito, ummm..."

"Hmm, what's up?"

Suzuna was very hesitantly trying to talk to me. Perhaps I'd had a harsh expression because of what I was thinking about.

But actually, that didn't seem to be the case. Suzuna's cheeks turned a little red, and she slowed her pace until she fell back to walk beside me. She whispered quietly to me so the others couldn't hear. Well, I say that, but anyone paying enough attention to us probably would have been able to hear.

"The monster we just fought made an ugly sound, which gave it control over Melissa...but Kyouka, the other members, and I weren't affected. I was wondering why... Do you know, Arihito?"

"Uh...ummm, well..."

The higher the Trust Level between me and the other party members, the stronger their resistance to the Charm status. Still, I was a little hesitant to discuss it so openly. I could tell them it was because they all trusted me—Suzuna included—but I felt like there was a lot of room for misinterpretation.

"I have a guess. I was wondering if it was right...," continued Suzuna. Did she see a similar display on her license? I didn't think everyone checked their license since it was the middle of battle.

"A guess...such as?"

"W-well... I used Medium to let Ariadne possess me when we needed it that one time, and you both exchanged a lot of magic... I th-thought that might be connected."

"W-well...I think it might be related at least. But if you think that process is weird, then it's probably better to find a different way to increase our devotion with Ariadne." I was concerned what might happen to Suzuna if we kept using the Energy Sync and Charge Assist combo because it raised Suzuna's Trust Levels along with Ariadne's devotion levels. Suzuna's feelings were paramount here, however. I could explain that to Ariadne, and we'd find another way.

Just then, Suzuna spoke again.

"...I...felt like you were protecting me, and that's what makes things okay... I—I know that everyone else feels the same, but I just..."

Even someone as slow as me could understand what she was getting at. She was so nervous because she was trying to thank me. And the fact that she was still so hesitant really did show that it took time to build a true trusting relationship. The Trust Level that you could see in numbers wasn't the whole story.

"It seems the stronger the person's ties to the party are, the more resistant they are to the Charm status. Melissa has been in the party the shortest—I think it'll take some more time for her... But that makes it sound like someone just needs to be in the party; that's probably not the case," I said.

"...I'm not sure that's true. Everyone always sees how hard you're trying... Both Ellie and I are so glad we joined this party..." Elitia heard her name mentioned even though she was in the lead. She left Igarashi and Cion in charge of the front line and quickly came over. But she didn't look annoyed; she seemed a little embarrassed if anything.

"...Sometimes I'm curious about what people are talking about in the back when I'm in the front," she said.

"I'm sorry, Ellie. It's rude of me to talk about this when you're not here," said Suzuna.

"I don't even know what you were talking about. Plus, you don't need to worry about manners so much with me..."

"I know we're still on an expedition, but with everyone from Four Seasons here, having a little chat once in a while makes it feel like we're on a picnic. It's niiice," said Misaki.

"......"

Theresia also heard, apparently, since she was in the midguard position, and she never walked too far away from us. I didn't know what kind of conversation she was interested in, but I knew she was always listening. It did seem, though, that her sensibilities were a little different from what I'd expect of a girl of the age I thought she was...but there was still very little that I understood about Theresia.

"We should make it so Theresia can talk again as soon as possible," said Suzuna.

"...Yeah. I want to see what it's like speaking with her," I said.

"Arihito, what do you think she sounds like? I think she'd be surprisingly gentle and mild-mannered," said Misaki.

"Well...I'm not sure." I tried to imagine what it would sound like when I did finally hear her voice, but my weak imagination still couldn't come up with anything concrete.

"......"

Based on how she fought, I had the impression she was fairly energetic, but that wasn't necessarily true. If we could find someone who knew Theresia before she became a demi-human... But a sudden question crossed my mind. Where did Theresia come from? Was she a reincarnate or a native resident of the Labyrinth Country?

"The leader of that Alliance is going to have the contribution points necessary to move up to District Six soon...but they haven't defeated enough Named Monsters yet, right?" asked Elitia.

"Yeah, that's what some of their members said."

"We can fulfill the requirements to move up to District Six without using the same method that they are. That said, encountering Named Monsters is really down to luck, so there's a chance we could end up stuck here for months if things don't go well... If the Alliance knew how to make a Named Monster appear but couldn't defeat it, we could think about moving in and taking it down ourselves. Although considering how prolific the Alliance is, anything they couldn't beat would be a serious threat to us, too..."

Twice we'd had to fight Named Monsters someone else had discovered: Redface and Juggernaut.

"They probably put surveillance on us because they want information on Named Monsters, too," I said.

"That was definitely part of it. Anyway, should we gather some information when we return to town?" suggested Suzuna.

"Is there anyone in town who might broker us some intel? That one clothing store owner looked like he could be the type."

"Misaki, that's rude...," Suzuna chided. But I'd been thinking the same thing, so I kept my mouth shut. I got the feeling that Luca hadn't exactly been on the straight and narrow his whole life. I'd felt like I was in some Mafia movie when he came out with the gun in its silver case.

"It'll take us a few days to have our equipment modified. How about we use that time to gather information in town?" I suggested.

"Oooh! Then Kyouka can get a massage to take all the stiffness out of her shoulders!" squealed Misaki.

"Wha...? What are you talking about?" shot back Igarashi. "All I'm doing here is keeping a close eye on things... Right, Cion?"

"Woof."

Igarashi's body had likely gotten much lighter since she'd become a Valkyrie, so I doubted if she even needed a massage. She could easily ask Louisa for one if she wanted, though.

As a former corporate slave, a day off sounded wonderful. Everyone else was probably burned-out from the continuous seeking as well. It'd be nice for us all to get a good rest.

"Mmm... That's one job down. Feels nice to be done with it," said Kaede.

"We were so on edge the whole time. Phew, I want to go straight to sleep without even taking a bath...," said Ibuki.

"Me too. But I need to go have the work started on my racket... Haaah..." Anna stifled a yawn as Kaede and Ibuki stretched when we made it to the square outside the labyrinth.

Ryouko saw the three of them and looked embarrassed. "Sorry, these girls...switch gears too quickly."

"You must be tired, too, Ryouko... Oh, are you all right without your coat?" I asked.

Igarashi had borrowed Ryouko's boa coat because her armor had broken during battle—leaving Ryouko in just her bikini when we made it out of the labyrinth.

"Ah...I—I... You're right; people will think I'm strange in this getup around town."

"Uh... It doesn't really match, but you can wear my suit jacket over it. You can give it back to me next time we meet," I offered.

"...Are you sure? Thank you. You're always doing so much..."

"I'm really sorry about this—I'm borrowing your precious coat. Thank you." Igarashi expressed her gratitude, but for some reason, Ryouko looked at me and smiled. Igarashi secured the front of the boa coat around her even further.

"I really hope we all meet up again, whether it's for seeking or something else," said Ryouko. "You can give back the coat whenever."

"Thank you, Ryouko."

"It's nothing... I should be thanking all of you. Atobe, are you sure I can borrow it?"

I had taken off my jacket and was holding it, then hung it over Ryouko's shoulders. It didn't really change much, though, because on top she was wearing a suit jacket and on the bottom she had her bathing suit. She still stood out quite a bit.

"...Must be nice... Aw crap, Arihito's gonna be annoyed with me if I get all giggly," said Kaede.

"His suit jacket is so baggy even on Ryouko...," said Ibuki.

"And the sleeves are too long... They'd hang down so low if I wore it," said Anna.

"Thank you, Atobe. I'll make sure it's nice and clean when I give it back. I'm quite skilled at doing the laundry," said Ryouko.

I was about to tell her she could just return it without having to go to the trouble of washing it, but then I realized that had its own problems. That's when Four Seasons left to return to their own home.

"If your suit was some super-awesome equipment, then you couldn't have taken it off," said Misaki.

"Not necessarily...but my suit doesn't have any special effects anyway."

"I feel like she'll draw attention for a different reason if she walks around with a man's jacket hanging on her shoulders...," said Igarashi.

"Well then, maybe you should have worn the jacket, Kyouka," said Elitia.

"Erk… Th-there's a lot that has to happen for me to be mentally prepared for that…"

"My jacket would be far too baggy on you anyway, which would sort of defeat the purpose… What? What's up with you guys?" Everyone was looking at me weirdly. Did I say something strange? The problem was that Igarashi's armor was broken, but the collar of my jacket was too open, making it a potentially dangerous solution. That should have been an obvious concern.

"Arihito, since it's become suddenly necessary, would you like to give me your spare suit to hold on to?" suggested Madoka.

"Suddenly necessary? What would it be used for…? Wait, Misaki's equipment didn't break or something, did it?"

"No, no. But everyone just said it was necessary."

"Um… Let's not take this conversation into a weird direction all of a sudden. We can sort out the suit thing later—let's go report to the Guild." Elitia shut down the strange topic and walked off to lead us toward the Upper Guild. I started to follow behind her.

"Igarashi, do you want to stop in the clothing store on the way?"

"Y-yeah… Even if Madoka did get some clothes for me out of storage, I can't really do anything without a changing room. I'd appreciate it if we could stop."

Igarashi changed from her armor into normal clothes for the time being, then we headed to the Upper Guild. When we entered the first-floor lobby of Green Hall, we saw a silver-haired man coming our way with a woman following closely behind. The woman looked like she might be pregnant.

"I'm sorry, Roland. It's such an important time, too...," said the woman.

"Don't worry about it. This is a gift from the gods. You can let us handle the rest," replied the man.

*Roland...Roland Vorn? Louisa said he's the leader of Beyond Liberty...*

The man was in prime physical condition but nearing middle age. The woman with him, possibly his wife, looked quite a bit younger than him. Her name was Daniella, if I remembered correctly. She had a bit of an exotic flair to her, and she clung closely to Roland. They noticed us and stared at each of the party's members in turn, their eyes finally falling on me at the rear. I stepped to the front, thinking that I should at least introduce us. Roland didn't show any particular emotion that might indicate if the members of his Alliance had told him about us.

"...That's a face I haven't seen before. I heard there were some powerful rookies who'd just come to the Upper Guild... Is that you lot?" he asked.

"It's nice to meet you. We started working at this Guild yesterday. My name is Arihito Atobe." I knew about them, but they didn't know about us. It seemed safe to assume that Gray had some plan in place if he hadn't reported our information to Roland yet.

"I'm Roland Vorn, number-one ranked in District Seven and the leader of the Alliance Beyond Liberty."

"I'm Daniella Vorn; I'm a member of Roland's party." She didn't introduce herself as his wife. Maybe they had a rule between them that she didn't when they were out together as a party. Daniella left Roland's side and stared at me cautiously.

"A hot older guy and a bronzed beauty… They make a picture-perfect couple."

"M-Misaki… Don't say that; they'll hear you…!"

Roland noticed Misaki and Suzuna talking behind me, and his brow creased slightly, but I was surprised when Daniella smiled.

"I thought you'd be ex-military or people with mercenary experience, but you seem like rookies without too much battle practice under your belts," said Roland. "Things must've gone well for you to come this far. Did you get lucky enough to find a lot of folks with top-tier jobs?"

"We've managed to make it this far by working together. Luck definitely did play a part as well," I replied.

"As long as you're aware of your own limitations, I don't think you'll try to push yourselves too far. The Labyrinth Country isn't a place where you can rely on luck alone to advance."

"…What are you saying, Roland? It's rude to lecture someone you've just met," said Daniella.

"Mm… Well, I suppose…" Roland sounded like he wanted to say more, but Daniella cut it off. Their relationship apparently didn't have the balance I thought it did. The wife was stronger in this case.

"I'm sorry—he's always like this. Your name was Arihito, wasn't it? Or would you prefer I call you Mr. Atobe?" asked Daniella.

"Either is fine. My family name is Atobe—my given is Arihito."

"Okay, I'll call you Arihito. I want to apologize. At the moment, we're sort of hogging the best hunting grounds that the Upper Guild oversees, but it's only temporary. I hope you're not too angry at us about it."

She seemed nice—not that it had anything to do with this conversation. At least she openly admitted they were taking over the hunting grounds.

"…Don't think less of us for it," added Roland. "You can't get up to the higher districts on luck alone."

"Of course… We're curious about the Beach of the Setting Sun, but we can always find another way to reach the top."

"I see. If that's the case, I suppose…we should say thank you."

"Aren't you always saying the best thing possible would be if everyone could move up to District Six without getting hurt? That as long as there's life, there's hope?" Daniella pestered Roland, and he scratched his head uncomfortably.

But when he looked at me again, his eyes weren't those of a person who'd been embarrassed in front of his wife. "Everyone has their own reasons for aiming for the top. If your party had come a little sooner, we would likely have invited you to join the Alliance…"

"We'll find a way to do things on our own. You don't need to worry about us." *If you guys get stuck, then we'll go on ahead of you,* I thought—but now wasn't the time to be provoking him.

"This is what I'm talking about. If this guy wasn't out fighting, he'd fill his time with drink and women. He's in no position to be

preaching to anyone. It's okay, I've reined him in; the ladies don't need to worry anymore," said Daniella.

"What are you talking about...? You're ruining my credibility. Stop making me sound like a dirty old man."

"...Roland, I'd like to ask you something—I hope this doesn't upset you," I said. "I've heard that a man named Gray, a member of your organization, has been upsetting female Seekers..."

"What...? Is that true? Has Gray been doing something behind my back...?"

"I told you, you can't put him in charge of recruitment," chided Daniella. "I'll ask everyone what's going on."

*Aha... Gray was abusing his position. If Roland wasn't aware of it before, he'll probably crack down on the guy now.*

If Gray was allowed to continue doing whatever he wanted, there was a chance it'd cause trouble. Talking to the Vorns turned out to be a good opportunity for us.

"Sounds like Gray's been a bit of a thorn in your side. I'll speak with him," said Roland.

"And let's both keep working hard, though I suppose we won't have much opportunity to see you once we move up to District Six," said Daniella.

The two of them left the building, and I heaved a heavy sigh. The encounter was much less antagonistic than I was expecting, but that didn't change the fact that they were our competition.

"Mr. Atobe... Oh, perfect. I saw you speaking with them and wasn't sure when I should start talking to you...," Louisa said. Apparently, our conversation had put her on edge. Seeing me talking with the Vorns all of a sudden probably made her worry something had happened.

"We were just introducing ourselves. Louisa, could I submit a report immediately?" I asked.

"Of course... Oh, my heart has already started racing..."

I wondered how much this report would shock Louisa; in fact, I was kind of looking forward to it. I could tell the others felt the same when I exchanged glances with them.


## Part II: Check


I parted ways with everyone in the lobby and headed farther into Green Hall's first floor with Louisa. She guided me to the familiar black doors and welcomed me into the room, then left for a moment to make some tea.

"I apologize for the wait," she said when she returned.

"Thank you for always doing so much for me, Louisa."

"It's my pleasure. Would you like to take a short break?"

"As long as it's brief, since I can't keep everyone waiting... Mm, very nice tea. It's different from what you've made before."

"It's made from the assam leaf plant, which is found in the labyrinth. It's quite similar to black tea. It was originally unidentified until a tea expert came to the Labyrinth Country, recorded its information, and named it. Apparently, the plant itself is completely different from a tree."

There was nothing remarkable about its color, and the aroma was that of good quality tea. The only difference was that when I drank it, my head felt clearer.

"Apparently the tea has components that can be used to make potions if it's concentrated enough. I feel like it has a calming effect...," continued Louisa.

"It does... It's quite effective. I feel calmer and more focused." The effects weren't expressed in numbers, but my shoulders relaxed, and I felt more comfortable. We had just gotten out of the labyrinth, though, so I started to feel a little sleepy.

*Crap, I'm gonna start yawning...*

"Hee-hee... Mr. Atobe, you don't have to hold back. You must be very tired."

"S-sorry..."

"How about I look at the report now, and you can check in with me later?"

"I'm all right. I want to get the things I need to do out of the way so I can relax... So if you don't mind..."

"Of course. To be honest, part of the reason I made this tea was to calm myself, since I'm always so surprised by your reports I feel like my heart's going to leap out of my chest." Louisa was embarrassed, but she didn't need to be. It really was best if the two of us could be relaxed with each other when reporting.

"All right, please allow me to view your results." Louisa prepared her monocle, and I showed her my license with the expedition results displayed. There were indeed a few points through the list when Louisa seemed about to cry out at certain items.

◆Expedition Results◆

> Raided Silvanus's Bedchamber 2F: 20 points
> Elitia grew to level 10: 100 points
> Arihito grew to level 6: 60 points
> Theresia grew to level 6: 60 points
> Kyouka grew to level 5: 50 points
> Suzuna grew to level 5: 50 points
> Misaki grew to level 5: 50 points
> Melissa grew to level 5: 50 points
> Cion grew to level 5: 50 points
> Madoka grew to level 4: 40 points
> Defeated 10 Aero Wolves: 350 points
> Defeated 48 Stray Sheep: 240 points
> Defeated 15 Darkness Blitzes: 640 points
> Defeated 1 Thunder Head: 80 points
> Defeated 1 bounty ★Silvanus the Enchanter's
  Messenger: 2,400 points
> Subparty defeated 2 Aero Wolves: 35 points
> Subparty defeated 2 Stray Sheep: 5 points
> Subparty defeated 1 Thunder Head: 40 points
> Party members' Trust Levels increased: 160
  points
> Subparty members' Trust Levels increased: 180
  points
> Conducted a combined seeking expedition with
  a total of 13 people: 65 points
> Returned with 1 Black Treasure Chest: 50 points
Seeker Contribution: 4,775 points
District Seven Contribution Ranking: 55

"…This is only your second expedition in District Seven, and you've already been given clearance. You and your party really are… You really are so incredible…" Louisa expressed nothing but admiration, and I could only scratch my cheek awkwardly.

"When you say *clearance*, you mean going up to the next district…right?"

"Yes. In terms of the amount of contribution points that you need to earn in District Seven, you're still a little short…but you've earned over seven thousand in just two days. I think that must be a record among all Seekers."

When we came up from District Eight, we skipped over the other Guilds and came straight to the Upper Guild, meaning we went into one of the more difficult labyrinths and were able to get these results. Even so, we were going into a labyrinth that was overseen by the Middle Guild and, as far as I was aware, it wasn't the easiest place in District Seven to earn contribution points.

*The Beach of the Setting Sun should be more efficient than this… The party leader has to earn a total of twenty thousand contribution points in one month, which is why the Alliance took it over to earn points.*

I understood why they did it, but I didn't have to like it. Roland said he didn't have any connection to what Gray was doing, but Gray was using the fact that they'd taken over the best hunting grounds to his own benefit.

"Our total contribution points have passed ten thousand, and we've gone into labyrinths in District Seven twice. Have we met the requirements to be allowed into three-star labyrinths?"

"Indeed you have—congratulations. Now you will be able to seek in any of the District Seven labyrinths." Louisa used my license to show me a screen that displayed our qualification for entering three-star labyrinths.

"Our next goals will be getting twenty thousand contribution points in one month and then defeat one more level-six or higher Named Monster. We'll do everything we can to achieve them."

I hoped we could move up to the next district even a little faster so we could accomplish our real goal of making it to District Five. Right now, we were doing it in about the shortest time imaginable, but we couldn't let ourselves get stuck here.

"Mr. Atobe… The results from this expedition are as incredible as I think is possible. Looking at your work so far, you have set yourselves apart from the pack of even the most talented new Seekers in the low number of days of rest you have taken compared to the high number of powerful monsters, such as Named Monsters, that you have defeated. I believe you are capable of maintaining a high standard of results even if you don't rush quite so much."

I was aware of it myself. If I didn't want to lose any party members when we encountered a powerful monster we hadn't planned to fight, the obvious choice was to use the first battle for information-gathering purposes only, then go back as many times as necessary to defeat them. So far, we'd fought battles where our lives hung in the balance every time we ran into something powerful. I understood how much that must've worried Louisa.

"You're right... I want us to climb the ranks as quickly as possible, but I want to make sure that's not the only thing I think about."

"I'm glad to hear it... Forgive me for pushing my advice on you. I resigned from seeking quite quickly, then become a Guild employee; I don't have any right to be telling such promising Seekers what to do..."

"If you put it like that, it makes it sounds like bigwigs can say whatever they want. Louisa, your opinion always gives me something to think about, and it would be really helpful if you continued to give me advice." I wasn't about to say that *slow and steady wins the race*, but we should at least take it easy after finishing a big job. I didn't know what it said about me that I was still learning what it took to be a good leader after I'd already become a leader, but I couldn't rob my party members of their free time with my orders.

"Very well... Then from now on, I will simply tell you what I think. However, I'm not sure suggesting you take a break could be considered advice. It might just be me being overly worried, so I do apologize for that."

"No, it's nice to have people worry about you."

"I'm not the only one. I think many of the people you met in District Eight think about you. If you'd like to let them know how things are going, I could introduce you to a Messenger so that you could send letters. If you have a special contract with someone, though, you can use your license to notify them of the situation at any time."

"Special contract...? I'm sorry, I've never heard of that before."

"The support member can pay a contracting fee to enter a contract with a Seeker, which provides a number of benefits, such as allowing them to accept requests for work in other locations when the Seeker moves to different districts. However, the support member can only be in a contract with one party. The Guild's policy is that they would like the support member to focus on work in the district in which they live and normally operate."

If they did have contracts with multiple parties, it would likely be difficult for them to get orders and have to keep moving all over the districts. The more jobs a craftsperson could get, the higher their income potential, but there was probably a lot of work where their shop was, too. I couldn't decide if it was a good or bad thing that they could only contract with one party.

"I see... Thank you for the explanation. By the way, Louisa, do you know of someone in District Seven capable of opening Black Boxes?"

"There was one here until just recently. Apparently, they received an invitation to rejoin their old party, so they've returned to seeking for now. Their apprentice is currently running the shop."

In order to safely open a Black Box, you needed Sleight of Hand 4 as well as accessories to increase your success rate of removing traps. I hadn't encountered anyone with a skill level higher than 4, so that meant people like Falma, who had Sleight of Hand 4, and perhaps this other Chest Cracker who left District Seven were really quite valuable. Shiori had said she couldn't open a Black Box, which meant that at this point in time, our only real option was to ask Falma.

"The Chest Cracker in District Eight is very skilled. Would you like to use her services again?" suggested Louisa.

"That's a good idea. I plan to take some time off from seeking in order to prepare, which means I can travel back to District Eight."

"It is also possible to contact a shop in a different district through the Guild to request they travel to your location instead. Whether they accept or not would depend on their own schedule, of course."

Madoka was also a member of the Merchants Guild, so she could contact Falma as well, as long as Falma was also a member. But it'd be best to ask Louisa now if I wanted her to contact Falma for us. There were also some other people whose services I'd like to use again—for instance, Ceres from the Mistral Forge. I wanted to ask her to do some modifications using runes since she was a Runemaker.

"Louisa, this may be asking a bit much, but would you be able to contact a few people for me?"

"Yes, of course. It takes some time to receive a reply. However, if I write who the request is from, I should be able to let you know tonight when we get home whether they accept the job... Oh, are you going to eat out again for dinner tonight?"

Louisa lived in the same house as us, so it was probably best for us to coordinate whether we were going to be eating out or at home. But first, I had to think about what we were doing for lunch.

"I'll ask everyone what they want to do. I'm sure they'll want to go home and take it easy, though, and it'd be a lot of work to cook for yourself after taking a rest."

There was a chance we'd get too dependent on Melissa and

her Cooking skill, but I wanted to try to spread the housework... Actually, thinking about it, I remembered there was housing in District Eight that had Maids, which meant there were Seekers who we could maybe ask to help out with the chores. My very first step as a Seeker was to hire Theresia as a mercenary, so hiring people wasn't a problem, but I shouldn't go overboard. If the eight of us in the party worked together, we should be able to handle the chores at the moment.

"Mr. Atobe, you could also personally request a housekeeper for your lodging. Would you be interested?"

"Ah, I was actually just considering that myself... I think we can manage on our own if we spread out the work among the party, but it would be nice to ask someone to handle the cleaning while we're out."

"I'll make the necessary arrangements so that you can request a Guild Maid to cover that if they have any availability. They very strictly follow regulations, meaning you can feel comfortable leaving them in charge of the home while you're away."

Guild Maids? It sounded like the Guild had a variety of different departments like the Guild Saviors. Well, we didn't need a Maid this very moment, though we should consider it if our household got any bigger.

"I wouldn't mind a little help with the housework," I said.

"Of course, don't hesitate to use their services. You will have to pay different amounts depending on the exact nature of the work, but the Guild covers eighty percent of the costs. The system is in place so that Seekers can focus on seeking without worrying about other issues."

It would mean coming home after a seek to a perfectly cleaned home and freshly made beds. Just thinking about it made me feel more at ease. It was a huge change from the house I'd used only as a place to sleep in during my days as a corporate slave.

I asked Louisa to contact Falma and the Mistral Forge for me and then went outside. When I did, my party came back from where they were killing time waiting for me.

"Nice work, Atobe. No surprise we racked up a ton of contribution points from beating such a powerful monster... Our ranks skyrocketed, and now everyone's super happy."

"My ranking is in District Five so that doesn't change much if I earn points in District Seven. Did you make it to the double digits, Arihito?" asked Elitia.

"Yeah, I'm at fifty-five now. Our earnings from this one expedition were really high, which brings up talk about our total contribution points, and our rank has gotten pretty high."

Louisa had told me that the Alliance had a total of twenty-four members, which meant there was a chance every one of them, even in their decent-sized group, was higher in rank than me, including Roland of course. Even so, we'd already gotten to a point where it seemed possible we could move up to District Six. I needed about another thirteen hundred contribution points in District Seven to meet the requirements, which meant we couldn't rest too much or my contribution points would fall. We'd also need a few more expeditions in the labyrinths.

However, there were surprisingly few parties earning contribution points with the goal of moving up to District Six. Yukari had told us this district was the *"real beginning of the Labyrinth Country"* when we'd first arrived, but perhaps that just meant it had vastly different requirements for moving up and far more powerful monsters.

"......"

"Ah...Theresia, what's—?" Theresia walked up to me silently, and as I started to ask her what was wrong, I heard her empty stomach gurgling. "Sorry, you've been waiting to eat for a while now, huh? True, the flow of time might feel different in the labyrinth compared to outside, but we did fight through the night."

Theresia stared at me, which I assumed probably meant she agreed. She pressed her stomach where it was visible from the slit in her bodysuit. It looked like she was quietly trying to show her hunger.

"Hey, Arihito, how 'bout we have an early lunch?" suggested Misaki. "Pretty sure I'm just gonna take a bath and pass out once we get home. Stuffing my face is a big no-no on a diet."

"You might as well eat a full meal whenever you can, though," said Elitia. "And it's not like you're hurting for exercise opportunities. Besides, I don't think dieting's something you need to worry about at your age..."

"That's not true at all! A girl's always thinking about losing another half a pound."

"Lately, I just fall apart if I don't eat right away... Same for you, right, Ellie?" asked Igarashi.

"It's because we're close-range fighters. And Theresia has Accel Dash. She's faster because she uses a skill, but it still counts as exercise. I imagine it burns a lot of energy."

I suddenly understood why I felt like Theresia was always hungry. It made a lot of sense once you thought about how much she ran around in battle.

"Arihito, these restaurants here are the ones nearby that would let us eat with Cion," said Madoka.

"Woof!"

The two of them came over, and she showed me her license. There were a few restaurants near Green Hall: Labyrinth Country cuisine, Thai food, and a café.

"Wow, there's Thai...," I marveled. "They probably use a lot of different herbs and spices—but then there's Labyrinth Country cuisine, too..."

"That restaurant is open in the evening. They seem to focus more on dinner," said Elitia.

"...Oh, Labyrinth Country cuisine," said Melissa. "I want to try some traditional District Seven dishes. Then I can tell Dad about it."

"Yeah, if Rikerton comes here, I wanna be able to recommend him some good places," I replied. "Okay, let's try that one, then." We all headed south of Green Hall. When we arrived at the location shown on the map, we saw a sign reading, HOUSE OF SEVEN SPICES.

# Part III: The Craftspeople

We looked at the brunch menu written on a board outside, and everyone chatted happily as they chose what they wanted to eat. I decided to go with the "Spiced Soldier Moose Sauté." I guessed this moose thing was some kind of deer. Theresia appeared interested, too, so we decided to order her the same thing. But since that probably wouldn't be enough for her, I had her pick another two or three small dishes.

"Arihito, do you think this 'Spicy Sand Crab Stew' is...?" started Misaki.

"That's probably the crab in the area the Alliance has taken over. Seems there's high demand for it as a cooking ingredient."

"It's one of the chef's recommendations," said Igarashi. "I am curious, but I feel like it'd taste better if we ate things we hunted ourselves as a sort of celebration."

She was right. Once the crabs' hunting grounds were free, we could hunt our own and eat them. It would probably taste better that way.

"We could also just go into other labyrinths to earn the contribution points we need. Four Seasons is still up for more seeking, and we should at least try not to meddle too much with the Alliance and their hunting grounds...," continued Elitia.

"Yeah. It's wise to avoid causing trouble if we can... But even if what the Alliance is doing isn't against the rules, that doesn't mean other Seekers have to go along with it. Anyone has a right to hunt those crabs," I said.

There was a huge demand for them as food and materials, and they were easy to defeat. That would of course mean there's a lot of Seekers who'd want to hunt them, but they thought twice about it because of the Alliance's monopoly. It likely left a lot of people fuming.

"I know you all probably saw it, too, but the leader of the Alliance didn't seem like a completely unreasonable person. If we do get a chance to go into the Beach of the Setting Sun, we can see exactly what the situation is with their monopoly of these crabs. If there really is no way for other Seekers to get in there, I think we can try to negotiate with him. Maybe we can get them to divide hunting times," I said.

"It wasn't just Four Seasons—even the Guild was aware of a problem. It sounded like the Alliance was constantly monitoring the area for crabs popping up…"

The fact that they'd go to that extreme must mean that Roland had his own reason for wanting to make it to District Six. It's possible that his experience of falling to the lowest rank in District Seven was related as well.

"No matter what we do, we need to make the party stronger. I was also thinking about our seeking pace in the future, and that we should aim for two days' rest every week," I said.

"I think that's a good idea, but I'm not even sure I'd know what to do with one day off," said Igarashi.

"We could go shopping or just sit around. Oh, Ellie said there was a theater, too, right?" said Misaki.

"Yeah, there is. People with acting experience put on the

performances, so I think it's worth seeing." While Elitia had given Misaki the suggestion, she herself didn't seem that interested in going. Perhaps she couldn't justify spending time on entertainment when her friend had been captured by the Shining Simian Lord.

"I think we should start putting our breaks to better use. As long as everyone is together, we can find a lot of different ways to have fun in our normal everyday lives," said Suzuna.

"I know, riiight? I never get tired of just watching Arihito. I'll probably spend my days off chasing him around everywhere," said Misaki.

"I m-mean, I know I'm not quite an old fart, but…is it really fun watching someone as old as me all day long?" I said.

"Woof, woof." Cion's bark made me think she approved of how I'd spend my days off…or she probably wanted to go for a walk.

"……"

"Cion seems to agree, but I also don't think Theresia has any problem with spending her days off like that," said Igarashi.

"…I'm fine with that, too. I also like sleeping," said Melissa.

"M-me too… I also think it'd be nice just to spend time with everyone at home taking it easy," said Madoka.

"Yeah, I'd also like to relax. Well, I say that, but I'll probably be running around on errands the whole time. Everyone else should think about how they want to spend their days off," I said.

"Yes, I know. I'll make sure I'm ready to leave anytime, so let me know if you need me to come along," said Igarashi.

"Oh, that's a good idea. We could get a schedule board, and

whenever we're going our separate ways, we could write where and when on the board. What do you think?" Everyone agreed with Misaki's suggestion. It brought back memories of the white board at work and how even my days off had *business trip* written on them. Igarashi smiled a little apologetically toward me; she must have remembered the same thing.

Once we finished eating, we decided to go back home and rest. When we arrived, we saw some familiar faces waiting for us outside. There was a small girl wearing a magician-looking robe. I say girl, but she was a race native to the Labyrinth Country who lived very long, and she was actually older than me.

"Ah, where have you been? I got your request, so I closed the shop for the afternoon and rushed here."

*"You've been on Master's mind since you last visited. Oh, you do remember me, don't you?"*

"Yeah, of course. Ceres, Steiner, Falma—I'm sorry for contacting you out of the blue."

Steiner was, as always, clad in their heavy armor, and Falma was wearing her apron even though she wasn't in her shop. It'd only been a few days since I last saw them, but their unchanged appearances brought back memories.

"Mr. Atobe, I'm just happy I'm able to still work for you. It's been a while since I've been to District Seven. It's changed a little," said Falma.

"Oh, that's right. You would have come here in your previous position."

"Yes, when I was seeking with my husband in our party... I don't know anything about any higher districts, but I can show you around this one a little bit. Although you contacted me for work, which means I can only stay for a little while."

"Mm, we don't have much time," said Ceres. "We need to make sure we finish our work. Though, they are sometimes flexible about allowing more time if we meet certain conditions." Those conditions must have something to do with the special contracts Louisa told me about before. I didn't want to spring that topic on the three of them since they'd only just arrived, though. First I'd ask them to handle the jobs I had.

I needed to think about where we should put the magic stones and runes once we got our new equipment. We'd start with Melissa dissecting the monsters, then checking whether we could use the materials on our equipment, then—

"...Ah." Melissa made a small sound, and I looked up to see a man coming up the sloped road leading along the rows of terraced houses. It was Rikerton.

"Ah, Mr. Atobe," he called. "Good, I managed to not get lost."

"...Is the shop okay?" asked Melissa. "We called you here out of the blue."

"Yeah, it's fine. I finished the orders I had before noon, then came over."

It had seemed like Melissa handled most of the dissection, but I knew that Rikerton's skills were just as good. Anyway, it was Melissa who had requested his support, and he seemed happy to come and help his daughter.

"Rikerton, did you come through the dividing wall? It wasn't too much trouble, was it?" I asked.

"The Guild let me use one of their teleportation doors, which is much faster than walking. But you're living in quite a nice place, aren't you? I'm always surrounded by the smell of blood; the air in a high-class neighborhood like this is so fresh compared to it."

"…I miss the air in the shop. But I think it grossed out Arihito a bit," said Melissa. It was true that I'd been surprised the first time I went to Rikerton's shop and saw Melissa dissecting, but it didn't bother me now. Maybe I'd gotten braver—or more confident.

"We also came using the Guild's teleportation doors, with Louisa's permission," said Ceres.

"I did as well. The children and my mother came to see me off… Mom told me to make sure I do a good job, and the kids wanted me to say hello to Cion and everyone for them," said Falma.

Cion, who was originally Falma's dog, was sitting and wagging her tail excitedly. She was looking at me, though, and seemed a little hesitant.

"Cion, it's a good chance to say hi, isn't it? Your tail gives away how happy you are." Igarashi loved dogs and could apparently understand what Cion was thinking just by watching her tail. How fond she was of dogs was so different from the strict manager I'd known before.

"Woof," Cion replied and walked to Falma, who leaned down and started petting Cion all over her head and body. Igarashi seemed to find the situation emotional, and even I felt a tug at my heartstrings.

"Your fur is very healthy. I can tell they're taking good care of you… Thank you, everyone," said Falma.

"It's nothing; Cion's the one who helps us out all the time. She's good at listening to commands, and she's so brave," I said.

"I'm sure she's happy to hear such kind praise about her, too… Cion, make sure you keep listening to what Mr. Atobe says." Falma spent a moment enjoying their reunion, then reluctantly pulled away from Cion. "I was told…that you called me this time because of a Black Box."

"What…? A Black Box…? I had assumed your previous rune had come from a rare box, too, but… What kind of monsters are you lot fighting…?" asked Ceres.

"One of our party members brings us good luck. That, along with a few chance encounters, has meant we've had quite a few opportunities to fight Named Monsters…," I said.

"Luck alone doesn't explain it all… There's supposed to be Named Monsters you can't find unless you know how to make them appear. I have heard that some of those will appear and attack many Seekers, but it's generally considered lucky to come across one Named Monster a month."

*"Master, I understand your shock, but our job is to make good equipment for Mr. Atobe and his party. If they have a Black Box, there is likely to be excellent materials or equipment contained within."*

"Hmm… I suppose it is no good to sit around marveling. Arihito, I assume you called us because you have found a new rune? Or would you like the magia rune…? What's this, you're using a katana in addition to your black slingshot?" Ceres went around behind me and looked at Murakumo with curiosity. I couldn't easily tell her about Ariadne or Murakumo, but it didn't seem like a big problem to let Ceres and Steiner see Murakumo and talk about it just a little. "What a fine blade... But it has a strange presence. I've never seen a katana this beautiful."

"I don't think you can upgrade this katana right now, but if we do find some materials that could be used to do so, I'd like to ask for your skills to do it. Then there's the runes. We've found two more, and I'd like to use them to strengthen our equipment," I said.

"...What did you say?" Ceres suddenly seemed disturbed, but I wanted her to tell us what kind of runes we had to begin with, so I guided them toward a nearby teleportation door, and we went to the storage unit.

When we walked through the door, Ceres saw the two runes we'd found in the Black Box that held Murakumo as well as a number of unused magic stones, and her entire body started to tremble. "...How...wasteful..."

"Uh...aah!"

Ceres violently turned around and rushed up to me, so fast I couldn't follow what was happening.

"You...agh! You have to use runes and magic stones more effectively! Leaving them to rot in storage is so terrible it'd justify a vengeful spirit coming to haunt you!"

"I—I thought the same thing... That it really was wasteful..."

"Hmph... Well, I suppose you're aware. There's only one

Runemaker in District Seven, and they likely are full up on work. Though, if it's like District Eight where few runes are found, they probably have more time than they know what to do with, like me."

*"Master, if Mr. Atobe continues providing us with his patronage, it may be a good idea to enter a special contract with him. If we do, we can always be in charge of working with runes or modifying equipment for him. Yes, I think that would be good!"* Steiner spoke with some excitement, as if they'd come upon a wonderful idea. It really would be a great help to us if they wanted to do that, but it would all depend on how Ceres felt.

"…It's been so long I'd forgotten about special contracts. But I remember now—such a system does exist. When I heard you'd moved up to District Seven, I thought I wouldn't ever see you again. When you called us to work here, did that mean you would become a regular client of ours?" Ceres spoke a bit jokingly. As a jade, she with her flax-colored hair was far older than I, but she looked exactly like a mischievous young girl.

I had assumed that my connections with the people of District Eight would become weaker the higher up the districts I went, but that wasn't necessarily true with the help of a special contract.

"I was thinking I'd like to ask you that. Ceres, Steiner…and you as well, Falma, if possible. Would you be interested in entering into a special contract with me?"

"Yes, I would be honored. That's such good news… I get almost no difficult chests to open in District Eight, and there's plenty of other Chest Crackers who can open wooden and red chests. Ah…I'm so happy I'll be able to open another Black Box so soon…"

The idea excited Falma, and her voice took on a sensual tone as usual. But I looked a little too much, and the others' glares stung.

Rikerton and Melissa had already headed to her storage and started working on dissecting. I of course wanted to talk to him about setting up a special contract as well afterward. That's as long as he wasn't already in one, though.

"By the way, Leila from the Mercenary Office seems concerned about you lot. She was asking about you when I arrived at the Guild. You've probably got a letter delivered from her," said Ceres.

"Oh, really? Thank you for letting us know. Theresia, we might have a letter from Leila," I said.

"……"

Theresia nodded. I owed Leila for introducing me to Theresia, and it looked like our relationship wasn't cut off, either. I felt even more grateful toward Ceres for telling me about Leila.

Was Ribault still helping novice Seekers at the Field of Dawn? I also wondered about Polaris. I decided I would try to ask Louisa to see if she could let me know how they were doing. Knowing they were doing well would be a huge boost to keep us going.

## Part IV: Mountains of Treasure

Apparently, it was an everyday occurrence for craftspeople from other districts to get called over, so there were workshops they could borrow to perform their work. Madoka made the necessary arrangements to borrow one near our house, and Ceres and Steiner started preparing for their work.

We had a lot of things to do, first of which was to choose an order. To decide how to use the materials from the monsters, we needed to open the Black Box and see what was inside.

"Falma, could I ask you to open the chest quickly?" I said.

"Yes, I'd be happy to. Mr. Atobe, have you used the services of any Chest Crackers since coming to District Seven? I'd like to ask them if I could borrow their teleportation door to go to a chest-opening room..."

"There's one called Shichimuan. They've opened a few chests for us. I can ask the owner there."

"Oh... What a classy-sounding name. It didn't exist when I came last time, so it must be fairly new... I'd love to make more friends in the industry. Thank you for introducing me to a new one." Falma was eager to get going, so I decided to ask Madoka to contact Shiori at Shichimuan for us.

We went to Shichimuan, and both Shiori and her brother, Takuma, greeted us. Apparently Shiori wanted to observe a Black Box being opened.

"I've heard the name Falma Arthur from my clients more than once. I've heard you're great at what you do, and you're an incredibly skilled Trap Master...," said Shiori.

"Oh, come now, that's not... Now I'm blushing. Shiori, what you're wearing is called a kimono, isn't it? May I ask where you bought it?"

"I bought it from a fabric store. They normally only have shops in the upper districts, but they open a store in the market a few times a year."

"If you don't mind, would you let me know the next time this market opens? ...Oh, that's not proper of me. I'm here on business for a client; I shouldn't be using the time for personal things..."

"Ah, um, you can send purchased items to other districts if you follow the procedure in the Merchants Guild," said Madoka.

"Oh really? How could an adult like me who's been running my store in the Labyrinth Country for so long not know about all this? How embarrassing!"

Madoka was always thinking about how to use the things she could do to help others. It impressed me. She was quite hesitant to jump into a conversation between two adults, but she did her best. She'd never seemed timid in front of adults when she was running her own stall before.

I thought about that while we went down the stairs behind the hanging scroll and came upon the teleportation door. The number displayed on the door was 35. A random room for opening chests was assigned, but just like before, I couldn't tell them apart merely by their appearance. The white stone floor was softly lit, allowing us to see in the room, but I couldn't see the ceiling if I looked up. The walls faded into darkness.

"This room feels as weird as eeeever. It's so big, and there aren't any lights, but it's lit up," said Misaki.

It was safe to assume that if we were under the Labyrinth Country, we were quite far down considering how horrific the damage could be when someone accidentally activated a trap on a Black Box. Either that, or they'd used some method for making sure what happens in this space doesn't affect anything outside of it.

"Arihito, what do we do if another Hidden God part comes out like last time? We can't win a battle like that if we don't have Seraphina." Elitia was right to be concerned. The only reason we beat Murakumo was thanks to Seraphina's defense. If something with similar attack capabilities came at us now with our current party, someone could end up getting hurt—or if things were really bad, they could die with one attack. We may have managed to come this far without anything serious happening, but I didn't want one moment of carelessness to ruin everything. But I had an idea.

"Shiori, can you check what traps are on the Black Box using Assess 3?"

"Yes. I can't remove them, but I can confirm what they do without any risk."

"Amazing... Your Assess skill level is that high? I've focused on disarming traps, so I've only acquired up to Assess 1," said Falma.

Melissa also had a skill called Assess 1, so it was safe to assume she could determine what traps were on a chest if she increased the skill's level. I didn't know if she could increase that skill that far, though. The different jobs might have different caps on how high, or they might have to learn it at different levels.

"I haven't really taken many skills for disarming traps... I decided it was unlikely I'd have a chance to go up a level, so I put my points into Assess instead," said Shiori.

"I see... I went toward increasing my success rate for disarming traps instead of increasing Assess. We're both Chest Crackers, but we lean different ways."

"If we can know what the trap is in advance and if it's going to be a monster, we can wait to open it and ask for assistance from someone who's helped when opening chests before," I said.

"Yes, that makes sense. Well then, please allow me to assess this quickly." Shiori gracefully pulled a folding fan out of the sleeve of her kimono once I placed the Black Box on the floor, then activated her skill with a dance-like wave of her arms.

```
◆Current Status◆
> SHIORI activated ASSESS 3
> Detected BLACK BOX's trap ⟶ Success
Traps: Teleportation Circle      Level 4 Trap
Teleportation Destination: ? 3-★ treasure
    labyrinth
```

"Treasure labyrinth...?"

"Teleportation traps can be on wood and red chests as well... but this is a different name from a normal labyrinth. I've never seen a treasure labyrinth come up before."

This type of trap was new to both Shiori and Falma. Elitia was the only one who knew what the display meant.

"This is one of the ways in which Black Boxes are very different from wooden and red chests...," she explained. "Sometimes there's a labyrinth within the Black Box itself. Apparently, you can't get out if you don't have a Return Scroll, but you're supposed to be able to find far more treasure than what was in the chest."

"...That's risky. If there are monsters in there, too, and if they're so powerful you can't do any trial runs against them, you might not be able to get out safely...," I said.

"But the treasure we've gotten from Black Boxes so far has helped us a lot, right? I think we might as well take a look inside rather than just give up... Actually, I understand if you want to take the safer path. We should discuss it as a group," said Igarashi.

Being teleported to another labyrinth did feel like a trap, but there'd be things there we couldn't understand unless we went. It was the same when we met Ariadne.

"It's a three-star labyrinth, so it's about the same difficulty as the labyrinths we can go in. I don't know how stars are decided, but it shouldn't be way out of our league as long as we prepare first, right?" said Misaki.

"I think so, too. If we make equipment and acquire new skills, then we can see what this labyrinth is like... I think it's dangerous to intentionally set off a trap, but it seems like there's a lot to gain," said Suzuna. They were both for moving forward on this. We had just gotten the qualifications necessary to go into three-star labyrinths, meaning it could be risky to go into this abnormal one first. But I still wanted to give it a try. We could go in so long as we left quickly if things got dangerous.

"While I'm undoing the Dimensional Barrier Lock, I can take off the trap by itself... Would you like me to try that? That way you can get everything in the box safely, other than what's in the trap," said Falma.

"You can do that? ...In that case, would you mind?" I asked. Falma nodded. She then placed her hand over the Black Box, and the magic circle expanded with the hologram-like Dimensional Barrier Lock. The previous ones had been cubes, but this one was a sort of octahedron.

The lock was woven into a three-dimensional maze path. Falma would send her magic down the path, which would unlock it. Every time I saw it, I admired how Falma did something so calmly that we would never be able to even try to do.

"This is the first time I've done one this difficult... It's such an important job, I will carefully finish it... Okay, here I go!" she said.

"And I will observe the work of such a famed Trap Master." Shiori watched Falma and her work with utmost seriousness as Falma sent her magic down the path. Even the smallest mistake would cause this to fail, but Falma tackled it with impassioned gestures and hand movements.

We sat in suspense as we watched Falma undo the lock, but our vision went blank when the chest opened and light flooded out. The next moment, the floor was covered in a layer of gold and equipment. Everyone present was thrilled.

It had taken Falma a whole fifteen minutes to unlock the chest, and she was now drenched in sweat from concentrating so hard the whole time, but Shiori went to help her recover. The rest of us also tried to go help, but Shiori insisted she do it because she'd been so impressed by the performance. She gave Falma a pillow to sit on with tears in her eyes.

"*Huff...huff...* I'm sorry it took so long... If I keep opening difficult traps like this, I'll be able to increase my Sleight of Hand someday..."

"Yes... If anyone can do it, it's you, Falma. I too will continue improving my craft, until I'm worthy of standing in your shadow."

I realized that Shiori seemed to respect Falma even more than before. Perhaps she had been so impressed because they had similar jobs.

"Look at all this gold and silverrr! And there's tons of women's equipment... Uhhh, is that because of that thing...?" said Misaki.

"Yeah...it's because Silvanus the Enchanter's Messenger targeted female Seekers," I said.

"You shouldn't think too much about where a chest's contents come from. If you focus on it too much, you might find yourself not using anything you find in the labyrinth," said Igarashi.

"Right. I want to use anything we find that seems useful. Just this much gold, though, is pretty nice."

If this gold also came from the labyrinth's levels, then the more victims the monster had, the greater the contents of the chest it left behind. I wasn't sure it was a good thing to think about, considering how many chests we'd opened, but I couldn't help feeling guilty.

"Atobe, what should we do? Should we gather everything that looks usable first?" asked Igarashi.

"Yes please. Falma, what happened to the trap you took off?"

"That magic item over there on the ground is the trap I took off. You can learn the details about how to activate it with an appraisal scroll; you should use one to check it out." Falma sat up and pointed to the magic item. I tried not to step on all the gold scattered around my feet and went up to it.

"Madoka, can you try appraising it?" I asked.

"Yes, I got ready for that in case you asked me to." Madoka gathered gold in a sack as she made her way over to me. The magic item was small enough to sit in the palm of my hand. It looked like a crystal cube set in a metal frame. I picked it up carefully and passed it to Madoka.

```
◆Trap Cube: Teleportation Circle◆
> Use sets Trap: Teleportation Circle
Teleportation Destination: ? 3-★ treasure
  labyrinth
> Can only be used once
```

*So...does that mean we can set a teleportation circle? We can't set it in housing we rent, so I'll have to ask Louisa where we could use it...*

"Thank you, Madoka. Now I understand what it is," I said.

"You're welcome. It's a very pretty item. It looks like a magic circle floating inside clear glass."

It appeared more like a decoration for a room than a trap turned into an item. Either way, it was obvious it had special value.

Removing the trap seemed to have been a lot of work for Falma, because she looked more tired than in the past. I had thought that we could ask her to turn future traps into items as well because they could be useful, but it might be best to try not to think about that as an option.

The fact that there was so much equipment that women could use was quite a boon considering the makeup of my party. Even so, I thought we'd be really lucky if we could swap two or three pieces of equipment, but we ended up finding way more usable items than I had expected.

"Ooh, magic cards! Sounds like something for meeee! I wonder if there had been a person with Magician as a job," said Misaki.

"Seems like it. We also found a silk top hat...but I don't think anyone in the party can equip that, so perhaps we should set it aside for now. Or maybe you want to try it on, Atobe? It might just suit you," said Igarashi.

"N-no... I don't think it would go well with my other equipment. And the effects...hmm?"

◆Spider Silk Top Hat +2◆
> Increases success rate for Magician skills.
> Increases maximum magic for Magicians.
> Abilities increase if equipped as a set.

Reading the effects again, I found that it had several different kinds. There wasn't anyone in the party at the moment who should equip it, but there were a few things interesting about it.

"This equipment is job specific... It looks like a Magician asked a craftsperson to make it on special request. There's some effects that would work for anyone, but it's definitely meant for a Magician," said Igarashi.

"I see. It'd be nice if we could make it usable for a different job... Anyway, I don't really get the impression it'd be useful for battle even if we had the full set," I said.

"There's *spider* in the name. Perhaps it's part of a set with the torn tights we found earlier... Since they're for a Magician, it's like a costume you'd wear when putting on a show or something." Igarashi smiled wryly, but it did mean that if we got the set, we might have someone equip it because it could have fairly strong effects.

"If I equipped just the top hat and the torn tights... Oh, come on, I get it! You don't need to actually pull away in disgust like that; I am actually a girl with a sense of modesty. It hurts when you do that," said Misaki.

"Anyway, there's no point making you wear them—they're for a Magician. Is there anything else usable?"

"There isn't anything better than what I currently have... There's a limit to how many accessories you can equip. I didn't find anything, but the others found things they can use," said Elitia.

Like Elitia said, we got a lot of equipment, but for some reason there wasn't a single rune or magic stone. Up until now, we'd found some in every chest we opened, but apparently that wasn't always the case.

"I didn't think we'd find any Shrine Maiden equipment... But some things do have effects," said Suzuna.

"There was some head equipment for me, and I found a weapon for Cion that has a star in the name. It doesn't even have any dangerous effects, so she'll be able to do even more now," said Igarashi.

"Woof!" Cion barked happily. She wasn't wearing her new equipment yet, but Igarashi was holding a set of gauntlet-type things with claws attached. That must be what she was talking about. We quickly ran through and appraised everything, ending up with this list of new equipment:

◆New Equipment — Kyouka◆
> Glow Gold Circlet +2
> Protection Necklace

◆New Equipment — Misaki◆
> Bat Leather Jacket +1
> Steel Magic Cards +2

◆New Equipment — Suzuna◆
> Silk Shaman's Clothes +2
> Leather Archer's Gloves +1

◆New Equipment — Cion◆
> ★Beast Claw
> Hound's Leather Vest +1

◆New Equipment — Madoka◆
> Merchant's Glass +2

◆New Equipment — Melissa◆
> Light Steel Apron +1

One thing worth noting was that we found a piece of equipment made of glow gold, which had come up in conversation before. Another interesting thing was that we found a necklace that made it harder for equipment to break, so we decided Igarashi should wear that considering how often her armor had broken. One thing I did notice, though, was that it only made it *slightly* more difficult for equipment to break.

I thought it'd be nice if there was some new equipment for me, too, but Silvanus the Enchanter's Messenger must have completely avoided attacking male Seekers. Unfortunately, we didn't find a single piece of equipment for me. If I could get the magic gun from Luca, though, I'd at least be able to change out my weapon.

"......"

And we couldn't forget about Theresia's equipment. From the collection of weapons we found, there was one that Theresia could use, and we also found her some armor.

◆New Equipment — Theresia◆
> Elluminate Short Sword +3
> Light-Shielding Bodysuit +2

"...Atobe, I was under the impression that Theresia could change out any equipment other than the stuff she can't take off, but changing for this skin-tight full bodysuit...is a bit of a problem, isn't it?" asked Igarashi.

"W-well, it's not like I want to make her wear that by itself.

The suit has a property that prevents light from passing through it. I thought it might work as a lining for the bodysuit that uses the camouflage stone..."

"I bet the original owner wore something over it. They were probably a Stuntman or a Diver or something." Elitia was right. The material was so thin that if someone wore this without something over it, it would reveal all of their curves. It wasn't like I hadn't considered that, though. If I wasn't thinking of using it as a lining for something, I probably would have decided to just put it in storage for now.

"......"

"Yeah, we'll take the magic stone off the sword you're using now and put it on your new one. Does that sound good, Theresia?" I asked Theresia since she was standing there staring at her current sword and the gaze stone in it. She responded with a quick nod. Her new sword was also a short sword, but it was made from elluminate and had a +3. Perhaps that's why it was a different shape and looked more powerful.

In addition to the equipment, we found 7,583 gold coins, 5,874 silver coins, and 6,960 copper coins. It was enough that it didn't seem like we'd run out of money any time soon, but together it was fairly heavy, so we sent it off to the bank. We called some Carriers to come and take care of the equipment we had no use for, and Madoka haggled a price for it with them.

Shiori was still shocked, perhaps since it had been the first time she'd seen a Black Box opened. Falma appreciated that we let her relax and recover while we worked.

"You've all been working so hard. I hope what you found from this chest will help you in your seeking," she said.

"Thank you, Falma. I was hoping I could offer you an additional payment on top of your normal fee," I said.

"It's enough knowing I'll get the opportunity to travel to the upper districts for work when you need me..."

"You opening Black Boxes for us is the reason we've been able to make it this far. And Cion's been such a huge help to us. I'd just like to thank you for that."

"But Cion is so energetic these days because of you; I'm the one who should be offering thanks... She's getting to see the world."

"Well, then... Since Cion can't spend her share of our money, please accept that at least. I feel like Cion would be happier knowing it went toward buying Eyck and Plum some nice treats rather than sitting around."

Falma finally accepted a gift of two hundred gold, though it was only thanks to Cion. She was incredibly hesitant to accept, but I felt like it wasn't nearly enough.

"Mr. Atobe, I am so grateful for this already, but...could I possibly ask you a favor as well?"

"Of course, you can ask anything you like."

Falma and Shiori looked at each other and smiled. The two had apparently been talking while Falma rested.

"Well...I took two days for this business trip, meaning I'll be spending tomorrow in District Seven as well. I plan to spend tomorrow picking up some souvenirs for the kids, but I haven't actually decided where I'll be staying tonight..."

In other words, she was hoping she could stay in our house. Everyone else agreed without a moment's hesitation, and I decided I should be ready to sleep on the couch if we didn't have enough beds.

## Part V: A Magic Gun

Falma wanted to stay at Shichimuan and chat with Shiori more, so we decided to come and pick her up when we were heading home. Our next stop was Boutique Corleone. Luca, the store owner, flashed me a wink while he wrapped up what he was doing with some other customers.

"I thought it would take you longer, but you really are a new star to keep an eye on. Either that or you wanted to come see me again so much you worked really hard," he said.

"Well, that might have been part of it, but a lot of things just fell into place. It's all thanks to the hard work of my party and the party we fought alongside."

"There you go again being so humble. You're as honest as they come."

I did get carried away sometimes, but I needed to always remember that what we managed to do in battle was all a result of cooperation.

"Right... Can I have you come with me, Arihito? Perhaps the girls can have a gander at some of what we have to offer. It's not really large enough back there for everyone to fit."

"Well, if that's what you're going to do, we can buy some of the things we couldn't last time... Ooooh, it doesn't look like they get bathing suits in that often," said Misaki.

"It's just a timing problem. Let's buy what we need and try not to waste anything." Igarashi turned to me and nodded as she chided Misaki. Luca attended to them before leading me into the back of the store.

The boutique's interior was bright and homey, but Luca's room for business discussion was dimly lit and furnished with leather seats and a table made of glossy black stone; it looked exactly like a room from a Mafia movie. It also smelled of musk, but maybe that was how Luca liked it.

"You're probably thinking this room is really used for secret conversations. Everyone's surprised at first. The shopworkers have gotten so used to it, they'll even come in here for a cup of tea while they gossip on their breaks."

"N-no... It definitely has a certain flair to it, but the decoration's spot on. It looks like something you'd see in a movie."

Luca smiled vaguely at my comparison but didn't respond. But it really wasn't like he was trying to pull me into a criminal underworld. That was obvious; there was karma, which meant you couldn't do anything really bad.

"This is where I went to get it before, the magic gun. It's in a hidden safe," said Luca. Hanging on the wall was a taxidermy monster that looked like a buck, but it was actually a hidden switch.

Luca slipped his hand into the creature's mouth, and a painting on the wall slowly slid to the side. Behind it was a safe.

*Uh... The recess where the safe is looks like it has burn marks around it...*

"Magic items are so useful, aren't they? You can do quite a few things with them that you wouldn't be able to without electricity."

"It'd be exciting to have a device like that in my house."

"Ah, you get it. It's important to never lose your childlike fascination, no matter how old you get." Luca twirled the dial on the safe to open it, and inside was the attaché case he had shown me before. I took out my license and pulled up the proof that we defeated the sheep monsters that seemed like they'd be a source of high-quality cloth. Luca activated the mechanism again, and the painting slid back into its original position. He set the case on the table, sat in a chair across from me, and folded his hands. There was a tension between us that said I'd get shot quickly if I let him down.

"Right... Arihito, do you have what I asked for?"

"It's currently being dissected. I believe we should have the materials in the next few days. Would materials from these monsters make a good suit?"

Luca examined the type and number of monsters my license showed we defeated, and his eyes went wide. He let out a shaky breath, took a cigar that was sitting on the table, and started to light it—but stopped as he looked at me with a wry smile.

"I'm amazed... I can't believe you'd go this far past what I hoped for. Fiber from a sheep's coat, wool, is considered the best material for cloth that you can find in District Seven. On top of that, these monsters... If I can use material from a Named Monster's body, I'll be able to make the best suit I've ever made."

"I'm glad... Wool is definitely a material used for suits, though I imagine it'll shrink if you don't have it dry-cleaned."

"Any clothing will get damaged someday. You can increase its life with proper care, though... I have a feeling your party will move up to the next district surprisingly fast. I'll do everything to repair and care for your clothing while you are here."

I'd bought clothing in District Eight as well, but it wasn't often that you met a craftsperson like Luca—someone who was mysterious but easy to get along with, who I could talk with about so much, and who worked so hard to make clothes for me. It was one of those strange twists of fate.

"Luca, I imagine you're already in a contract with someone, but if not, I was wondering if I might be able to have an exclusive contract with you. It would include maintenance of my suits of course, but I'd also like to talk to you about everyone else's clothes as well."

It wasn't that unheard of to continue using the services of an establishment that made you a suit once, but Luca looked like he didn't know what to say. He seemed confused, but he didn't outright reject the offer.

"...Right. I can't be certain how strong the equipment will be without seeing the materials first, but since my apprentice is working on making other clothing, I can commit myself to your suit. I'll finish it within a week. Why don't you reevaluate my work once its complete?"

"One week... That's amazing. I wouldn't be surprised for a custom-order suit to take over a month to make."

"With all my years of experience, I should be able to make it work. We normally have a lot in the shop, but there's all sorts of equipment that can't be mass-produced just like suits. There's a lot of crude items out there, too, so I'm not about to tell you to treasure your average leather armor or buckler."

A craftsperson had made every single piece of equipment. Thinking about it made me want to find someone to look at all the equipment we'd found in a chest.

"First, I'll use the Thunder Head wool for the lining; that will give it lightning resistance. Then there's these Darkness Blitzes... They're incredibly rare, and their wool is perfect for a suit since it's dyed from the start. Normally, I'd dye Stray Sheep wool, but the color is completely different."

"Really... The suit I'm wearing now feels pretty comfortable, but it doesn't have any special effects. It'd be nice if I could have that as well."

"One problem with wool is its breathability, but I can fix that with materials I have on hand. Since you wear armor over your suit, it's probably best to think of it as a sort of gambeson you'd normally wear under armor." Luca's eyes shone as he started talking about the suit's details. It was that childlike fascination he was saying you should never lose. "Were you thinking that an adult like me shouldn't get so carried away?"

"No, I was happy that you'd be this excited to make my suit. I wore a suit every day before I reincarnated, but I didn't have a single one that had that much put into it. It's a nice change."

"I appreciate you saying that. I'm normally making ready-made clothes; it's rare that I get a chance to make something one of a kind like this."

The clothing options in the boutique were all excellent, but I suppose as a fashion designer, that wasn't enough. I was thinking that when Luca opened the case on the table. Apparently we'd reached that point in the conversation. Inside was a gun made of black metal that shone dully. Since it was a magic gun, though, loading and using it was likely very different from a normal gun.

"This magic gun... How do you use it to fight?" I asked.

"I can tell you that it comes at a high cost. If you can equip the gun, you can shoot it by 'charging' it with magic stones."

"Charge... I see. But if that's the case, how is it different from applying a magic stone to a weapon and using a special attack?"

Luca smiled as if I'd asked a good question, then picked up a clear magic stone that was inside the case and showed it to me.

"Arihito, do you know what magic stones are made of?"

"They appear to be produced by the labyrinths. They grow in the labyrinths, then monsters carry them around either in chests they have or somewhere on their bodies, I guess."

"That's right, but also slightly wrong. Whenever a skill is used inside the labyrinth, the energy seems to disappear, but apparently, it's actually gathered into the labyrinth. For example, regardless of whether its friend or foe, if something keeps using skills with a water attribute inside a labyrinth, a lot of water-related magic stones will be produced. There are magic stone deposits as well, but they're completely different from gemstone deposits."

I was very interested in what Luca was telling me, and he seemed to like that because he smiled as I listened intently.

"I make myself sound like an expert, but this is all information you can learn if you do some research in the Guild's data repository."

"I have heard that there's one in District Seven. I haven't had a chance to go yet..."

"You can even manage to get a little information about District Six and higher in District Seven. There is a limit on what you can access in the data repository based on what district you've made it to, which is pretty annoying. Some people spend a lot of time in the repositories, but I can only recommend you go when you need to... And I think that's enough off-the-topic chitchat."

"It was very useful information, though. So then, this magic stone..."

Luca handed me the magic stone. Inside the clear stone was what appeared to be a white mist. When I stared closely at it, it looked like it was swirling slightly.

"This has no fire or wind or whatever attribute; it's an attribute-less magic stone. There are a few floors in a labyrinth where all the monsters use attribute-less attacks. Based on the monsters' level, you can find this kind of magic stone. This is the lowest grade 'white crystal' there is... You can check out the specifics on your license."

◆White Crystal (3)◆
> Cannot be used unless the user has the skill
  Magic Stone Operation 2.
> Can be charged with skill level 1 magic-type
  skills.
> Power increases if charged with the same
  skill multiple times.
> Breaks once charges are used completely.

"It seems like it'd be incredibly hard to get a magic stone like this, or something like the magic gun, in District Seven…," I said.

"If you understand their value, then go ahead and use it as you like. I'd prefer for the Seekers I like to stay alive for a long time to come." Luca tried to say it lightly, but there was a somberness to his tone he couldn't hide.

Supporters worked with a lot of Seekers. It wasn't surprising that some of them would lose their lives. It was supporters, not Seekers, who encountered people's deaths most often.

"If you want this white crystal, you'll have to agree to my conditions for how you seek in the labyrinth. If you don't, you can make friends with a magic stone salesman. These stones are in high demand, so they tend to get sold in the higher districts," said Luca.

"Do you mean they're like potions…? They sell out in the higher districts so they're expensive and hard to find?" When I said the word *potion*, Luca got a distant look in his eyes that I could have missed had I blinked.

"…Let me say one thing. Even if you find yourself in a difficult situation, don't do something that'll have negative consequences later down the line."

"Of course… Well, I hope I can keep that one. I tend to get reckless when I'm in the heat of things. I need to be more careful about that."

"It's good to keep a level head. I don't get the impression that you're reckless just because you want the fame of having accomplished something, Arihito." Luca seemed to want to express something during the time that we spoke. I finally understood what that was. Luca had used this magic gun when he'd been a Seeker in the past. By accepting it and using it, I was carrying on with his goals.

◆Light Mithril Revolver +3◆
> Can be charged and fired when a magic stone is attached.
> Allows charging with magic stones that require Magic Stone Operation 2.
> Slightly decreases gun's required cooldown time.
> Durability recovers slightly over time.
> Created using a Gunsmith's abilities.

The gun itself actually gave you the Magic Stone Operation 2 skill. That meant that even I could use it without a problem.

"If you charge and fire this magic gun with a normal magic stone, the attack is more powerful than it would be if you put that magic stone into equipment and activated a special attack. And if you can use that white crystal, well, you'll find a lot more situations you can break through. There are some magic stones that are easily used as ammunition, so you could use those instead. When you find yourself in a real bind, you can use rare magic stones to get yourself out of there."

"So that's what you meant when you said it came at a high cost. It has its risks, but it seems like it'll work well as a trump card."

"Yeah, it'll do you well if you keep it concealed. Sometimes I miss the smell of lead bullets and gunpowder, though... Yeah right!" Luca said it jokingly, but he definitely wasn't a normal guy before he'd reincarnated. I decided to just leave that to my imagination.

Now, Luca ran an outstanding tailoring business, and soon I'd be the one evaluating his work. I was certain that no matter what suit he made, it would be a fine piece that I could wear and know it was worth it.

"The gun won't stand out if you put it in the inside pocket of your suit. A man should always have a whiff of danger about him... Right, I should start taking your measurements now." Luca pulled a tailor's measuring tape from his pocket, stretched it out, and showed me. I didn't think they'd have something like that in the Labyrinth Country originally; perhaps Luca made it himself or received it from somewhere.

"...By the way, Arihito, I had my reasons, but did you notice that I've used that gun in this room?" he said. As the very last thing, he pointed out the secret. How exactly had the holes in the wall that hid the safe gotten there? They weren't small holes. If the gun had made them, I had a feeling it would become very useful in future battles.

# CHAPTER 2
# Reliable Supporters

## Part I: A Meeting in the Workshop

I met back up with everyone, and we left Boutique Corleone where I saw three men I recognized. It was the three-member party Triceratops that had watched our fight with Silvanus the Enchanter's Messenger from a distance. Their leader, the bearded guy, waved weakly when they saw me.

Elitia noticed the wave since she was walking in the front. She turned back to me and said, "Arihito, those people..."

"Oh, right, I'll go say hi. I also want to ask about what the Alliance is up to."

They seemed like they wanted to talk as well, and the leader walked over to meet me halfway. He shrugged with a pained smile in my direction.

"You don't look very well. What happened?" I asked.

"Well... It's sort of our own fault. The main party said we were out if we didn't give them information on you lot. Well, the leaders were actually pretty forgiving about it, but we put our foot down and said we weren't willing to do any more of their dirty work."

"...Oh, I'm sorry."

"Nah, no need to apologize. We always got treated worse since we were a group of three guys. We wouldn't have joined if we'd known it was that kind of organization... But it's poor form of me to complain."

Listening to what he was saying, I could only think of one person in the main party he could be referring to, and apparently my prediction was correct.

"It's that ass Gray. He joined the Alliance after us, but he just does whatever he wants. We were trying to contribute to the Alliance in our own way, but since he's been in the main party, we've been treated like his servants. Why would Roland let someone like him in the main party...?"

"I've met this Gray person once... It really is strange that he's in the main party even though I've only gotten a bad impression of him."

"So you know Gray? The only thing he's good at is words... But even though he might not be one of the warriors of the Alliance, he's stronger than us. He's a cunning man. Never let your guard down around him."

"Thanks for the advice. What are you going to do now?"

"For now, we're going to play it safe and go where we know we can beat the monsters. We plan on trying out some of the less popular labyrinths. We're all right on living expenses thanks to you for buying those binoculars from us." He showed me a pouch with gold in it and smiled. He was telling me not to pity them—that they would work hard at seeking. People like him always gave a good impression.

"Oh, by the way... There was something I wanted to tell you. The leader of the Alliance is getting very close to getting the contribution points he needs. After that, they're supposed to work on increasing the contribution points for the leaders of the other parties, but the leaders have directly ordered for contribution-point farming to end soon," he continued.

"Really... I was interested in how they were doing things."

"It's simple. Keep out any parties not in the Alliance and get a group of Seekers to keep an eye on a number of locations where monsters appear. That way you can farm the most contribution points possible in a day in District Seven and do it safely, too. I have heard talk that if you do it too much, though, the contribution points for a crab will drop."

No matter how efficient it was, if you kept doing the same thing over and over to defeat the monsters, the crabs' threat would go down and with it the contribution points they gave. There were very limited circumstances in which you could use this type of repetition to earn experience, and the fact that you earned less meant it wasn't in line with the Guild's intentions.

"I know it's not right of me to talk bad about an organization I belonged to up until now. Roland has just chosen a method for moving up to District Six safely, which I get, considering his past."

"I heard he once fell to the bottom ranks in District Seven due to illness..."

"Yeah… That'll give you a certain drive. We're not really in a place to be giving you lot advice, but never let yourself get in a position where you're forced to stop seeking for a long period of time."

"I'll keep that in mind." When I said that, the bearded man looked at me a little regretfully.

"If you were the leader of a group like that, I'd be willing to join despite the bad experiences I've had with alliances."

"I—I mean… I haven't exactly thought about making a group like that or anything."

"Ha-ha-ha, very well. But I really do think you've got what it takes. You've already managed to get the party members you did… Anyway, see you around," he said and left. They say that even a chance encounter can lead to a strong bond, and in that vein, I hoped I'd be able to see him again somewhere. I watched as he walked away, until he turned down another street and was lost from view.

Everyone else had been watching, but they now came over to me.

Misaki smiled mischievously. "Arihito, you look sooo serious when you're talking to another guy."

"M-Misaki…," said Suzuna. "You're making it sound like Arihito's usually…"

"It was a serious conversation, and I approached it with the appropriate amount of discipline. Does it not suit me?"

"No, that's not it. You've always been really good at handling people when you first met them. Not like me; I'm always shy around people I don't know," said Igarashi.

"A-actually, Igarashi...I feel you've always been really open."
When Igarashi complimented me, I could think of times before we reincarnated that she'd complimented me, but I felt a lot prouder now than I had then.

"......"

"Sorry to make you wait, Theresia. You're probably getting hungry about now, right?"

"......"

Theresia didn't respond; she just held on to my suit jacket sleeve. I thought maybe she was trying to express that she was concerned that I'd gone off on my own to have a conversation.

"What would we do if those men asked you to support them and you left us...? N-not that there's a single tiny part of me that thinks that's possible, but I feel like they might have asked you." Elitia was surprisingly a bit of a worrywart. But thinking about it, I probably would help out another party if they were really in a bind.

"It's all right. I would never go support another party without talking with everyone first," I said.

"There aren't any rearguards better than you, Atobe. You don't want people to start talking about that... You sure those guys are okay?" Igarashi whispered so people around us couldn't overhear. I replied in kind, and Misaki put a finger to her lips to indicate we should stay quiet.

"They didn't report on us, and so they were forced to leave the Alliance. That's why I don't think they said anything about me," I said.

"Trustworthy men, then… I wonder if part of that was from seeing you, Atobe."

"I think anyone would have been moved if they saw Arihito then. Just thinking about it makes my heart…"

"…Suzuna, are you okay? Do you need a Healer to do a checkup?"

"Oh, Elitia, you're waaay more innocent than I thought you were!"

"Uh… Don't you think it's a bit of a leap to assume it's that simply because she said her chest hurt?"

Misaki and Elitia argued, or maybe it was more accurate to call it bantering. Anyway, as an adult, the only thing I could do was scratch my nose awkwardly and watch.

"It's not only women who admire you—men do, too. That's a sign that you've got what it takes to be a leader," said Igarashi.

"U-uhh… Igarashi, do you think you could rein it in a bit where I'm concerned?"

"Why? I'm just speaking my mind."

Were we to a point in our relationship where she didn't feel the need to only compliment me in roundabout ways? Standing by Cion was Madoka, who also seemed like she wanted to say something, but she averted her gaze in embarrassment when I looked at her.

"Everyone's thinking how they aaaaall wanna talk to you," said Misaki.

"You don't have to be so hesitant about it. Madoka, could you contact Melissa for me? I'd like to see a material list if we can, even if it's a preliminary one."

"Y-yes... Actually, that's also what I wanted to talk to you about; I've been waiting for a while!"

*Also* meant there were other things she wanted to talk to me about, but Madoka was as work-focused as always and started by showing me the monster material list that Melissa had sent her. Apparently, Melissa and Rikerton had left the storage for the time being and gone to the workshop that Ceres and Steiner had rented. Since the materials would be used for equipment, I decided it would be better to have a meeting with all of them at once.

We went to the workshop, which was a few minutes' walk from our home, to find Ceres and Steiner had completed their preparations for work. Melissa and Rikerton were sitting down for a cup of tea.

"We've been waiting, Arihito. Well, actually we've only just finished preparing this workshop for our work," said Ceres.

*"Master, it's impolite to stand while holding your teacup."*

Ceres wasn't wearing the hood she normally had on. She was a native to the Labyrinth Country and did resemble someone from another world. Her appearance was fairly close to what I imagined an elf to look like. Her ears were long, and she appeared far younger than she actually was. She said she didn't normally show herself in front of customers. That and the fact that she was willing to come to a different district to do work for me made me feel very grateful.

"Wh-what...? You're making me uncomfortable looking at me like that. Are you that happy to see me again? If so, I would have wanted you to not make me wait like you did."

"I just really wanted to thank you. Thanks to you and Steiner coming here, we can finally figure out how to use the materials we have that have been sitting around." I thanked her again, and everyone in the party bowed their heads. It made Ceres blush a little, but she used Steiner's hand as a platform to climb up onto his shoulders, where she sat down. She looked down at us from her newly gained height.

"Hmph, it's nothing... I just wanted to try saying that."

*"Master has been concerned ever since your party moved to District Seven. She was very happy that you requested she come. That, and a craftsperson always feels blessed when they're requested to work exclusively with a party."*

"W-well... All my clients up until now have taken me lightly when they saw me or been afraid of Steiner. I don't feel good about my work when we're treated like that. I've worked in the forge for a long time, though, so it's not like I've never seen a Seeker with promise."

It was a compliment in and of itself to have Ceres see that much potential in me, considering she'd lived for more than a century. I was thinking that when I realized it was strange she would decide to set up her forge in District Eight where runes were practically unheard of. There must be a reason she did.

"I'm sorry, there's something I want to ask... Ceres, why did you and Steiner live in District Eight?" I asked.

"Hmph, and a good question it is... Truthfully, there's no particular reason. After I stopped seeking, I traveled around to find a place to live that I liked. The area around the forge I'm in now is quiet, and the canals are beautiful, so I decided it would do."

So Ceres had been a Seeker before, too. As a jade, a native of the Labyrinth Country, was she required to seek the same way we reincarnates were? I was curious, but I didn't feel like she was going to let me ask any more right now.

"Right... About the magic stones you have. You're not going to leave them in your old equipment, are you? You'll become stronger if you think of how to use them effectively, instead of letting them sit around. It's best to use them as much as possible," she said.

"Yes. Melissa learned a skill that lets her merge magic stones, so I also wanted to try that out."

"There are some that can be merged and some that can't. Right now, I can only merge once. Choose two, and I'll merge if I can... Tell me if there's something that looks like it would be good," said Melissa.

"I haven't learned Magic Item Creation 2. Instead, I can create runes if you gather enough magic stones of the same kind...but you need ten stones to do that. It's difficult to get that many," said Ceres.

I started to think that it would indeed be difficult to gather ten of the same kind of magic stone, but Melissa brought over a sack that clattered with the sound of stones inside it.

"...We found a few magic stones while dissecting."

"Thanks, Melissa. That's quite a few..."

"Sometimes monsters will use magic stones as a source of their power, if they're the kind to use magic. And you just defeated quite a lot of monsters as well." Rikerton showed us a list of the magic stones that were inside the sack, but it was too early to talk about making a rune.

First and foremost, I saw that it wasn't only magic stones in the list—there actually was a rune already. I didn't know what it did just by looking at it, but it would surely help us get more powerful.

◆Discovered Magic Stones and Runes◆
> Trans Rune × 1
Dropped by ★Paradox Beetle
> Gale Stone × 1
Dropped by Aero Wolf
> Elastic Stone × 18
Dropped by Stray Sheep
> Lightning Topaz × 1
Dropped by Thunder Head
> Dark Bullet Stone × 12
Dropped by Darkness Blitz
> Fornia Rune × 1
Dropped by ★Silvanus the Enchanter's Messenger

"Hmm, elastic stones and dark bullet stones can be added to the projectiles from long-range weapons. They can't be compressed into runes," said Ceres.

"I've actually gotten a magic gun, and it uses magic stones as its bullets. It'd be nice if I could use them for that," I said.

"Wh-what?! A magic gun... They say only a person with the

Gunsmith job can make those. I never thought I'd meet someone who had one…" Ceres trembled. I thought it was more from shock than from being impressed. I placed the silver case on top of the table and showed the gun inside to her.

"This is it…"

"Hmm… I think it could be strengthened, but it doesn't seem like it has been. It won't be easy to get the metal you can use to strengthen it; it's best to leave it as is for now. I'll need to study to make sure I can work on it in the future."

*"I specialize in metalworking. I think I can strengthen it without a problem. But I agree with you; it is complete as is. It would be best to leave it until we find the materials necessary for modification."*

"Good, I'm glad to hear it could become even more powerful in the future," I said. I needed to try shooting it sometime, but we had a lot of elastic stones, so I could use those for test shooting. My first chance to use it would have to be our next seek.

"So can you tell me about what equipment we can make from the materials we got?" I asked.

"Yes. Melissa, how far have you gotten in dissecting?" said Rikerton.

"The big one will take until tomorrow, but we have a dissection plan. I can propose ways to use the materials."

"The Paradox Beetle has some marks on it where the outer shell fell off partway through the battle, but the largest section of shell remains and can be used for a large shield."

Theresia used a targe, but we didn't have any members in the party who could use large shields. If we could only use it for

the one thing, though, it might be a good idea to have the shield made and store it for later use. If we got someone who used large shields in the party later, we could have them equip it then. The topic of people who used large shields made me think of Seraphina, but it would be almost impossible to get her to join the party. She had her duties as a Guild Savior.

"Sometimes you'll come across a powerful monster that, unfortunately, only a part of it can be used for equipment... How about the Paradox Beetle's horn that Melissa chopped off?" asked Elitia.

"It'd be good if we could use that for something... I still have no idea how she managed to chop off something so hard in the middle of battle, though," I said.

"It's quite likely that this horn couldn't have been cut off unless done in battle. The makeup of a monster's body sometimes changes after it's been killed. That can make it unsuitable for working with, but the lopped-off horn was preserved in a condition that is workable," explained Rikerton. There were a lot of mysteries about monsters' characteristics. If we could only work with a portion of it, we needed to decide how to use it.

The whole party considered our options and we decided how to use our materials.

◆Aero Wolf Materials◆
> Suzuna's Ashwood Bow: Use Fang to add increased attack, strengthening to +1

> Suzuna's Silk Shaman's Clothing +2: Use Pelt to add increased speed, strengthening to +3
> Cion's Hound's Leather Vest +1: Use Pelt to add increased speed, strengthening to +2

◆Grand Mole Materials◆
> Use Head Shell to forge two-handed hammer ★Hammerhead
> Use Claw × 2 to forge Mole Knuckle

◆★Paradox Beetle Materials◆
> Theresia's Elluminate Short Sword +3: Use Horn to strengthen to Elluminate Razor Sword +4
> Use Shell to forge ★Mirrored Shell Pavis

◆Stray Sheep Materials◆
> Kyouka's Light Steel Ladies' Armor +3: Use Wool to add slightly increased Breath Resistance, strengthening to +4
> Misaki's Bat Leather Jacket +1: Use Wool to add slightly increased Breath Resistance, strengthening to +2
> Madoka's Cotton Turban: Use Wool to add slightly increased Breath Resistance, strengthening to +1

◆Thunder Head Materials◆
> Kyouka's Elluminate Cross Spear: Use Thunder Horn to add effect that increases lightning attack's power, strengthening to +1

> Melissa's Denim Overalls: Use Wool to add
  medium lightning resistance, strengthening
  to +1

◆Darkness Blitz Materials◆
> Elitia's Unicorn Ribbon +1: Use Black Wool
  to add Darkness Status Resistance 1,
  strengthening to +2
> Arihito's Elluminate Mountaineering Boots
  +2: Use Black Wool to add Darkness Status
  Resistance 1, strengthening to +3

◆★Silvanus the Enchanter's Messenger Materials◆
> Arihito's Hardened Ox Leather Armor +2: Use
  Black Wool to add medium darkness resistance,
  strengthening to +3
> Elitia's High Mithril Knightmail +4: Use Black
  Wool to add medium darkness resistance,
  strengthening to +5
> Use Curved Horn to forge ★Silvanus's Flute
> Use Claws to forge Anti-Charm Charm

There was apparently a limit to the number of materials that
could be used on a single piece of equipment, so we couldn't focus
on strengthening one thing a lot. That's part of why we decided
to spread the improvements around as much as possible. If there
were certain materials that could only be used to make a specific
piece of equipment, I asked Ceres and Steiner to make the equipment even if we didn't have a way to use it at the moment. I also

had them divide up a portion of the sheep's materials for use in my suit. It would take a lot of the materials we had, but everyone agreed to it.

"It's harder to add the necessary resistances when you need them. It's better to add resistances whenever you can just in case you need them later," said Ceres.

"Yes, especially considering they are in effect without you having to think about them," I said.

"*It's not often we get to strengthen this much equipment in one go. I'm itching to get started. Don't you agree, Master?*" Steiner looked like a heavy suit of armor, but their excited tone reminded me of a boy. I was told there wasn't a person inside the armor, but they seemed fairly young.

"Melissa and I will help since you'll be working with monster materials. Arihito, do you have plans to use the strengthened equipment today?" asked Rikerton.

"No, not yet."

"*The work will take some time, but we're ready. Could you please allow us to take your equipment?*"

I assumed we wouldn't be able to use the modified equipment for a few days at least, but Ceres raised a finger.

"One day."

"Uh... It'll be ready tomorrow?"

"We will finish all the work tonight and deliver the finished products tomorrow. It's not that difficult. We'll be using skills, so as long as we do something about supplying magic, it should be simple. Right, Steiner?"

*"We ought to avoid drinking mana potions wherever we can, though. Potions are convenient, but they can have side effects if you use them too much."*

A mana potion recovered magic, but the license didn't display *mana*; it displayed *magic*. They seemed to mean the same thing... I started to wonder about it but wanted to keep listening to Ceres and Steiner talking as well.

"I won't use such cheap products... I say that, but all potions have side effects, regardless of the quality. They're not all supposed to be bad, but I don't feel like testing them."

I had the idea that I could use Charge Assist on Ceres instead, and I could drink the potion, but then I remembered that time I drank too many energy drinks and got really strung out. Energy drinks were definitely potions to me.

"Atobe, what's wrong?" asked Igarashi.

"Uh, i-it's nothing... I was just thinking about something from a long time ago."

"Oh... W-was it that time when...?"

Now that she mentioned it, I remembered a time when Igarashi gave me an energy drink. I talked to my coworker, and for some reason he was jealous that our beautiful manager gave one to me. I wondered what flight of fancy had captivated him.

"...Arihito, I'll make Theresia's bodysuit, too. The leather bodysuit I made from the material from Death from Above. The design won't change much, but its abilities will increase a lot," said Melissa.

"Yes, please. If you use the Light-Shielding Bodysuit as a

lining, I think it'll solve the problem of it being transparent when you use the camouflage stone."

We wouldn't know if it worked well until we tested it, but I was hopeful. It would probably be a good idea for them to test the active camouflage in our home the first time, just in case.

"Next, we have to decide how you're going to use the magic stones and runes. This could take a while," said Ceres.

There were the magic stones already installed into our equipment, the magic stones and runes sitting in our storage unit, and the ones we just received. We had a lot of possible combinations of equipment and magic stones. We also had more options for merging stones, but first I wanted to approach it from the assumption that all the magic stones would be used for the party's equipment. It was a pain to add and remove stones constantly, so it was a good thing we couldn't change our set magic stones.

"It could be nice if we give one person multiple stones with attributes so they have more options, but it could also be a good idea to give each member of the party a different attribute attack. It's a hard decision." If Elitia herself could change swords, we'd be able to use magic stones on it. She'd be quite powerful if she could use her sword skills along with the attribute the enemy was weak against. "We won't be able to merge stones with special attacks right now. We can only merge stones with the same attribute or that have good compatibility..."

"And we can only merge once—it's such a haaard decision! I sort of only want to merge things we have more than one of...," said Misaki.

"Don't you think it'd be amazing if we could merge a gale stone and an explosion stone?" I said.

"The life stone increases vitality... It seems like the kind of thing that could protect the user if it comes down to it. If we merged that and put it into Arihito's equipment...," said Suzuna. I appreciated her concern, but it was generally the vanguard's vitality you wanted to increase. Merging that stone was fine, but if we did, it should go to our foremost vanguard: Cion.

"Arihito, I put the materials we can't use for equipment up for sale like you said. This is the estimated price." The report Madoka showed me said 5,300 gold. I was pleased with that, considering we'd used what we could, and this was only the cost of what remained. Before I realized it, we'd pretty much gathered enough money to buy a house.

I checked how much money we'd gotten so far, and we had around thirty thousand gold. If we converted our silver and copper into gold, we'd have even more. Our priority was improving our equipment, but I wanted to use that money effectively where I could.

**Part II: New Magic Stones**

Unless you focused on defeating the same monsters to get magic stones, it was fairly rare to find multiple of the same stone. But we all agreed we wanted to try merging stones since we had the opportunity. We started thinking about what combination we wanted to try.

"If we merged an explosion stone and a vitality absorb stone, we could attack a lot of enemies and recover a lot of vitality at the same time...or would that not be possible?" I asked.

"If you read the explanation of what the stones do, you can get a feel for what they might do after we merge them," said Elitia, and I looked it up.

◆Explosion Stone◆
> Execute an explosion-attribute attack on a
  group of enemies.

◆Vitality Absorb Stone◆
> When equipped to a weapon, the user absorbs
  a portion of vitality from an enemy attacked
  with the weapon's physical-attribute attack.

"Hmm? Suzu's arrow has the explosion attribute, but does that mean it's not a physical attack?" said Misaki.

"It appears so... It seems like I would only absorb from the actual arrow's attack, not the explosion portion of Blast Arrow. Besides, I'm in the back so I'm low priority for vitality absorb." I did always want to keep her vitality at its maximum if possible, but her opinion took into consideration the party's formation. Unlike my Recovery Support, this was a type of recovery that took effect immediately. Pretty much anyone would benefit from that.

"Ellie has so many attacks, maybe... Oh, we can't put any magic stones onto that weapon, can we?" she continued.

"Yeah... It would be nice if I'd taken a hit, then I could use a lot of attacks to recover, but I can't take any magic stones right now."

With that being the case, I wanted to put it on the other vanguards—either Cion or Igarashi—but there were other stones I wanted to prioritize for Igarashi anyway.

"I thought this when I first saw the situation, but you're doing well enough with the stones you currently have on your equipment. The party has attribute attacks such as fire, wind, and lightning, then you have status abnormality attacks as well. How about you take the magic stones on your old equipment that you no longer need and try merging those?" suggested Ceres.

"Yeah, that does sound like a good idea. All right, what if we try merging the blaze stone that was on my slingshot with the wind agate?"

"Blaze and wind have good compatibility. Wind attacks are generally popular with Seekers as they can put distance between you and the enemy."

Theresia could use her dirks with Double Throw to attack from a distance, but since her short sword had just been upgraded to a razor sword, it might be good to give her an opportunity to attack with that, then put distance between her and the enemy. Even if the fire didn't have any effect, she could blow them back with the wind. If the fire has an effect, the attack would have quite a lot of power.

"Melissa, could you please merge those two stones?" I asked

Madoka to get the first slingshot I used out of the storage unit. She used her Take Inventory skill to see what was in storage, then used Unpack Goods to pull out what we needed. Thanks to those skills, we could get any of the magic stones or equipment we needed right here.

"Okay...I'll try. It's my first time, so everyone step back. It might explode," said Melissa.

"Don't worry—I can use my power to suppress anything even if there is an accident. Runemakers don't only compress stones to runes, you know."

*"I've never heard of a magic stone merge going wrong; I think it'll be fine. Though, there are very few people who can make magic items."*

Melissa herself didn't actually seem truly concerned, because she stuck her tongue out a little. It was a catlike gesture that you'd only expect from a werecat. Apparently, she had been joking just now—that was unusual for her.

"...Wind agate, blaze stone. Two powers become one."

◆Current Status◆
> Melissa activated Magic Item Creation 2 ⟶
  Merged Wind Agate and Blaze Stone
> 1 Blue Flame Stone created

Melissa held her hands over the stones set on the tabletop, recited an incantation that perhaps only people with the skill learned, and the two stones began to shine brightly before merging into one. A new blue magic stone was created.

"...Finished," she said.

"Wow... You can see a little blue flame inside this stone," I said.

"It really was like watching a magic spell... Melissa, are you okay?" Suzuna patted Melissa's cheek with a handkerchief. It seemed that since she could only merge once, it took quite a bit out of her. I looked at my license and saw that Melissa had lost more magic than Madoka did when she used Unpack Goods. Merging did use a lot of magic.

"...I'm a little tired, but I'm okay. Dissecting and modifying equipment doesn't take magic," said Melissa.

"I can't believe my own daughter learned such an incredible skill... I guess this is what they mean when they say you blink, and your kid's all grown up." Rikerton was very impressed by the display while Melissa said something quietly to Suzuna. Perhaps she was thanking her. Misaki and Elitia also smiled at it.

"I'll put this new magic stone into Theresia's new sword. What do you want to do with the rest of the stones? You should use the runes as well, if you can," said Ceres.

"Yes. We don't have too much time. We need to hurry up and decide."

We prioritized the strongest stones out of the ones we'd gotten, then assigned the rest. This is what we ended up with:

◆Changes to Magic Stones on Equipment◆
> Affixed Lightning Topaz to Kyouka's Elluminate Cross Spear +1

> Affixed Vitality Absorb Stone to Cion's ★Beast Claw
> Affixed Life Stone to Cion's Hound's Leather Vest +2
> Affixed Blue Flame Stone and Gaze Stone to Theresia's
  Elluminate Razor Sword +4
> Affixed Camouflage Stone to Theresia's ?Leather Bodysuit
> Swapped Explosion Stone affixed to Suzuna's Ashwood
  Bow+1 with Gale Stone
> Affixed Explosion Stone to Misaki's Steel Magic Cards +2
> Affixed Confusion Stone to Melissa's Denim Overalls +1

We had Igarashi specialize in lightning-type attacks. Her skill and the magic stone seemed to go well together. The fact that she could use Thunderbolt meant the skill she could use with the lightning topaz would be even stronger.

Cion got the life stone and the vitality absorb stone, which would increase her max vitality and let her absorb vitality when she attacked. We did have another absorb stone left over, but we didn't have any weapons to equip it to and decided to just set it aside for now.

Theresia got the stones we had planned for her. Stun was usable in pretty much any situation, and she could use the blue flame stone to get at the enemy's weakness when needed.

Stones that gave status abnormalities had different effects if put into armor, instead giving the wearer resistance to the enemy's status abnormality attacks. Since Melissa had such high potential for incredibly powerful single attacks, we decided to give her resistance against Confusion.

Next, we swapped out the magic stone on Suzuna's bow for the gale stone. Since Misaki's new Steel Magic Cards had an effect where they returned to her after being thrown, we were able to add a stone to those. We put in the explosion stone that had been on Suzuna's bow.

"A-are you sure...? I could go really overboard if you let me use this," said Misaki.

"You'll need to watch your remaining magic. You can die if you collapse from using up all your magic," warned Ceres.

"Okaaay! I think even I can handle using it just once!"

It was decided that Madoka would take a break from our next expedition. She'd helped out incredibly during our fight with Silvanus the Enchanter's Messenger, but it was still dangerous to have her hide during a battle so that she could use her Morale Discharge. Even if the enemy didn't know where she was, they might indiscriminately throw around area attacks that could still catch her.

"Hmm, if that's the case... Once I've been formally accepted as Arihito's specialized craftswoman, I'll be able to stay here for a while. I'll join you, Madoka," said Ceres.

"Y-yes... I appreciate the offer, Ms. Ceres."

"Ha-ha, and she's polite enough to treat me with respect as her elder."

Everyone felt better about leaving Madoka behind in town since everything seemed to be going well between the two already.

"If we formed multiple parties, we could go into the labyrinth with everyone, but there are some labyrinths with entry limits. It's best not to get too used to having large numbers. There's some where you can't even go in with a full eight-person party—you can only take six," added Elitia.

"Certain monsters have territories that they prevent any Seeker from entering until they meet the requirements. Those monsters have a set number of how many exist, and they don't cause stampedes, which is good," said Ceres.

Which meant that stampedes were most likely to originate from labyrinths that the average Seeker could go in but had difficult monsters and therefore people avoided it.

*"The Guild works to prevent stampedes, but they're always short on people for it. That's why they have no choice but to rely on Seekers and their personal decisions."*

Speaking of personal decisions, the Sleeping Marshes in District Eight had been the source of a stampede, but we never did go in there. After a stampede occurred, there were fewer monsters in the labyrinth from which it originated, and it took some time for it to return to normal. You couldn't go in during that waiting period.

Even so, I still thought there was a chance we'd go back to the Sleeping Marshes someday. We were currently focused on moving forward, but there was probably a clue to Theresia's past in one of the labyrinths in District Eight. If we could turn her back to a human… But part of me thought it would be cruel to make her remember her past and how she turned into a demi-human by asking.

"Arihito, don't push yourself. You don't need to solve every single problem yourselves," said Ceres.

"Yeah…but we'll probably come across situations we can't just walk away from."

"That inability to walk away from something is both a strength and weakness of yours. This may be an overly heavy statement, but

I want you all to see parts of the Labyrinth Country far beyond what I've ever seen... Anyway, pep talk's over. All of the runes you have seem to have serious drawbacks. You should carefully consider whether you will be using them or not."

We had a total of four new runes including the ones we found from the Black Box Murakumo was in and the ones we'd just received. Here's what they did:

◆Alter Rune◆
> Adds half of user's magic to their maximum
  vitality, creating an Alternate Body.


◆Hollow Rune◆
> Inflicts Angry status on target, adding an
  additional attribute weakness. Cannot be
  stacked.


◆Trans Rune◆
> Consumes magic to create equipment for an
  equipment change.


◆Phonia Rune◆
> Gives ability to enhance strength of effects
  from sound-based attacks and skills.


Used effectively, they could all be powerful, but the situations in which they could be used were limited. Then there was one other hurdle preventing us from using runes.

"We don't really have many open rune slots... Does anyone have any equipment with open slots?" I asked.

"Kyouka's armor does. What if we put in the trans rune so she could change equipment when hers breaks?" suggested Elitia.

"Th-that's... Well, I have the Protection Necklace now. I think it'll be fine..."

"It doesn't matter if you're twenty-five years old—you can still change into magical equipment when we're in a pinch!" said Misaki.

"Look... I'm no magical girl or anything."

I admired Misaki's imagination in times like this. Perhaps that's what it meant when it said it created equipment to change, though I had a feeling it just modified your current equipment.

"All right, we'll give Igarashi the trans rune, and let's put the hollow rune in Misaki's cards," I said.

"Drawing the monsters' attention does sound like a role I'm suited for, but you have to remember to protect me!"

"I think we should just hold on to the other runes until we can find a way to use them."

The alter rune would go to best use when we found someone to be our tank. The phonia rune would have to depend on what Silvanus's Flute did, or we could use it when someone learned a skill that used sound.

"Right, I will apply these two runes. Words of power, become one with this object... *Enchant Rune!*"

◆Current Status◆
> CERES activated ENCHANT RUNE → Success

```
> Light Steel Ladies' Armor +4 transformed into
  Variable Armor +4
> Steel Magic Cards +3 transformed into Jester's
  Wildcards +3
```

"Ooh... The design on my cards has gone sort of see-through."

"My equipment doesn't look that different... Maybe it'll change when I use the ability?"

Magic stones were simply placed in a recess in the equipment, but runes fused with the entire item, becoming one. It could be hard to tell there was a change just by looking at the item, but the process provided abilities unattainable with magic stones. That might be why it gave the item a certain name.

"Now then, the rest is up to us craftspeople. We'll be focusing on work, so you lot should go relax. You'll overwork yourselves if you don't even rest when not in the labyrinth." Ceres's warning was spot on. We decided to treat ourselves like she said and went home to rest until dinnertime.

My dreams were neither good nor bad. I usually had weird dreams if I took a nap, but I just had one about Silvanus the Enchanter's Messenger, which was no surprise. Of course I would—I had almost died then, but I wished I could have dreamed something more peaceful.

"......"

"S-sorry... Was I talking in my sleep?" I woke up to see Theresia standing next to my bed, bathed in the evening sunlight coming in through the window.

"Did you sleep well, Theresia?"

She nodded. I felt better knowing that. I would have felt bad if she'd been up the entire time, worrying about me.

I went down to the first floor of the house, and the others got up as well. We got ready to go out, then headed to a restaurant we'd found earlier. It was near the Upper Guild, a short walk away from where we were staying. We met up with the support people, Falma, Louisa, Ceres, and Steiner, making us quite a large group. When we'd considered what places would be good to eat with this many people in District Seven, we eventually found a do-it-yourself barbecue joint that served lamb and mutton.

"I invited Shiori as well, but she said she didn't do well in noisy places...," said Falma.

"It'd be nice if there was a place we could eat in peace and quiet, but we have so many people it's likely to get rambunctious anyway," I said.

"I told her to come have fun sometime. We talked all the way until evening; there's so much to talk about with her since we're in the same business." Falma was in a good mood, but she did seem to miss her children. Her eyes would lock onto any child she saw, though the sun had almost set and there were mostly just adults walking around.

"Oh, Atobe, that's Four Seasons over there," said Igarashi. If they came over here, we'd have even more people... Kaede and Ibuki spotted us while they were looking for a place to eat and waved as they came over.

"Ryouko was right; she said you all would be around here probably," said Kaede.

"You're the one who said you'd like things to get rowdy since we're going out to eat, right, Kaede? You were pretty worked up, too, Ibuki," said Ryouko.

"Oh, let's not get caught up on who said what," added Ibuki. "Arihito, would you like to eat with us?"

"Please do. I think Ryouko will run to the nearest bottle of alcohol if you say no." Anna nodded vigorously, and Ryouko's face turned bright red, but alcohol could be a good way to relieve stress, so I wouldn't have said no to a nice drink, either.

We entered Ordo Banquet, a hot pot restaurant, and started off with a drinks order. No one seemed to notice what the restaurant name meant, so I decided not to bring it up myself. Wasn't an *ordo* a group of people kind of like a harem that the leader of a certain type of nomadic people would have?

"Sheep's milk alcohol... It's called kefir. This is the first time I've tried it," said Ryouko.

"Mm, me too... How about you, Atobe?" said Igarashi.

"I had it once at a Mongolian restaurant. It had quite a strong flavor, but the one this place has is much smoother."

"What, won't you be drinking this 'magic nourishment alcohol'? It's a special drink that recovers spent magic," said Ceres.

*"Master, you must work when we return; you shouldn't be drinking. I'm just having tea...but you're not going to listen to me, are you?"*

"I'll be fine. I won't get drunk if I have only a little."

I started to wonder how Steiner was going to drink, then saw that he had a straw ready-made from the stalk of some plant. That made sense.

"Mr. Atobe, I think everyone has their drinks now...," said Louisa.

"Oh yes, if I can have everyone's attention... Everyone, good job seeking! And thank you to everyone who came from District Eight to help us; I hope we can work together for a long time to come! Cheers!"

""""Cheers!!!"""""

""""Cheeeeeers!!!"""""

"Woof!"

"......"

Joyous voices filled the large room, but I got uncomfortable whenever I did a toast, no matter how many times I've done one. "Ummm... So, Igarashi, would you mind doing a rotation for who makes the toast starting next time?"

"Atobe, your shoulders are still so tensed up. Theresia's worried, too."

Theresia stood up and placed her hands on my chair's back. Did I look that upset? Perhaps she could tell I was uncomfortable?

"There's nothing you need be worried about; you're among friends," said Ceres.

"It's just how I am—I'm not good at getting up in front of people."

"Mr. Atobe, sorry to interrupt... But can I...?" Louisa held up her glass. I felt awkward again, but it wasn't just her—everyone brought their glasses together. Theresia had a glass of the milk alcohol, but it was watered down so much with juice that it had essentially zero alcohol content, and she also brought her glass in to clink. Madoka was still underage, but she also ordered the same drink.

"Arihito, you've done so much today. We're going to keep doing the best we can until you need us again. Just let us know when you do," said Kaede.

"I'm sure we'll have the chance to fight together again. I look forward to it."

"It's thanks to your party that I was able to make my new racket. It lets me do lightning attacks."

"I'm glad we helped you reach your goals. I'd like to see that lightning attack someday."

After Kaede and Anna, Ryouko and Ibuki came up to speak with me. Ryouko looked at Ceres and then at Falma. After a moment of smiling at them, she finally turned to me.

"S-so… Falma is a Chest Cracker from District Eight who's helped us out a lot. She came to District Seven to open a chest for us…," I said.

"I was certain you'd made more…*friends*…," said Ryouko.

"Oh, it looks like Arihito really does prefer mature women…," said Ibuki.

"Ah… Wh-what are you talking about, Ibuki? Did you accidentally drink some alcohol?" said Kaede.

I was about to respond to Ibuki when Falma stood from her seat and came over. "Mr. Atobe is a customer of my store. I've been thinking I'd like to introduce him to my husband, when he returns, since Mr. Atobe's also been caring for Cion so well."

Ryouko and Ibuki were relieved when they realized what Falma meant by mentioning her husband. They'd probably been worried about what my relationship was with Falma, but Falma's calm reaction showed her maturity.

"S-sorry, I was thinking such rude thoughts… Arihito probably thinks I'm annoying," said Ibuki.

"I also need to apologize. I got carried away. Can I introduce myself properly?" said Ryouko.

"Of course. My name is Falma Arthur. I specialize in opening chests, and I would be happy to open one for you if the chance ever arises."

Falma, Ceres, and the others who were meeting for the first time introduced themselves. Everyone was surprised by Steiner, but Ceres told them about "the person inside," and they all felt better.

"Mr. Atobe, the meat has just finished cooking. Please take some," said Louisa.

"S-sure, thank you… Ah, have Theresia and the others already started eating?"

There were so many people in the group that we had four hot pots set on the table to cook the meat. Theresia and Melissa were already munching away at the meat cooked in one of them. Everyone noticed, then took what they liked and started eating. The food seemed to suit Rikerton's tastes as well because he was chowing down quite happily.

I had been under the impression that mutton was quite gamey, but it must have been well prepared or something because it wasn't at all. Everyone enjoyed it way more than I'd expected.

"It's so juicy... Ah. Do you think those Stray Sheep grow up to be sheep eaten like this?" said Misaki.

"No, this isn't monster meat. It's mutton sourced from elsewhere. Supporters in the Labyrinth Country have established some ranches and farms in order to stabilize food supply to a certain degree. Maintaining food production in District Seven here is actually quite a big issue... The food brought back from the labyrinths would never be enough to sustain the district," explained Ceres.

I had monsters in the Monster Ranch that were part of our team, but apparently there were ranches with a different purpose. The fact that we had fresh eggs and dairy products meant there was dairy farming going on somewhere.

"It wasn't just the blessing of the labyrinth that brought us this food—it was from the hard work of people... Thank you," said Suzuna.

"Thanks! Mm... All the extra fat was trimmed off before we cooked it. It's really nice because it's not too greasy." Elitia seemed to like the food—same with Suzuna—and they both ate away.

Igarashi was eating, too, but she suddenly looked over at me. "Atobe, eat plenty of meat and get your vitality—"

"Arihito, I'll get you some meat. Would you like a refill on your drink?"

"Oh, yes please."

Igarashi started to talk to me, but Madoka suddenly came by to take care of me. At this rate, I wouldn't have to cook any meat myself. It's not like I wanted to be in charge of cooking it all, but it would have been fun to do a little.

"...G-get your vitality b-back up, is what I was saying. We all need to make sure we get enough to eat. Madoka, have you had enough?" asked Igarashi.

"Yes, just eating with everyone else makes me feel full already!"

"You're still growing, so you need to make sure you eat enough. None of this eating like a bird," said Ceres.

"Meat's full of protein, which your body needs to grow properly. I'm making sure I eat plenty," said Anna.

"I only did kendo as an extracurricular activity, but Anna was probably on her way to being a pro tennis player. I bet she's been eating right to build muscles for a long time," said Kaede.

I had thought Anna was capable of leaping high to launch serves when I wouldn't expect that of her small frame; perhaps she was just that promising a player. Anna noticed I was focused on her and surprised me when she flashed me a peace sign.

"Theresia, you can't eat only meat. Make sure you're eating vegetables, too... Are you eating properly?"

"......"

"Theresia always seems to enjoy her food so much. It makes me happy just watching her." Suzuna was watching gleefully as Theresia ate. Some people felt relaxed when they watched girls eat a lot of food. I had a feeling this was that kind of thing.

"Oh, Atobe. They serve all sorts of other food, too..."

"Indeed, this soup is fairly tasty. You can try a taste if you like," said Ceres.

"And this shish kebab has a lot of nice seasonings; it tastes wonderful. Would you like one?" asked Louisa.

"Oh...Mr. Atobe, you look a little hot. You're sweating...," said Falma. The three of them kept coming at me; they were trying to be helpful but taking it too far.

"Kyouka, I know how you feel, but you can't panic in situations like this," said Ryouko.

"P-panic? I'm not panicking... Are you sure you're not drunk, Ryouko?"

"I am, but just a little. And now...how are you doing, Kyouka?" Ryouko's tanned skin was flushed, and she held a bottle of alcohol. It made me think of that time Louisa got hammered. It wasn't good to let things go down that road again. It was fun to have a drink, but a healthy and productive member of society needed to make sure they only drank in moderation.

I readied myself to say something harsh. I had to. I was thinking I would say, *There are members here who aren't of drinking age, so you need to show restraint as an adult, and—*

"Kyouka, are you not a big drinker, either?" Ceres said, interrupting my train of thought.

"N-not really...but I do enjoy a drink quite often."

"Now that you mention it, I've never seen you drunk... I suppose I'm the only one who will have that embarrassing experience," said Louisa.

"It's a special occasion. Won't you have another drink? I'd love to keep chatting with you while we drink," said Falma. Apparently, it wasn't just opening chests that got her excited—she also enjoyed drinking. Her gestures had become really sensuous. There was a good chance Igarashi would get pulled into their celebrating, or she would have a hard time saying no since they'd all done so much for us. I was surprised, however, to see her make the decision to give in without them pressing too hard.

"Maybe I'll just have one more. This is my first drink; I don't want it to hit me harder than I expect," she said.

"Ha-ha… If that happens, we'll have Cion take you home."

"Ryouko, you can drink if you want. We'll manage somehow," said Kaede.

"Kaede… Don't make me sound like I get sloppy drunk."

I was starting to think it was likely I'd get pulled into all of this, then Falma poured me another drink. I didn't exactly have any boys in the party who could help me out if I needed it—I needed to get through this with my own willpower.

## Part III: The Alliance's Miscalculation / Reviewing Skills

Everyone got happier as they drank more. The younger party members happily chatted with the adults. We were getting pretty boisterous, but that was good.

"Hey, hey, Arihito, were you dating anyone?" asked Kaede like it was a great opportunity to bring it up, though I had a feeling this kind of topic would come up in a situation like this. She already knew that Igarashi and I had only been coworkers before, so she must have been asking if there had been anyone else.

"I didn't have much of that going on since it was all work, work, work... Though that sounds a bit like an excuse."

"No, not at all. People who throw themselves into their work are really cool."

I think the normal person would call me a *corporate slave*, and I was aware of that. I had assumed that most people would decide I was boring because I did nothing but work. Kaede would probably just think how hard it was to be a salaryman if she'd really seen me at work.

"Mr. Atobe, you always wear these suits... Was that a uniform in your former place of employment?" asked Falma.

"I always wore suits, but we were free to wear what we wanted. There were quite a few people who dressed casually."

Falma seemed interested in my clothes since she was born and raised in the Labyrinth Country. She was seated next to me, asking about it. I'd loosened my tie a bit shortly after we started eating, but she seemed curious about how it was tied. She placed a hand on her cheek as she stared at it.

"You don't stand out too much in your suit, since people in the Labyrinth Country dress in so many different ways."

"You're right. I'd thought he would stick out like a sore thumb in it, but he doesn't. Then there's Ryouko with her swimsuit, which she wears into battle as equipment...," said Igarashi.

"But it suits her, what with that tanned skin. You just need to be careful that it doesn't break, because that would cause problems," added Ceres.

*"It would mean my life if my armor were damaged. I must always be careful that it doesn't break on accident."*

At that moment, everyone was probably thinking about how they'd like to look into Steiner's armor, but no one actually said it. There are some secrets that you just can't ask about.

While we chatted, Louisa and Anna returned from where they'd gone. I decided to get out of my seat for a bit. The pot of meat was almost completely empty anyway, but Theresia stopped eating to stand up and join me.

It might be rude to leave the table while sharing a meal with everyone, but I'd unfortunately had a bit too much to drink and needed to clear my head. There were apparently quite a few other customers in the same situation, because there were people in the hallway.

"…Wait, Theresia."

"……"

The hallway was only dimly lit so I hadn't noticed from far away, but when I got a better look at some of the people who had left another large dining room, I realized I knew them. It took me a moment, though. It was Roland, the leader of the Alliance, with a gray-haired man in tow. They walked to the end of the restaurant, and I was absolutely certain that the other man was Gray.

I was surprised the Alliance had yet again chosen the same restaurant as us to eat in, but that must have been because the selection was limited if you needed a restaurant that could accommodate large groups. It was wrong of me to stand around and listen to others' conversations multiple times, but I didn't even need to listen that closely to hear Roland's voice, raised in anger, or even Gray's.

"Nothing should have changed for us until tomorrow. We should have been able to keep waiting for and hunting crabs... What the hell happened today? Why weren't they appearing...? Goddammit!"

"Please calm yourself, Roland. Today may not have gone well, but we have multiple courses of action left to us."

"Multiple? Then tell me about them. The monsters won't come out—do you have a way of making them?"

Roland had said that he would be done farming contribution points in the next couple of days, but apparently something unexpected had happened, and it ended in failure. It didn't seem impossible for monsters to do something you hadn't planned for. But apparently, Gray had a way of solving the problem of monsters not appearing. They had turned a corner in the hall, and I heard an excited voice over there.

"There aren't many Seekers in the Labyrinth Country with the Summoner job, but Summoners can make a monster-summoning charm. If we use one of those where the crabs normally appear, it should pull out all the ones that have gone into hiding."

"...And how do we get our hands on something like that?"

"I'll use my particular methods. I've got influence with a fence."

"Hmph... I wondered what you were doing while you weren't helping us fight. Did you think I wasn't aware of the rumors that you were off in the shady parts of town doing something?"

"N-no, of course not. Don't misunderstand, Roland. I wasn't just skipping out on you, really."

There was an unusual amount of force behind Roland's voice, but Gray's sounded half full of laughter and half cringing.

"Fine, whatever. Can you get enough of these monster-summoning charms to achieve our goal?"

"Of course I can. This should be able to get the job done."

*This* must be some cash. I heard the sound of heavy coins clinking together. Perhaps a pouch of gold had been handed over.

"We will achieve our goal tomorrow, without fail. If things go well here…"

"I'd be honored if you would consider me to be your next assistant leader. It will definitely go well."

"…There are other members who have contributed for longer than you. I can't treat you differently, especially considering you joined this party late. All I can do is talk to everyone about what you've accomplished."

Roland ended the conversation there and left. Theresia and I shrank into the shadows because Gray looked like he was going to come where he could see us. That's when—

"Can't do shit on your own but think you can act all high and mighty… Old buffoon. Your time was over when you retired the first time!" Gray's voice was raised in anger and filled with venom as he punched the wall. Immediately after, his expression changed, going back to his normal light smile, and he returned to his party's room.

It was less that Gray was two-faced and more that he was simply hiding his true intentions as he worked his way up the ladder.

I wasn't one to judge someone else's way of doing things, but it didn't sit well with me.

"......"

"Sorry to drag you into this, Theresia. I think hearing that has sobered me up a bit, though... Let's head back soon."

Theresia nodded. She'd activated her Rogue Silent Step skill without me saying anything, and I could barely tell she was walking next to me. There wouldn't be anyone better than her if we ever needed to do any spy work.

"......"

"Yeah, I'll tell everyone about what we just heard. I'm curious about what the Alliance is up to, so tomorrow we might check out our enemy's...well, our rival's plans." I wasn't sure that's what Theresia wanted to ask about, but I wanted to tell her. She nodded. Communication between us would never be hindered that much as long as she could nod or shake her head. But I still thought all the time that I really wanted to hear her opinion in her own voice.

While it might be wrong to think this was exactly what I thought would happen, I was right, and Ryouko did end up so drunk she was unsteady on her feet. That's why I ended up taking her and the other members of Four Seasons back to their home.

The Middle Guild was also divided into a number of buildings, and we made our way to the apartment buildings near one of them where they were renting two apartments. We arrived in front of their apartments on the third floor, and Ibuki shook Ryouko awake where I was carrying her piggyback.

"Ryouko, hey, we're home. You'll have to walk the rest of the way."

"Mmmm... I'm not that drunk... I'm not drunk at all..." Ryouko was practically delirious. She struck me as a lightweight. The rest of her party hadn't even seen her like this, either.

"It seems like it'd be fine if we drank here, too, in the Labyrinth Country, but Ryouko's so proper about these things. She said we'd go out and drink once we're old enough," said Kaede.

"...Alcohol...can only be drunk in moderation once you're an adult...," muttered Ryouko.

"I can never tell if she's nervous or relaxed around you, Arihito," said Anna.

"Nervous...?"

"Oh, it's nothing. Anna, that's our relationship with Ryouko; we're like sisters," said Kaede.

I had noticed that Ryouko was stiff when she was pouring my drinks since we hadn't known each other for very long. I wasn't exactly that skilled socially, either, so I felt bad if I'd made her feel nervous, but...I couldn't stand here with her on my back all night.

"Kaede, which one is Ryouko's room...?"

"Ryouko shares with me. This way, Teacher," replied Ibuki as she opened the door, and we entered. The room was only big enough to fit two beds. The kitchen and bathrooms must have been shared among all residents, because the apartment only had what you needed to sleep.

"Here we go..." I wasn't sure if it was fine to just put her down, but Ibuki indicated I should, so I laid Ryouko on her bed. Last time we'd gone out together, she'd changed her clothes, but this time she was wearing only her bikini and something over it. She rolled on her side, and if I was quite honest, there wasn't anywhere safe to look. And then.

"...So hot..."

"Ryouko, are you okay? Hold on a sec—I'll go get you some water." Ibuki dashed out of the room, leaving me behind. I couldn't very well sit on the bed, nor could I just stand in there the whole time, so I decided to go stand outside for now.

"...Mmmm."

While I did that, Ryouko rolled over to face me. She must have been uncomfortable because she started groping around to find the buttons on her shirt and started undoing it.

*Wait...*

My first thought was that I should stop her, but then I realized that actually, the most important thing was that I didn't see anything. I really did need to leave the room for a minute.

"...Atobe... Where'd you go...?"

*That's not good...* There was no way I could do what I wanted to when she was talking so helplessly to me.

"I just want to talk to you a little more... But I can't think. The alcohol got to my head too much..."

"Uhhh... Don't worry about it. It's good that you enjoyed it. I like to drink, too, but I don't really get drunk. Sometimes I'm jealous of people who can."

"...Good. I didn't want to cause you trouble or disappoint you... I was so weak, and your whole party saw it..."

"I think everyone understands. It's fine."

Falma had gotten pretty drunk as well. We had to put her on Cion's back so she could carry her back to our house. I was taking too long; they were probably starting to worry. Not that I really thought they'd worry about a full-grown adult like myself.

"...Um... All my other equipment is bathing suits, too, so I look like this... Sorry you had to carry me..."

"I-it's all right... I'm the one who should apologize. I know it was necessary, but I just carried you without asking if it was okay."

Carrying her meant I had to touch her in various places. It was wrong to think of it as a perk of the job, but if someone asked me what I thought about, it'd be a lie if I said I hadn't noticed at all.

"...I was competing with Louisa and Kyouka when I was talking to them... You probably noticed... Didn't you, Atobe?"

This topic suddenly came up. Well, I guess it wasn't actually that sudden. She was asking because we were alone together.

"I—I... Well, how should I—?"

"Sorry I took so long, Ryouko...huh? Teacher, why are you there?"

"I-Ibuki, we were..." I couldn't keep myself from panicking. There wasn't actually anything wrong with me talking to Ryouko while she was in bed wearing her bathing suit, but I suppose it wasn't good, either.

"Welcome back, Ibuki."

"Oh, you're up, Ryouko. Did Arihito look after you?"

Ryouko pulled a blanket around herself to cover her body and calmly greeted Ibuki. She stood up and took the glass with water, then guzzled it.

"Mm... Nice and cool. Would you like some, too, Atobe?"

"Arihito, will you stay a little while longer? Kaede and Anna said they'd like to talk to you a bit more... Oh, they've even brought their pillows."

"...We only brought them because today's the day we all sleep in the same apartment," said Anna.

"Oh, since Arihito's here, we could have a pillow fight. But whatever team he's on will have the advantage. As long as he's in the back, we'd get the strength of a hundred men," said Kaede.

Anna was wearing a nightcap and looked more like a child than usual. Kaede had on something that resembled a *yukata*. If we tried having a pillow fight with her dressed like that, I felt like there was a high risk of something getting exposed.

*With our age difference, there wouldn't be any improper thoughts or anything, but...thinking about it rationally, it's just a bad situation to be in.*

"Arihito, I'd like to continue our discussion from earlier... Is that okay?" asked Ibuki.

"You can't keep asking him about his girlfriends. He won't like you if you're too pushy. Anyway, why don't we play some strip poker or something?"

"Kaede, you're too caught up on doing something special. You don't need to make yourself do that—you're bright red," said Anna.

"Strip poker... Things would get dangerous after about the second hand if I played..." Ryouko was considering it. They would never trust me if I actually wanted this. The only reason they thought I was harmless was because I'd been so careful about acting proper up until now.

"I want to hear about all of you. How did you meet? How did you end up in a party together?" I asked, and the four looked at one another. They smiled shyly, then told me about what had happened to lead them here. I had to head home, though, so unfortunately, I could only listen to about half the story before I had to say good-bye. Kaede and Ibuki walked me out to the front of the apartment building, then I left, the sun's warmth still remaining in the city streets as I walked.

Since Falma was staying with us that night as well, I ended up sleeping on the couch in the living room on the first floor. Thankfully, it was big enough that I could easily stretch out to sleep.

"You're the one who needs to get the most rest, though. I'd be happy to take the couch, and you can have my bed," said Elitia.

"I appreciate the offer, but I feel bad making a girl sleep on a couch."

She was in the living room, having just finished her bath, her license in hand. The two of us ended up looking at her new skill options.

"...Do you think it's wrong of me to not show everyone what my skills can do?" she asked.

"Perhaps... It does seem a little unfair that I'm the only one who's seen your skills. It might be a good idea to share them with the group at a party meeting sometime, but that can probably wait until after we've broken the curse on your sword."

The reason she wanted to talk with me separately was because she didn't want to show others her Cursed Blade skills. Even so, her skills had saved us on a number of occasions. I was certain the others wouldn't fear her or anything even if they knew about her skills.

"That's what I keep telling myself...but if I really trusted them, I would tell them. Sorry..."

"You've never once attacked us, even in Berserk mode. We can keep the worst aspects of the Scarlet Emperor in check. We can't say we've overcome them just because we've beaten enemies without triggering it, but I trust your strength. Including the risks it comes with. I think that's what it means to be in a party together."

"...Thank you, Arihito. I feel better when I talk with you about it... I'm sorry for causing you trouble."

Her curse meant that she couldn't equip any weapon other than her cursed sword while in battle. Outside of battle, she could set it aside as long as she was within a certain distance from it. That probably helped Elitia feel more relaxed right before going to bed, though a part of her attention did still seem hung up on the sword that was on the second floor.

Elitia came up to where I was on the couch and showed me her license. It displayed her new skills.

◆New Available Skills — Elitia◆
Level 3 Skills
Scarlet Dance: Consumes magic while using Red Eye
    to execute a chain of attacks. Power increases
    with each attack. Effects stack until defense
    reaches zero. (Prerequisite: Red Eye)

Level 2 Skills
- ✕ Pierce 2: Pierce distance increases as well as number of attacks. (Prerequisite: Pierce 1)
- ✕ Reckless Raid: Rushes toward distant enemy and attack, hindering enemy's movements.
- ✕ Blade Aura: Accumulates SWORD AURA when user defeats enemy with a sword.

Remaining Skill Points: 4

She had four more available skills, most of which she couldn't learn because they were Swordswoman skills she couldn't acquire as a Cursed Blade. There was only one Cursed Blade skill that she could take.

"Looks like you start getting four skill points at level ten," I said.

"Oh... You're right; I didn't even notice. That must mean level ten is a milestone."

"Seems to be. It's a bit of a waste that there's some interesting skills, but you can't take them... Not just the new skills here—there's a lot of Swordswoman skills, too."

"I've thought the same thing so many times. I would at least have liked the ones that give me more mobility as a Swordswoman... I really am better with a rapier, you know."

As a Swordswoman, she could learn Dual Wield, letting her take two weapons into battle. If she was able to change from the Cursed Blade job, her fighting style could change drastically, since she would be able to equip two different kinds of swords with that skill.

"Even if we do remove the curse from the Scarlet Emperor, it's a powerful weapon, so it might be good if you could still use it."

"Yeah... The Brigade thinks that cursed weapons are powerful because they're cursed. They never once considered removing the curse, but maybe, just maybe..."

"There's a chance. No, there's definitely a way."

"Right. We won't get anywhere if we give up before we start." Elitia's expression softened, then she pointed to the single skill she could take. "I'll take this Scarlet Dance. It'll likely come in handy as a trump card."

"...Elitia, how is Red Eye activated?"

She looked like it wasn't easy to answer my question. Even if the Cursed Blade skills didn't have the ▶ mark, they still had some inherent danger.

"It's different from Berserk in that there's no risk of indiscriminate attacks. But...it activates when the user is bleeding."

"...Wow..."

It was too dangerous to aim to use a skill like that, but Elitia smiled even after putting that particular risk into words.

"Everyone who wields a sword will end up getting injured. And didn't Kyouka use Ambivalenz, which makes her more powerful the lower her vitality?"

"...That took some courage. Igarashi's the kind of person who can do that kind of thing when it's needed, but..."

"So are you, Arihito. You won't hesitate to put yourself in danger for all of us. I want to do as much as I can to prevent you from having to do that. I've been prepared for it for a while now."

She predicted my trite line of trying to tell her I couldn't let her push herself over and over, and I could only smile awkwardly that she beat me to it. When I did, she suddenly brought her hand to her mouth at a sudden realization.

"...S-sorry, I shouldn't preach like that. I know you save me so often, but I worry..."

"N-no, it's okay. I know I put myself in danger. The most important thing is making sure we stay alive..."

"You...really are a rearguard, but you put yourself so far ahead of everyone when we're in danger." As she spoke, her expression was that of a girl her age, which she rarely showed. No matter how strong she was, I couldn't keep making a girl as young as her worry.

"Uuuuhhh, don't you think you two are getting a little toooo cozy for a silly skills meeting?" came Misaki's voice.

"Ah... We're not cozying up... We're just talking normally. Arihito, I'm going to take the skill I mentioned earlier. Good night."

"Oh, night. Misaki, Suzuna, sorry to make you wait."

"N-no, it's okay. I told Misaki we should wait until you call for us, but it...ended up this way."

"Everyone's just sitting in the room waiting for Arihito to call them, though. We need to make sure we stick to the assigned time. Suzuna and I are together, so we should get twice as much time!"

Considering how everyone had to wait their turn currently, it did seem better for us to have a full-party meeting where we decided skills, but we'd sort of settled on our current style of individual discussions.

Misaki sat down on my right without any hesitation while Suzuna sat across from me. Misaki felt too close, and I wished she would learn from Suzuna, who had kept an appropriate distance.

"Arihito, this might go late—is that all right?" asked Suzuna.

"I want to finish this tonight, though it's tough on everyone else to make them wait until late…"

"Everyone else is chatting with Falma. They were talking about you," said Misaki.

"I-it's…stuff they can't talk about when you're around, but it's not anything weird. Falma was a bit curious, so they're just…"

It was quite possibly the least helpful explanation ever, but I couldn't really push Suzuna for more. What exactly could they have to talk about that they couldn't talk about in front of me…? But this wasn't the time to be trying to guess that.

"There's still a lot of people, so I want to hurry up and pick," said Misaki.

"Yeah, if we select our skills quickly, Arihito will have more time to relax," said Suzuna.

They had said something about wanting twice the time since they're really two people, but they'd probably be considerate of the others and try to finish quickly. The two winked to each other, and Misaki held out her license, which I politely accepted and started examining her skills.

After about an hour, I was finally able to finish looking at everyone's skills, except Theresia, who was last.

"Thank you, Arihito! See you tomorrow!" said Madoka.

"Good night. I'm gonna rest a bit and then go back to work," said Melissa.

"If our equipment's ready tomorrow, I think we'll be going into a labyrinth. Melissa, I think you should take a break from this one along with Madoka."

"...I will. But bring me along if you go against another big one."

It was a huge burden on Melissa to have her seek right after having finished dissecting. She said she'd take a break, but there was potential for another target to pop up anytime. If we didn't find anything, she could take the time off, but she might not be able to relax all day thinking about it.

Something unexpected had happened to the Alliance, and they'd ended up stuck. It sounded like they had a way to get out of it, but I wasn't certain things would go as they expected.

Melissa and Madoka went back to their bedroom, and I decided to go outside to see Cion. Guard dogs apparently took their skills on their own, meaning I had no say in the matter.

*...Still, where has Theresia gone? Is she already asleep?*

I'd told her we were selecting skills, but she didn't show even when it was her turn. My license display showed her inside the house, so she must've been resting in one of the other rooms.

## Part IV: New Skills / A Vague Premonition

Cion was lying half in, half out of the doghouse in the front garden, and she opened her eyes when I came out.

"Sorry I woke you."

"...Nnn."

"What's with that whine? That's not like you."

She made a sweet little sound, and I started petting her head when I got closer. She pressed her cheek against my hand and licked the back.

"It's nice you got to see Falma again... Oh, she's going home tomorrow—are you sad she's leaving? That must be it..."

"Woof."

"Hmm... That's not it? Are you going to stay with us from here on out, too?"

It wasn't like she would understand what I was saying anyway, but she stared at me when I talked to her. It made me think she was picking up some of what I was trying to say. Thinking back, Cion had also had the Trust Level bonus against being Charmed. That meant she was fairly attached to me.

"Anyway, I should go to sleep soon. Will I get to see your new skills in battle?" I asked, but Cion was focused on licking my hand. She was a clever dog—or more specifically, a clever silver hound. I had a feeling she'd learn new skills when she needed to use them.

I went back inside and decided to have a bath before going to bed. I got undressed in the changing room and headed to the bathroom, using a towel to cover my front as I opened the door. There, I looked up at the ceiling only to learn I no longer needed to wonder where Theresia was.

"......"

"T-Theresia… I'm not gonna run away or anything, so you don't have to make yourself practically invisible."

"So this is the kind of relationship you and Theresia have. I knew it."

In front of me was Theresia, and now, behind me was… Well, I knew their voice, but I was afraid to turn around.

"Oh, you don't need to be that embarrassed. You're like a little brother to me, Mr. Atobe."

"Uh… L-little brother…? B-but I'm twenty-nine… And, Falma, your children are still young, so there can't be that big of a difference in our ages…"

Actually, there was definitely a possibility that I was older than Falma. Either way, it really made no difference in a situation like this.

"Whoa… F-Falma, what are you doing?" came another voice.

"Oh, I just wanted to thank Mr. Atobe for being such a good customer…"

"Mr. Atobe, Falma is a little drunk right now. I would like to respect your intentions, but Falma is married, so…" This other voice was Louisa. The first was Igarashi. She and Louisa had thankfully come to stop Falma from doing whatever she was trying to do and led her away. I just wanted to profusely apologize to Falma's husband if I ever met him. I couldn't exactly argue that it was perfectly fine because all she saw was my back.

"……"

"Sheesh… *Ahem.* Theresia, be careful not to stay in the hot bath too long."

Theresia nodded, then brought a stool over. She set it down and knelt behind it. It was like she was telling me to sit.

"……"

I wanted to hear what Theresia was thinking in times like this. I still found it too bold to say that it was fine for us to take a bath together because she was wearing a bathing suit. That could be said about Igarashi and Elitia as well.

Even a slight change in the bath's temperature could mean death for Theresia, so I made sure she was careful. I personally thought it was understandable that I'd become overprotective, considering the time she almost passed out.

"Theresia, sorry for making you get out of the bath so quick, but I'd like to select your new skills and then get some rest."

"……"

Since Theresia didn't have a license, I had to select them for her. I poured her a glass of water and had her replenish her moisture while I sat on the couch and considered her skills. She stood behind the couch and looked at them from there.

"Can you see from there? You can sit next to me if you like—it's fine."

"……"

I knew she wouldn't really listen even when I said it and didn't push it too much. I pulled Theresia's skills up on my license, saw something I was interested in, and was about to ask Theresia her opinion when she reached her hand over my shoulder to point at the display.

"......"

"Ah... You're interested in that skill?"

She was leaning over from behind, so her face was fairly close to mine. Her eyes were covered, and I couldn't gather any emotion from her mouth, either, but she responded to my question with a nod. As I looked at her new available skills, I couldn't help thinking how weird Theresia's standards were if she was hesitant to sit next to me on the couch but perfectly fine with this situation. I'd also need to choose my own new skills later.

The next morning, Falma helped prepare breakfast as thanks for letting her stay with us. There was pan-fried bacon, soup, and salad, all of which more than satisfied our morning hunger. I brought up the special contract with her again while we ate, and Falma reassured me that she would be happy to. That meant we could ask her to open Black Boxes for us in the future, too. She made some packed lunches for Ceres and the others in the workshop, and we waved good-bye from the front of the house as she headed off to the Guild's teleportation door.

"I pray for your good fortune in battle! I hope to hear from you again."

"Thank you so much, Falma. Really. Tell Eyck and Plum I said hello."

"Of course. Oh, and Mr. Atobe..." Falma seemed like she wanted to say something else. I looked at everyone around me, but for some reason, none of them would meet my eyes.

"...They all said it doesn't matter whether you're on the first or second floor—you're always protecting them. They really admire you," said Falma.

"Uh…" I hadn't thought anything of sleeping on the first floor, but apparently, that put me in a position where I was behind everyone else.

"Last night was a lot of fun. It felt like I was back in my seeking days. Everyone, make sure you stay good friends with Mr. Atobe like this from now on as well."

"W-well, I think we are all slowly getting closer as friends, but I'm not sure about anything more than that, Falma…," said Igarashi.

"You said you definitely wouldn't say anything… You really are a mischievous one," said Louisa.

Igarashi was flustered, and Louisa seemed confused but smiled. Madoka, Melissa, and Suzuna all turned bright red for some reason. Falma smiled contently as she looked at them all.

"All right, well, please feel free to use the services of Arthur Chest Cracking anytime." Falma's last words were a graceful salutation before she turned and walked away. We were also ready to go out, so we left then as well.

"…Oh, Atobe. Did you sleep okay last night?" asked Igarashi.

"Y-yeah… I slept pretty well. Did I talk in my sleep or anything?"

"N-no, you slept very quietly…," said Suzuna.

"Arihitoooo, you can't tempt Suzu! She is such a pure young girl!" cried Misaki.

"Oh, uh…I'm still half-asleep; I don't really remember what

happened. I feel like there might have been something inappropriate with Arihito…," said Suzuna.

Igarashi had seemed like she was probing for something when she asked me how I slept, but all I could really say was that I slept well. But there was something about what Falma said that caught my attention.

"……"

"Wh-what's that—? Theresia, what are you…?" Theresia's hand lightly touched my arm. Was she saying I shouldn't worry about it? On top of that, her lizard mask was slightly red.

"Moving right along… Arihito, should we go see what the Alliance is up to?" asked Elitia.

"Yeah, let's change into our new equipment, then we can head out. Madoka contacted me earlier to say Ceres and the others were done with their work."

"The Beach of the Setting Sun… Even if we do just go to check up on the Alliance, we might run into the powerful monsters that live inland. We need to stay on our toes." Igarashi was right; there was a high probability that we could run into both those spiders and mantises. We might be able to avoid fighting them if we scouted well, but I also wanted a chance to try out our new equipment and skills. There wasn't any need for us to avoid battle altogether.

I looked over the new skills everyone took again while we headed to the workshop where Ceres and the others were. I grew more and more excited as I considered how we could use them most effectively.

◆New Available Skills — Kʏᴏᴜᴋᴀ◆
Level 2 Skills
☆ Lightning Rage: Adds Lightning attribute
  to attacks along with random additional area
  attacks. (Prerequisite: Thunderbolt)
Lancer's Protection: Enemy's piercing attacks
  are nullified when skill is activated.


Level 1 Skills
Evasion Step: Dodge rate increases the more
  user evades enemy attacks. (Prerequisite:
  Mirage Step)
Throw 1: Attacks by throwing a spear. Increased
  hit rate compared to normal throwing attack.

Remaining Skill Points: 3—→0


◆New Available Skills — Tʜᴇʀᴇsɪᴀ◆
Level 2 Skills
Hidden Viper: Special demi-human skill. Allows
  user to bind target when attacking from a
  Hidden state.
Pickpocket 2: Steals multiple specified items
  from target without their knowledge.
  (Prerequisite: Pickpocket 1)
☆ Activate Trap: Activates a trap without
  touching it. Has a chance of trap affecting
  nearby people or objects. (Prerequisite: Trap
  Detection 1)

Level 1 Skills
☆ Trap Detection 1: Detects when a trap is
  nearby.

Remaining Skill Points: 3→0

◆New Available Skills — ELITIA◆
Level 3 Skills
☆ Scarlet Dance: Consumes magic while using
  Red Eye to execute a chain of attacks. Power
  increases with each attack. Effects stack until
  defense reaches zero. (Prerequisite: Red Eye)

Remaining Skill Points: 4→1

◆New Available Skills — SUZUNA◆
Level 2 Skills
Exorcism 2: Effective against undead-type
  monsters. (Prerequisite: Exorcism 1)
Dance of the Shrine Maiden: Draws target's
  attention with a dance. Increases dodge rate.

Level 1 Skills
☆ Archery Master: Increases damage from shooting
  a bow using proper archery techniques.
☆ Resonant Sound: Allows user to use musical
  instruments as weapons.
Sacred Words: Houses written characters in
  equipment, temporarily granting it the Holy
  attribute.

Remaining Skill Points: 3⟶1


◆New Available Skills — MISAKI◆
Level 2 Skills
Surrender: Makes it easier to retreat from
    battle by reducing monster's hostility. User
    is unable to re-engage target before exiting
    the labyrinth.
Extra Turn: Takes one action on behalf of
    indicated party member.


Level 1 Skills
☆ Fake Hand: Creates the illusion to the enemy
    that user's next attack will be powerful,
    canceling the enemy's action.
Small Bet: Divides user's vitality and magic
    among others during battle. Recovers twice
    the given amount when battle ends.

Remaining Skill Points: 3⟶2


◆New Available Skills — MADOKA◆
Level 2 Skills
Trade: Determines whether an item in the
    target's possession is valuable to your party
    and conducts trade negotiations for said item.
Cart Attack: When a cart is equipped,
    skill inflicts an attack whose damage is
    proportionate to the amount of goods in the
    cart. (Prerequisite: Equip Cart)

Level 1 Skills

☆ Equip Cart: Allows user to equip a cart.

☆ Bargain: Negotiates purchase of goods currently excluded from a store's available stock.

Remaining Skill Points: 4→2

◆New Available Skills — Melissa◆

Level 2 Skills

Break Bones: Adds Bludgeoning damage to attack regardless of weapon type. Inflicts greater damage than normal attack.

Loud Voice: Emits a threatening cry that causes target to faint and reduces their magic.

Level 1 Skills

Cat Walk: Allows user to pass through extremely narrow spaces.

Sharpen Nails: Increases damage of attacks inflicted with user's nails. Heals any psychological status ailments.

Remaining Skill Points: 3

In the end, there were a lot of skills that we felt could be useful, and we weren't able to immediately assign all the available points at the moment. The skills with the ☆ mark next to them were the ones we selected. We decided to hold off on the rest for now. Being unable to choose a skill among all the ones we wanted wasn't a bad problem to have.

Igarashi began to specialize in attacks so she could be the second-best attacker after Elitia. Theresia started focusing on dealing with traps, taking a role in the party that only a Rogue could. Suzuna, Misaki, and Madoka all had specialized jobs and, along with them, a lot of skills that would only be effective in specific situations. Since skill points were limited, we decided to take a few priority skills, and then the others they could take if they became absolutely necessary. I wanted to have Melissa focus on skills that would help her with her job as a dissector, but she didn't have any skills like that among the new ones she could learn. Instead, we decided to hold on to all of her skill points. She could take any appropriate skills when she was fighting with us if need be.

Then there was me and what skills I should take. As always, the decision came down to what was necessary. Cooperation Support 1 was the only one that I'd been wanting for a long time, so it was the only one I took right away.

◆New Available Skills — ARIHITO◆
Level 2 Skills
Command Support 1: Makes frontline allies
    accurately strike your current target.
    (Prerequisite: Cooperation Support 1)
Back Slip: Temporarily increases user's speed,
    allowing user to move first.
Back Order: Activates a skill with insufficient
    magic by taking a portion from your
    allies.

```
Level 1 Skills
☆ Cooperation Support 1: Activates a frontline
  ally's combined skill.
Pass Back: Passes an attack onto target behind
  you. Can only be used when there is an
  available target.

Remaining Skill Points: 3—→2
```

I'd have a hard time using Pass Back even in an emergency. I could tell it was a powerful skill, but I was generally the very last in formation in our party anyway, and we shouldn't really be making a situation in which there was someone behind me. It'd be fine if it were an enemy, but I didn't really want to get flanked like that, either. It was hard to decide which skill was best out of the level-2 ones as well. I could imagine situations in which each of the three would be useful, so I decided to take the first one that became necessary.

"I feel all excited thinking about taking a skill on the fly when I need it, you knooow? Oh, can I be all like, *You haven't seen my true power!* or something?"

"Misaki, I really hope we don't find ourselves in a situation where we need your Surrender skill, but it could end up being effective. That and Extra Turn," I said.

"If I can gain one more level, I can take them boooth. But then, I'll probably get new skills I can learn that seem good, too. Haaah. Oh, but you're so cool now, Suzu! You can use an instrument to fight."

We had Silvanus's Flute, and it would be nice if we had some-one who could equip other types of instruments if we came across them. I had suggested that, and Suzuna had agreed.

"I used to practice a few different instruments so I could play them during the kagura performances we dedicate to the gods. I should be able to use a flute, too. I don't really know how it'll be useful just yet, though..."

"You might be able to attack with the sound, since Silvanus's Messenger had an attack like that."

"I've seen a few people who could use instruments as weapons, but they often have special effects depending on the characteristics of the tone. I think if you don't have any musical performance skills, that special effect is entirely dependent on the instrument itself." According to Elitia, Guitarist and Minstrel jobs existed, but they weren't very common. That meant Suzuna's Shrine Maiden was also among the few jobs that could equip musical instruments.

"New equipment and new skills... With all this, we won't need to be afraid of any of the monsters in District Seven."

"But, Igarashi, you're getting pretty focused on attacking..."

"Atobe, I should be fine staying in the front lines and fighting as long as I can use Evasion Step effectively. I couldn't evade chain attacks with just Mirage Step."

"O-okay... But you don't need to stay up close the whole time. You have Thunderbolt, too."

"You don't have to worry about me; I won't get in too deep." Igarashi smiled as she walked ahead, but I really did worry. A

Valkyrie could be in the vanguard position, but it wasn't actually specialized in vanguard fighting.

"......"

"Woof."

"...Yeah, maybe I am just being a worrywart."

Both Theresia and Cion acted as our vanguards, making a total of four. Igarashi probably wouldn't get too far ahead of them anyway.

*"Ah, good morning. We managed to get everything done today like we promised."* Steiner was out front of the borrowed workshop waving as we approached. Ceres must have been tired and was resting. I really wanted to thank her for all her hard work.

## CHAPTER 3

# The Labyrinth Strikes Back

### Part I: Brand-New Equipment / Beach of the Setting Sun, First Floor

We entered the workshop, and the rest of the party went into the women's fitting room. I was glad coed parties were accounted for in this workshop. I could hear the girls' happy chatter from the fitting room while I put on my Hardened Ox Leather Armor +3 and Elluminate Mountaineering Boots +3, both strengthened with the materials we'd found. They now possessed medium darkness resistance and Darkness Status Resistance 1, but those attributes would only be useful against certain enemies.

*"How is the fit on the equipment, Mr. Atobe?"*

"It's really nice. Fits perfectly, unlike before... Thank you so much for finishing these in one night. You need to make sure you rest plenty today, too, Steiner."

*"I am but a simple suit of armor. Going one night without rest does not bother me."*

"What are you talking about? You were half-asleep earlier, but you didn't wake me up. Really, I can't take my eyes off an assistant like you." Ceres grimaced, still clad in her pajamas.

Melissa came out around the same time. I would've thought she'd have spent the night dissecting, but she didn't seem tired at all. "...Morning. I had breakfast with Dad and walked him to the Guild teleportation door. Arihito, is my equipment done, too?"

"Yeah, everyone's getting changed now. You can go join them." Right as she turned to leave, Theresia came out of the fitting room before the rest of the girls. Her equipment didn't look all that different, but her bodysuit was different from what she had before.

◆★Hide and Seek +3◆
> Leather bodysuit made of materials from ★Death from Above.
> Light—Shielding Bodysuit +2 used as materials to strengthen.
> Camouflage Stone allows wearer to use Active Camouflage.
> Wearer can become undetectable for a set period of time, even during battle as long as wearer is not targeted by an enemy.
> Increases ease of movement.
> Slightly increases resistance to Light attribute.
> Slightly increases resistance to reductions in defense.

Its abilities were so far beyond Theresia's previous leather bodysuit. On top of that, it was made from monster materials but had a ★ on it. Silvanus's Flute was the same, which made it seem that equipment made from materials received from Named Monsters were likely to get the star. That meant it was possible that any starred equipment we found in the labyrinth was made from materials someone got when they defeated a Named Monster.

*"We made this with both Melissa's and Rikerton's assistance. I am the only one who has skills that can bring together two pieces of equipment. Master and I spent the night sewing in the lining."*

"You did all that and more in one night... I'm sorry to make you do such taxing work, but thank you again for it." I bowed my head once more, and Steiner put their hand to their helmet in embarrassment while Ceres puffed out her pajamaed chest in pride.

"A good craftsperson always meets the delivery dates they give their clients," she said.

*"Master, you've used quite a lot of magic. You need to keep resting."*

"You're the one barely able to move your armor."

"I'm sorry to bring this up again while you're both so tired, but...I wanted to readdress you entering a special contract with us," I said, and Ceres and Steiner exchanged a glance. They both looked at me and nodded in unison. I couldn't help smiling at how perfectly in sync they were.

"From this day forward, I, Ceres Mistral, and my assistant, Chiara Steinweg, will provide for all your workshop needs..."

"...Uh, huh? Umm, Master?"

"Chiara... Is that Steiner's real name?" I asked.

"I couldn't let you keep going without knowing Chiara's real name despite entering a contract with us. Chiara's not the same race as me but is from *this side* of things."

Steiner was shocked that their real name had been revealed. Their large armored body was shaking.

"*Uh... It's not what you think. It's not like I absolutely didn't want you to know my real name; it's just that...*"

"I informed you of their name to show our sincerity in entering a contract with you, but could you continue to use the name Steiner? I apologize for asking," said Ceres.

"I know how uncomfortable you can feel if someone calls you something you don't want to be called. I look forward to working with you, Steiner," I said.

"*Y-yeah... Thank you, Mr. Atobe.*"

I shook hands with Steiner's simple suit of armor, as they called it. Next, I shook hands with Ceres. A contract could be verbal here. It would display on your license as long as both parties had confirmed that they accepted the contract.

"Hmph, we did a good job. I am very satisfied... *Yaaawn.* Indeed, I have become quite tired now that I am certain things have turned out so well," said Ceres.

"*You sound a bit like a happy king when you get that satisfied... Oh, I still feel as if my heart will burst from my chest. Anyway, Mr.*

*Atobe, I hope you don't mind if we excuse ourselves for another rest. We'll be spending the rest of our time here with Madoka, until we return to District Eight."*

"Right, thanks for looking after Madoka and Melissa."

Ceres and Steiner went back to the sleeping area of the workshop. The girls seemed to need a little longer to get changed; perhaps it was going to take longer because Melissa had arrived.

"......"

"Theresia, you'll definitely put your new equipment to good use." I was trying to say that I trusted her, but she just tilted her head to the side a little. In the moment I spent trying to figure out what that gesture meant, I saw her body suddenly *melt* into thin air.

"Ah...T-Theresia, what are you...? Aah!"

It was so fast that I could have missed it had I blinked, but there was a brief moment that Theresia's bodysuit literally turned invisible. I saw the Light-Shielding Bodysuit for a brief moment before she turned completely invisible. The whole process lasted less than a second.

"It works...really well, doesn't it? But..."

It wasn't like the heat stone, which confused the enemy's sight. This actually made her blend in perfectly with the scenery. I had no clue where she was no matter how hard I looked. This was the power of the camouflage stone. It could bring out more of a Rogue's potential for spy work.

"......"

"Um...Theresia? Where are you...?"

I sort of had the feeling that she'd moved. I called to her, but

I had absolutely no idea where she was. The invisibility was so perfect that I was starting to get worried she'd never come back. Active camouflage was a really cool idea, but I was starting to see a scarier side to it.

It was right then that I felt a tug on the sleeve of my jacket near my right elbow. I looked back to see Theresia coming out of her invisibility. Perhaps she decided to come out of it because it used magic.

"Oh, you scared me... With that suit and your chameleon boots, you're completely invisible. I wouldn't be able to find you if you went far away while using it."

"......"

Theresia shook her head and took my jacket sleeve in her hands.

"Right... I was being a worrywart again. I guess that's a bad habit of mine..."

"......"

This time she neither nodded nor shook her head. I smiled a little, thinking that she meant she couldn't deny the fact that I worried too much.

"Arihito, sorry we took so looong! My new equipment feels soooo good!" Misaki was excited as she bounced out of the fitting room, followed by each of the others. There didn't appear to be any issues in size. They all seemed a bit self-conscious but showed off their new equipment to me.

The Beach of the Setting Sun was a labyrinth located in the northeasternmost corner of District Seven. When we approached

the square in front of the entrance, we saw a large number of people who looked like the Alliance entering the labyrinth. There weren't many other people; I wondered if other Seekers avoided showing up around the Alliance. I was thinking about it while I checked our surroundings and noticed Seraphina and another woman in the square. Based on her appearance, I guessed the other woman was a Guild Savior like Seraphina.

"Good morning, Seraphina."

"Good morning, Mr. Atobe."

"Ah... You and Seraphina have spoken before, haven't you? It's nice to meet you. I'm Adeline, a member of Seraphina's squad." Adeline held out her right hand as she greeted me, and we shook hands. Seraphina was her superior, but Adeline seemed younger to me since she was a bit smaller. Her skin was dark brown, but the Labyrinth Country had people from all over the world, so that wasn't really something that made her stand out at all. Her red-tinged brown hair hung to her shoulders, and one small section was braided. If she was a reincarnate, she probably did marksmanship sports because she had a crossbow slung across her back.

"Mr. Atobe, are you planning to enter this labyrinth?" asked Seraphina.

"Yes, that's the plan."

"I...see. Oh, make no mistake—we have no intentions of interfering, but we have been asked to check the situation in this labyrinth as part of our duties."

"Seraphina, should we ask them to assist us? There's a limit to how much we can investigate, and considering the size of Beyond

Liberty...," Adeline suggested, and Seraphina looked as if she was considering it. I didn't quite understand what the two of them were doing, but it sounded like what Beyond Liberty was doing was starting to cause problems.

"I believe it would be inappropriate to ask Mr. Atobe and his party for assistance at this point in time. As a general rule, we need to complete our duties on our own."

"If there's any way we can be of assistance while we're nearby, just let us know. You've helped us out quite a few times, Seraphina," I said.

"That's right—we depend on each other. You're always too proper, Seraphina," said Adeline.

"...Really, don't get all puffed up because Mr. Atobe said he would be willing to help," snapped back Seraphina, and Adeline straightened up in fear. But it did seem like she listened to my proposal. "Very well... We will do our utmost not to interfere with your seeking. Might I ask for your assistance if we find ourselves with no other options?"

"Of course. All right, we'll go on in ahead... You two be careful."

"I'm a bit nervous because it's been so long since I've gone into the labyrinth on a mission as a party. But I should be completely safe with Seraphina as my vanguard," said Adeline. They didn't have anyone else; it was just the two of them. Seraphina, and Adeline as well, really were a step above any of the Seekers in District Seven.

The seven of us went into the labyrinth, knowing the two

Guild Saviors would be following after. We passed into the cave-like entrance and walked down a long declining slope. Partway through, I felt the teleportation sensation, and the air around me felt completely different. There was absolutely no doubt about it—I could smell salt water.

There was definitely a sea in this labyrinth, but we couldn't see it right after entering. We found ourselves in a field filled with short grass, and the cave we came through was smack dab in the middle of it. A short way ahead, there stood a practically vertical stone wall. It was formed of strange stone shapes, like stalagmites thrusting up from the earth, creating a natural barrier.

"I smell the ocean, but I can't see it... I wonder if it's on the other side of that stone wall," said Elitia.

"Woof."

"Cion seems like she's saying it's that way. Atobe, what should we do? There's a passage over there—looks like we could get through to the other side, but... Oh." Igarashi and I realized the same thing at about the same time. There was a place where we thought we might be able to pass through, but we could see Seekers nearby. They were some of the Seekers we saw earlier that looked like they could belong to the Alliance.

"That's pretty bold of them... I don't think it would be impossible to get past them, though," I said.

"Guess they're not just watching over where the monsters show up. I feel like they're gonna tell us to cough up a toll for passing!" said Misaki.

"They can't do that because their karma would go up, but if we try to force our way through, then there's a chance we'll also rack up karma," said Elitia.

"I'm sure the Alliance has its reasons... If they won't let us pass no matter what, we want to at least avoid the situation coming to blows." If we did give up on going to the other side of the stone wall, like Suzuna suggested, and instead went seeking in the fields, the Alliance member would be able to observe us fighting from far off. Considering the fact that Gray had Triceratops spy on us, there was a good chance that they'd keep their eyes peeled for our party. Granted, that was if Gray had secretly gotten to all the Alliance members.

"We shouldn't work in a way that we reveal our hand to the Alliance, but the field isn't perfectly flat, and there's some thickets and trees. There's a chance we'll end up in battle somewhere that they can't see us. When that happens, we'll fight safely and carefully," I said.

"And sometimes, we'll fight boldly! I'll fire off my explosive cards!"

"Misaki, I think you should only use your explosion stone when it's necessary. The most important thing for you is to make sure you don't run out of magic," said Elitia.

"Okaaaay, I'll be careful!" Misaki really did seem keyed up over having new equipment. I was a little concerned things wouldn't be entirely fine, but I couldn't say anything to dampen her spirits.

Seraphina and Adeline had entered the labyrinth after us and huffed when they saw the Alliance member near the passage through the stone wall.

"Mr. Atobe, if you can't pass because they're blocking the way, we can try to negotiate with them…," offered Seraphina.

"No, that sounds difficult. We couldn't pass that pregnant lady without pushing by, and even Guild Saviors like us would get a penalty for bumping them," said Adeline.

"I never said anything about *pushing by*. We could persuade them to let us pass; there's nothing wrong with that."

"Ah, Seraphina… Hey, don't just rush in!"

Seraphina had already left Adeline behind and was walking up to one of the Alliance members. She was approached by Daniella, who was assisting the Alliance in their battle strategy because of her pregnancy.

"Hello, my name is Daniella Vorn. I am second-in-command of Beyond Liberty. May I ask why the Guild Saviors are here?"

"We've received multiple reports that you have set up hunting activities here. There isn't any penalty for doing so, but we would like to ask that you allow as many Seekers as possible to hunt here." Seraphina's tone was cold and had a certain force to it, but Daniella didn't flinch at all. She simply smiled.

"District Seven is known as the elimination district. There aren't many Seekers who make it up to District Six. We have no intention of giving up on our dreams of making our way higher, and that's why we chose to work this way. I hope you can understand that."

"I do understand your intentions. However, the question is, if you use this method to move up, will you be able to establish yourselves in District Six and continue working? Is there a chance that some of your members won't be able to act unless they're hunting in safe conditions?"

They could potentially move up to District Six but then come back to previous districts if need be. It wasn't unreasonable, though, to consider if all this standardized seeking of theirs had made them unable to handle District Six's labyrinths. But it did look like the Alliance had considered that possibility. Seraphina's words seemed to bother Daniella and the Alliance members behind her.

"We, as Seekers, are aiming for somewhere, and we are going to get there our own way. There's nothing wrong with moving up to District Six safely. There's no coming back if we end up dead or turned into demi-humans. No one's going to be giving us a prize if we take a risk and some of our members lose their lives. Right?"

"…I see. But what you are doing is an infringement on other Seekers' freedom to do as they will. Please be aware that there's a chance the Guild will…adjust the contribution points of the monsters you are focusing on."

"I know. I also know that it takes at least a month to adjust it."

The Alliance members smiled like Daniella's last remark was a good retort. Seraphina didn't show any anger, but she did turn on her heel to leave.

"…It's no simple task for the Guild to revise contribution points after a monster is defeated. It may not require a whole month, but it's unlikely that any changes would take effect while they're still here in this district," Seraphina said to us after returning.

"It'd mean that other parties couldn't use the same method as them to earn contribution points. That makes the whole thing a bit complicated... What should we do, Seraphina?" asked Adeline.

"We carry out our duties. We will monitor Beyond Liberty, and that will prevent them from keeping tabs on other parties."

That meant they would be keeping the Alliance from interfering in what we did. They weren't overtly backing us, but as long as they were here, the Alliance couldn't inspect us too closely.

"Thank you, Seraphina."

"We may have monsters coming our way here; we'll handle them when that happens. I believe we should be able to manage between the two of us, so you please continue to act freely, Mr. Atobe... We'll see you around."

The rest of the party said their good-byes to Seraphina, and we started to walk across the field. We came over a gentle hill and saw a beautiful landscape dotted with trees.

"Huh? Arihito, there's some white flowers in bloom around here," said Misaki.

"...Are they just flowers?" said Suzuna.

Like they said, there were what looked like white flowers scattered across the field. Elitia stopped Cion and faced me with an expression that seemed to ask how we should proceed. Everyone was probably suspicious because the flowers weren't growing in one concentrated area—they were spaced out fairly evenly. It felt like they floated throughout the entire area because there wasn't anything to obstruct them.

"We could hit one from a distance with something. Seems a bit mean if they're just normal flowers, though...," I said.

"What if I use my Decoy to get closer?"

"Oh, that's a good idea, Igarashi. Please do."

Igarashi pulled a doll from her pouch and placed it on the ground before reciting the incantation.

"Human form born from the earth, imbued with my magic! Rise up and be the vanguard to draw the demon's gaze."

The mud doll absorbed Igarashi's magic, then grew to almost the same size as a human. It moved in closer to the white flowers and...nothing happened. The rest of us approached one of the blossoms. The white parts appeared to be cotton; maybe these were cotton flowers or similar.

"This looks like it could be used as a material for something...," said Igarashi.

"There's a lot of them. Maybe we should grab some? Though, I'd rather fight a monster and do some trial runs than collect materials."

We split up and gathered a number of the cotton flowers. We didn't know what they could be used for, but we didn't need to be afraid of them for now.

But right when we started to feel at ease, Theresia stopped as she was nearing one of the flowers.

"Theresia, what's wrong?" I asked.

"......"

I could tell from her gaze that there was something, and I

checked my license. There was an entry other than us collecting this pure-white cotton wool.

```
◆Current Status◆
> THERESIA activated TRAP DETECTION 1 ⟶ Trap
                                           discovered
Capable of activation
```

"Ah… Everyone, watch out. Theresia's found a trap."

"In the middle of a field…?" asked Elitia.

"Maybe the white flowers are supposed to lure people in and then catch them in the trap…?" wondered Igarashi as the two of them looked where Theresia was staring.

*Should we…attack? Actually, maybe we should make it catch nothing with Activate Trap if that'll work at a distance…*

"All right… Let's try activating the trap with Theresia's new skill. We shouldn't get caught in it if we're far enough away."

"Oh my gooosh, this is so exciting… Traps are set by somebody, right?" said Misaki.

"I think a monster might have set it. I doubt the Alliance has any reason to come all the way out here."

"If it was a monster, they probably set the trap and are lying in wait…"

We got into our battle formation, and Theresia held her hand out in front of us, to something that just looked like more white flowers. The next moment:

◆Current Status◆
> THERESIA used ACTIVATE TRAP
> TRAPDOOR WEB trap set by ARACHNOPHILIA activated

"—Aaaah!!"

The ground rumbled and shook. Centering on the white flowers and spreading out across the ground was what looked like a spider's web.

"Aaah... Wh-what is this?!"

A pit was dug into the ground, then a lid was made of spider's silk. The top of the lid was covered in dirt and flowers to blend in with the surrounding, but the monster must have had a special skill for it because the camouflage was perfect. We could have easily fallen in if we'd been caught in the trap. That wasn't the end to it, either. A number of sharpened talon-like appendages fiercely struck out at the center of the web.

"That's Arachnophilia... The spider monster!" cried Elitia.

The monster in the bottom of the pit finally realized it had missed its prey and appeared before us. It was a spiderlike creature massive enough to easily eat a human whole.

## Part II: Cooperation Support

◆Monster Encountered◆
ARACHNOPHILIA

Level 6
In Combat
Dropped Loot: ???


The monster leaped from the pit, seemingly unhindered by the threads it created, and landed in front of the trap. The multiple eyes on the shell-covered section I assumed was its head looked our way.

"GII…GIIGIII…"

It wasn't a Named Monster, but it was so enormous and menacing that it rendered the entire concept of an "ordinary monster" pointless. This thing was far more intimidating than something like a Grand Mole.

There was a large lump on the creature's back that made it resemble both a spider and a scorpion. I couldn't even fathom what purpose it served.

"It kinda looks less like a spider and more like a robot with scratchy fur… Urgh," said Misaki.

"There are a lot of tough monsters in District Seven… But as long as Arihito's here…," said Elitia.

"First, I'm going to attack from afar! Everyone, brace yourselves!"

"Okay!"

I used Morale Support 1 to increase everyone's morale, then loaded my magic gun with an elastic stone. I wanted to first test it with a normal single attack to see if it would be effective for using with Attack Support 2.

"—Take this!"

◆Current Status◆
> Arihito loaded Magic Gun with Elastic Stone
> Arihito fired Soft Bullet ⟶ Hit Arachnophilia
Delay added

I aimed my gun and pulled the trigger. The hammer struck, and the magic from the stone I used to charge the gun was fired. The spinning light roared as it struck the spider's head, exploding with an incredible sound.

"—GIIII!!"

Perhaps it was a special effect of the elastic stone, but the impact didn't stop at the creature's surface. It seemed to reverberate throughout its body. I scanned my license and saw the spider had been delayed. The shock had passed through its body, slowing its actions.

The magic stone was ejected from the gun like a spent cartridge, now useless after being shot. Considering how powerful it was, though, there was plenty to be gained from using the magic gun in the appropriate battle conditions.

"Now's our chance... Kyouka, Cion, let's go!" cried Elitia.

"Right! ...Let's do this, Cion!"

"Awooooo!"

◆Current Status◆
> Kyouka activated Wolf Pack ⟶ Kyouka's and Cion's
  abilities rose

```
> ELITIA activated SONIC RAID
> CION activated BATTLE HOWL ⟶ Vanguards' attack
  power rose
```

Cion used a new skill to increase the three vanguards' attack power, and then...

*The three of them can make a good combination attack... I wonder what'll happen if I add that skill here!*

"—Cooperation Support...vanguards!"

Since the skill was level 1, I pretty much just expected it to increase the damage after everyone had attacked.

"Ah... Is this...Atobe's orders...?"

"Cion will break through, and we'll push forward!"

I didn't know all of Cion's skills, but it occurred to me a chain of attacks, including Cion's own, would cause a lot of damage.

"—Booowwow!"

"I'll cut you down!"

```
◆Current Status◆
> ARIHITO activated COOPERATION SUPPORT 1 and ATTACK
  SUPPORT 1
> CION activated SHOULDER TACKLE ⟶ Hit ARACHNOPHILIA
Reduces defense
Combined attack stage 1
> ELITIA activated ARMOR BREAK ⟶ Hit ARACHNOPHILIA
Reduces defense
Combined attack stage 2
```

The first attack was Cion coating her shoulder in magic and crashing into the spider.

"GIIIII!!!"

Afterward came Elitia, lashing out with Armor Break, a strike that could pierce into an enemy's armor. Cion had thrown the spider off balance, reducing its defense, and Elitia reduced it even more.

They weren't done yet, though.

"Kyouka!"

"Here I go...hyaaaa!"

◆Current Status◆
> Kyouka activated Spiral Lightning ⟶ Hit Arachnophilia
Caused Electrocution
Combined attack stage 3
> Combined attack: Tackle, Brake, Spiral
36 support damage
12 additional cooperation damage

The last to add on her attack was Igarashi. She blasted off Spiral Lightning using the power of her lightning topaz.

"—GIIIGIIIGI...GAA...GAGAAAH!"

◆Current Status◆
> Arachnophilia was immobilized
Continued Electrocuted state

* * *

Electricity ran through the spider's whole body, making it stagger. It took support damage for the three attacks, and it looked like another attack's worth was added in. I couldn't believe the fight was going this well. Even Suzuna, who had activated Archery Master and was preparing to fire, glanced at me to ask if she should fall back.

"I want to finish it off here. Next, us rearguards will do a combined long-range attack…"

"—Mr. Atobe, don't let your guard down! That spider's—!"

"Huh…b-but it can barely move at all…"

The voice that had called out to us was Seraphina's. Apparently, she could see us even at a distance. She probably had experience fighting these creatures given how she was able to warn us of an incoming attack.

*Can we…beat it to the punch…? No, right now it's—!*

"—Everyone, pull back from the spider!" I cried.

Elitia and the others had been about to strike again, but the spider's many eyes glittered in anticipation.

◆Current Status◆
> Arachnophilia canceled Play Dead ⟶ Electrocuted and Delay statuses removed
> Arachnophilia activated Web Spinner

"Wha—?!"

A massive stinger unlike what you'd expect from a spider

grew from the monster's body and pierced the ground. The next moment, its legs, which had been planted firmly, lifted up, and it began spinning around violently, spewing white silk everywhere.

"Ack!"

"Booow!"

"Aaaah!"

The only way a rearguard could prevent the vanguards from getting pulled into an attack was if they staggered their attacks with the vanguards', but this counterattack forcefully prevented us from doing that. There was no way to avoid it from the moment we saw the stinger.

"Oh no… A-Arihito, what do we do?!" asked Misaki.

"Arihito, it's transforming!" said Suzuna.

◆Current Status◆
> Kyouka, Elitia, and Cion were captured
> Arachnophilia activated Shape Change ⟶ Changed into Arachnomage

"Wh-what is that…? Part human, part spider…?"

The lump on the spider's body had in fact been the upper half of a human form, bent over and concealed. It appeared to be wearing some sort of hooded robe, like that of a sorcerer. With my Hawk Eyes skill, I could see that what looked like clothing was in fact the same material as the spider's body.

"Mr. Atobe!" Seraphina started rushing toward us. Even if she was coming to assist us, our captured members were sure to take an attack before she arrived.

"Dammit... I can't get these threads off me...!"

"Elitia, stop! You'll just get more tangled if you touch them!" I called to her.

We needed a way to cut the threads. If we couldn't do it with physical attacks, we'd have to use something else. We could use magic stones, but what would be most effective?

◆Current Status◆
> Arachnomage began casting a spell

The human part of the spider started emitting a purple light from its hands. I couldn't hear its voice, but I could see with Hawk Eyes that its lips were moving. It must have been reciting some incantation.

Magic gun, slingshot, Suzuna's bow, Misaki's cards... None of our different attacks were fast enough that we could guarantee they'd cut off the spell. Even so, we were all prepared to shoot out of sheer desperation when I realized something.

*There... She's there, I can tell. Theresia!*

I couldn't see her, but she was waiting for my orders. Even though she was invisible, I could tell she was in front of me.

"—Theresia, I'll support you!"

◆Current Status◆
> Arihito activated Attack Support 2 ⟶ Support Type:
                                    Force Shot (Stun)

```
>  THERESIA activated SNEAK ATTACK  →  Damage to
                                         ARACHNOMAGE doubled
>  THERESIA activated ACCEL DASH  →  Canceled ACTIVE
                                        STEALTH
```

Theresia had decided to use her camouflage stone to activate Active Stealth, then circled around the enemy. Since the enemy wasn't aware of her, she could use one of her new skills: Sneak Attack.

The Paradox Beetle had used its horn for a skill called Razor Horn. Now, that horn had been put into Theresia's sword, and it glowed with a blue light from the blue flame stone.

"......!"

"—KIIIAAAAA!"

Even from where I was, I could see where Theresia had circled behind the spider and attacked. There was a flash of blue light, and the human part of the spider screamed in agony before falling over forward.

```
◆Current Status◆
>  ARACHNOMAGE partial destruction
>  ARACHNOMAGE burned magic
Slight knockback
>  ATTACK SUPPORT 2 activated  →  ARACHNOMAGE was STUNNED
Action canceled
```

"Wow...Theresia, you've gotten soooo strong!" cried Misaki.

"—Theresia, evade! It's going to counterattack with silk!" I shouted.

"......!"

◆Current Status◆
> ARACHNOMAGE activated REVENGE SPIRAL ⟶ Skills can activate immediately
> ARACHNOMAGE activated WEB SPINNER
> THERESIA activated MIRAGE and SHADOW STEP
> THERESIA evaded WEB SPINNER

Theresia's form slowly wavered. She wasn't reactivating Active Stealth, which had stopped when she attacked. Instead, she was cleverly combining her evasion-type skills to draw the enemy's attention and dodge the threads it shot out. If the enemy had been completely unable to see Theresia, it might have targeted Elitia and the others who were trapped in its web. But Theresia couldn't keep up using these skills or she'd run out of magic.

"Suzuna, Misaki! It's our turn now!" I called.

""Got it!""

Suzuna had finished preparing Archery Master, and Misaki was once again raring to go. There was absolutely nothing wrong with that now. By using the attacks of us three rearguards in tandem, we could use another combined attack. Theresia was drawing the spider's attention, and by the time it realized we were making a move, it was too late.

"Cooperation Support...rearguards!"

"—!"

The human-half body part of the spider spread its hands, and with Hawk Eyes, I could see that its mouth was moving again. But I was already pulling the trigger of my magic gun before the spell could take effect.

*Can I support two people with one bullet…? However this goes, just let this be where we finish it off!*

```
◆Current Status◆
> Arihito activated Cooperation Support 1
> Arihito activated Attack Support 2 ⟶ Support Type:
                                         Soft Bullet
> Arihito fired Soft Bullet ⟶ Hit Arachnomage
Delay added
Combined attack stage 1
> Suzuna activated Storm Arrow ⟶ Hit Arachnomage
Delay increased
Speed reduced
Combined attack stage 2
> Misaki activated Blast Card ⟶ Hit Arachnomage
Arachnomage fainted
Dropped 1 material
Combined attack stage 3
```

My bullet struck the human part of the spider, causing it to stagger. Suzuna's gale-wrapped arrow hit its body, the strong winds whipping around it and slowing its movements. Like an attempt to make sure it was finished, Misaki's card flew into the spider and exploded around it.

"GIIII…AAAAH…"

◆Current Status◆
> Combined attack: Bullet, Storm, Blast ⟶ Hit
                                           Arachnomage
Fainted state extended

When the third stage hit, the combined attack added another attack, leaving the spider completely unable to move. The strength suddenly went out of its legs, and it collapsed to the ground. The robe-like section that covered the human part fell open, exposing the skin beneath. I tried to tell myself it was definitely a monster, but it resembled a human in the same way as the Demi-Harpies. I didn't have it in me to make the move and finish it off. Elitia had her sword ready, but she was waiting for my decision.

"I can't keep showing mercy to monsters just because they have parts that look exactly like humans, but…," I said.

"Well, we could also capture it. We can still get materials from it after we send it to the Monster Ranch anyway," suggested Elitia.

"Won't the people in the ranch be afraid of such a gigantic spider? Hmm, but this part looks like a woman… Oh, it's my fault she went through so much…urgh," said Misaki.

"Oh… A-Arihito, please turn away for a moment. I have a towel; I'll cover her," said Suzuna.

"Wait. Her skin might be poisonous. My shoes have Poison Resistance 2, so I should be fine if I climb up and only touch her with my shoes." Elitia took Suzuna's towel and jumped up on the spider, laying the towel over the human part to cover her. I couldn't watch this part.

"Atobe, what should we do? Have the Demi-Harpies put her to sleep, or...?" said Igarashi.

"Having them continue that for a long time would be tough on their magic. Considering how powerful the spider is, too, I'm hesitant to leave the Demi-Harpies to keep an eye on her..."

It looked like our only option was to take it to the Monster Ranch for them to take care of her, but right when I was thinking that, Seraphina hesitantly approached from where she had been watching.

## Part III: What Emerges from the Ocean's Depths

"Mr. Atobe, everyone, I apologize. It's inappropriate for an outsider such as myself to barge in..."

"No, it's wonderful actually. Thank you for watching over us," I said.

"I-it's nothing... I don't deserve such kind words. I requested again from the Alliance that they allow us to observe what is happening on the beach, but it does seem at this point that the only thing we can do is advise them not to take over the hunting grounds..."

"Today's apparently an important day for the Alliance; they just turned us away again. Does being a Guild Savior really mean that little?" Adeline shrugged as she followed Seraphina over to us. The same thing would probably happen to us if we went, but it was pointless if we left the labyrinth now.

"...Oh, are you not going to finish off this spider?"

"No, we were thinking we wanted to capture it... We were just trying to decide if we should leave the labyrinth for a bit."

"You can bind it safely with a capture rope, though you need a skill to use it," said Adeline.

"Oh... Well, we don't have one. I have used normal rope to capture Demi-Harpies before, though. Sorry I couldn't use your advice."

"You used normal rope...on Demi-Harpies... You say that with such a straight face. Atobe, I didn't realize you were into that kind of thing."

"Adeline, stop chatting while you're on duty. Mr. Atobe, would you allow us to bind this Arachnomage with a capture rope? I imagine it will be out for another couple of hours, but it will slowly regain consciousness," said Seraphina.

"That would be a great help, if you don't mind."

"Understood, Commander Seraphina. I'll do it properly; no need to get so angry with me." Adeline actually called Seraphina *commander* when obeying orders. She pulled a rope from her pouch-like inventory and bound the spider before you could say *spiderweb*. Apparently, she used a skill called Rope Bind in the process.

"Assuming they come collect the spider as soon as possible, what should we do next...?" I said.

"Arihito, should we try to find a way to go see the beach side? I'm sure we could find a back way through so the Alliance wouldn't notice us...," suggested Elitia.

"We could try, but how should we do it...? What if we ask the Demi-Harpies to carry us through the sky?" Igarashi said as she pointed to the sky. Right around then I was thinking about the Demi-Harpies and realized something: We couldn't tell how high the stone wall was from the bottom, but the Demi-Harpies should be able to fly over it. Spiders were good at climbing walls, too, actually. If we managed to train this spider enough that it would help us, we could ride on it to get over the nearly vertical wall. But right now, that wasn't an option, and the only other option we really had was to negotiate with the Alliance and try to pass through.

"I am sorry—if only I was better at negotiating...," said Seraphina.

"No, there's not much you can do since the Alliance isn't actually breaking any rules. But we didn't come to this labyrinth solely to hunt crabs. At least we've accomplished something by defeating the spider. It's because we went through that process that we can argue against fighting monsters in the same way over and over..." I didn't think they'd listen to our argument just because things went well for us, though. It'd be hard to talk to them because they'd probably think that all we wanted to do was hunt the crabs ourselves.

"You've considered that much when dealing with the spider... Mr. Atobe, you are a very logical person," said Seraphina.

"N-no, actually... To be honest, it's just a reason I added on after the fact."

"Arihito's blushing... He's so cute when he does that, right, Suzu?" said Misaki.

"Uh... C-cute isn't really something you say about a grown man..."

"Woof!"

While Suzuna was flustered by Misaki's statement, Cion barked happily. Maybe she was agreeing with Misaki...or maybe I was overthinking.

"Seraphina, we can't leave after only having a staring match with the Alliance. Should we use my skill to investigate what's happening on the other side?" suggested Adeline.

"But it's inappropriate to meddle too much in the Seekers' affairs..."

"Generally, yes, but there are exceptions, aren't there? I believe it's fine to approach this instance like that. Even if we're wrong, rule one of being a Guild Savior is to consider all possibilities in order to prevent disaster."

Seraphina turned around and stared up at the cliffs after Adeline made her argument. She closed her eyes and took a breath, before turning to face her subordinate again.

"You're right... Adeline, can you do a search to see what the leader of the Alliance is up to?"

"No trouble at all. My job's Hunter; that's our bread and butter. All right, let's move around so those people from the Alliance can't see us. The closer to the cliffs the better."

We followed Adeline until she reached a certain point, pulled the crossbow from her back, and set it up on the ground pointing toward the top of the cliffs.

"Okay... Step back just a little, please." Adeline turned the handle on the crossbow's grip and pulled the string taught. The tension was so great it looked difficult for a human to pull it back by hand.

"Arrow filled with my magic, take this momentary life and become my obedient familiar!"

◆Current Status◆
> ADELINE activated ARROW FAMILIAR ⟶ Created 1 ARROW
                                              FAMILIAR
> ADELINE activated SEARCH ARROW ⟶ Fired ARROW FAMILIAR

Adeline poured her magic into the arrow and fired it into the sky. Just as it looked like it reached the height of its trajectory and was going to start losing speed, it flew off as if it had wings and climbed even farther.

"That cliff is so high...but it got past it somehow. It might be a feature of this labyrinth, but it appears infinitely high when you're at the bottom, even though it's really only about a third of a mile high."

"Adeline, what is the Alliance doing currently? And their target monster...?" asked Seraphina, and Adeline put a hand to her mouth in shock.

"Wh-what are they doing? They're... They didn't have to go this far; there's other ways... Ah, S-Seraphina!"

Seraphina's expression clouded over as she looked at Adeline's license.

"...It must be because their hunting has been abnormally stable until now, making it very efficient. But...there's a tiny chance that this could be part of the 'conditions' necessary to..."

"What's going on?" I asked, and Adeline let me see her license. It showed what the Arrow Familiar could see the Alliance doing on the other side of the wall.

```
◆Current Status◆
> GRAY used MONSTER-SUMMONING CHARM —→ Failure
> GRAY used MONSTER-SUMMONING CHARM —→ Failure
> GRAY used MONSTER-SUMMONING CHARM —→ Success
> 1 GHOST SCISSORS appeared
> ROLAND's party defeated 1 GHOST SCISSORS
> GRAY used MONSTER-SUMMONING CHARM —→ Failure
> GRAY used MONSTER-SUMMONING CHARM —→ Failure
> GRAY used MONSTER-SUMMONING CHARM —→ Failure
```

"What is this...? It's like the monsters are..."

"...being lured out and hunted. They're not waiting for them to appear naturally."

"Seraphina, this *Ghost* part... The priests say you shouldn't hunt undead-type monsters unless you have the proper countermeasure against them... This really isn't good!" said Adeline.

I was curious what this countermeasure was, but I had the impression that you could end up cursed if you killed dozens of a monster with *ghost* in the name. I wasn't certain if that kind of curse existed in the Labyrinth Country, but there was the job Shrine Maiden, which came along with a lot of ghost-related skills. It wasn't entirely impossible.

The rest of the party was also looking at Adeline's license, lost for words. Only one Ghost Scissors appeared. They must have already defeated the monster they called the crab. Now, we only saw displays that they used a summoning charm, with the occasional monster appearing and being defeated.

"Based on the information we received, they started using those summoning charms today. If they're resorting to using items to force monsters to appear, they must have already hunted a significant number of them...," I said.

"Ah... Atobe, look! The display changed!" said Igarashi, and I felt my blood run cold. Shivers of dread greater than I'd ever experienced running down my spine.

"What...? Ugh...I feel like my head's going to explode..."

"Suzu?!"

It wasn't just me—apparently everyone was feeling it, but Suzuna was the most sensitive of us all. She turned pale, and her hair stuck to the sweat slicking her cheeks.

"Arihito... There's something...sinister on the other side of the wall...," said Adeline.

"Woof, woof! Grrrrr..."

"......"

Cion barked toward the cliffs, and Theresia stared in the same direction. That's when I saw that Theresia also had a cold sweat on her face. Just like Suzuna, she seemed to be sensing something menacing.

"Is the monster...trying to get revenge for its fallen companions...?" asked Elitia. She, Igarashi, and Adeline were staring wide-eyed at Adeline's license. I felt so terrible I thought I might vomit, but I pushed the feeling aside and forced myself to look at the license's display.

◆Current Status◆
> Roland's party defeated 1 Ghost Scissors
> Ghost Scissors activated Ocean's Grudge
Unidentified Monster appeared
> ??? activated Bubble Laser

"Ah?!" Adeline cried out, and her license's display automatically changed. It showed that the familiar she'd made with Arrow Familiar had been destroyed.

"What is going on over there...? Is this terrible feeling... because that unidentified monster appeared...?" asked Igarashi.

"It's most likely...a Named Monster. The Alliance used summoning charms to kill an excessive amount of one type of monster, accidentally fulfilling the special requirements to make it appear...," answered Seraphina. The unforeseen circumstances changed nothing for the two Guild Saviors.

"Seraphina, we should call the military!"

"I have decided that at this point in time, we have reached the requirements necessary to justify stepping in on Beyond Liberty's actions. Adeline, you leave the labyrinth and report on the situation. I will go see this unidentified monster," said Seraphina. Adeline looked like she wanted to say something, but she saw Seraphina's expression and swallowed back her words.

"...Understood. But, Commander Seraphina, if you go alone..."

Seraphina looked at me. Knowing her, she'd be hesitant to ask us for help even though we talked about it before. But this wasn't the time to stand around deciding what to do.

"I'll go over there with the members of my party who can run quickly if need be. We have a way to get past the Alliance members blocking the way," I said.

"...Please, Mr. Atobe."

"Fast party members... So Cion, Elitia, Theresia...Atobe, and me...," said Igarashi.

Considering the number of Demi-Harpies we had, we could only take three people over, including me. Cion was too big, so she'd have to wait. We needed to choose two more.

"Arihito, I can use my own skills to get past the Alliance. Take Theresia and Kyouka with you," said Elitia.

"All right. Igarashi, do you mind? And, Theresia...you don't have to push yourself."

"......"

Theresia shook her head. Did she mean it wasn't pushing herself to do it? Igarashi smiled when she saw it, too, then nodded to me to accept the task.

"Misaki and I will go with Cion toward the path to the beach.

Even if we can't get through, our skills might be able to reach," said Suzuna.

"It looks like the Alliance has gone all crazy since we've been talking." Misaki was right, they seemed to be arguing about something. Daniella was trying to go over to the beach, and the other members were stopping her.

"Let me go; I can fight, too! Roland would—he plans to fight!"

"Calm down, please. Roland said not to come... He's confident he can handle it—that's what that guy said!" yelled one of the young men in the Alliance. They hadn't yet realized that we'd come close. Elitia was in the lead and aimed for a crack in their lines where they'd stopped focusing on blocking the path, speeding up even more.

"Mr. Atobe, could you handle things in the front? I'm not far behind you!" said Seraphina.

"Understood!"

She seemed to want to try persuading the Alliance one last time. I ran after Elitia as I pulled out my summoning stones, gripped them tight, and called, "Come forth, Demi-Harpies!"

◆Current Status◆
> Arihito summoned Asuka, Himiko, and Yayoi

"Ah... Y-you—you're in the suit-wearing guy's party!"

"—Stay right there. Don't you move a muscle!" said Elitia.

◆Current Status◆
> Elitia activated Sonic Raid

For a brief moment, it was completely impossible to follow Elitia. She rushed between the seven members of the Alliance so fast they couldn't even lay eyes on her. The big man blocking the path leading to the beach reacted too slowly. By the time he looked up, Elitia had bounded off the stone walls of the path and somersaulted over him.

"...Huh?"

The District Seven Seekers had never seen someone move like Elitia and couldn't even perceive her she was moving so fast. The moment the large clueless guy cried out, Theresia, Igarashi, and I followed after Elitia, carried higher by the Demi-Harpies.

"Y-you!" The man holding back Daniella shouted after us, but we didn't have time to worry about them.

We passed through the narrow gap between the towering rocks and could tell that the saltwater smell really did come from the beach we saw before us. But that wasn't all: We were still far away, and it was hard to get a good look, but the previously pure-white sand was dotted with red marks around Roland's party.

"That attack from earlier even got them!"

"I don't know if they were just caught up in it, or if the monster aimed at them...but either way, they're in no condition to keep fighting!"

A gash cut the beach in two and continued up the cliffs. Something in the ocean had unleashed an attack. That was what had destroyed Adeline's arrow, and it had left Alliance members with horrific injuries.

"You're asking for harm when you use harmful methods!"

"—Elitia!"

The Demi-Harpies would likely die if they took a single hit, so I couldn't use them to cast Lullaby. I undid the summon and followed Theresia and Igarashi as they rushed after Elitia. It was still quite a way to where Roland and his party were even for Elitia and her high Sonic Raid speed.

```
◆Current Status◆
> ARIHITO activated HAWK EYES ⟶ Increased ability
  to monitor the situation
```

Even from this distance I could see dozens of felled human-sized crabs—most likely the Ghost Scissors—each with one massive overgrown claw. Nearby was a gaping hole in the beach. That must be the monsters' nest that the Alliance had staked out.

Near the hole stood Roland, with what looked like a saber in his hand. Gray's legs had given out from under him in fear, and he was staring at the ocean. I followed his gaze and saw another crab breaking the surface of the water. It was ten times bigger than the ones on the beach.

```
◆Monster Encountered◆
★MERCILESS GUILLOTINE
Level 8
Variable Resistances
Area Effect: FEAR
Dropped Loot: ???
```

*   *   *

*That area effect... Does that mean it inflicts Fear on people in the area just by appearing? That's gotta be the source of this feeling of dread!*

"Why...am I so scared? We don't have time for that..."

"......!"

Luckily, Elitia wasn't affected by Fear, but Igarashi and Theresia were. They slowed, losing their will to fight.

"Igarashi, use Mist of Bravery please!" I cried.

Igarashi realized what was causing the strange feeling and quickly pulled herself together. They could use their morale to recover from the status effect, but it was better to use a skill to keep the morale for later.

"Theresia, Atobe, come close to me!"

◆Current Status◆

> Kyouka activated Mist of Bravery ⟶
  Kyouka's and Theresia's Fear status was removed

Using Mist of Bravery once can continue to suppress Fear for a period of time. The fact that most of the Alliance members were unable to move, though, meant they had neither resistance to Fear nor a method for removing it.

The only one among them not affected by Fear was Roland, and he didn't look back toward his companions. He stood, staring down the massive crab in the sea. I assumed it was a Named version of the Ghost Scissors, but it had some differences in its shape.

Its left pincer was abnormally large, but its right wasn't the shape of a pincer at all; it seemed more like a scythe. Maybe the right one was formed in a different shape for a different purpose, like taking advantage of openings made with the oversized left pincer.

The creature hadn't even come on land yet, but it'd managed to devastate Roland's party with a single long-range attack. Five of them were injured while Gray and one other member managed to get by without a direct hit, but they'd already lost their will to fight.

"Run, all of you! Thomas, give me just one setup, though!" called Roland.

"—M-morons...urgh, this is ridiculous. Like hell I'm gonna fight against a monster like that!" Gray shouted as Roland rushed ahead. Thomas, the only other member with minor injuries, knew what skill he should use.

"—Haaaaaaaaah!"

◆Current Status◆
> Thomas activated Springboard —→ Produced a temporary launchpad
> Roland activated Sky High

The sky was so blue it chilled you to the bone. Roland let out a battle cry that echoed across the entire beach and leaped higher than I ever believed someone could. That must be a combo that they knew was sure to bring them victory. Thomas's skill made footing for Roland, regardless of the fact that they were on soft sand, and Roland increased his jump height to fly high in the sky, attacking the enemy from directly above. Louisa had said his job was Air Trooper. That meant that even in the Labyrinth Country, he was specialized in aerial attacks.

"Wait! If you miss—!" Elitia's shout didn't reach him. Gray was surprised when he realized Elitia had come near and skittered backward on the sand. He finally got up and ran away, panicked from Fear and screaming the whole time.

"AAAaaaaaah, aaaaaah!!"

*He's just...ugh, he's just going to leave Roland and the others!*

I had no obligation to assist with Roland's attack, but I couldn't leave him there alone, fighting against a monster ten times larger than him.

◆Current Status◆
> Arihito activated Outside Assist
> Arihito activated Attack Support 2 ⟶ Support Type:
                                           Force Shot (Stun)
> Roland activated Vapor Dive

I considered the possibility that the set damage would make it through the massive creature's defenses, but my highest priority was making an opening for Roland to get away after he made his attack.

From the corner of my Hawk Eyes' expanded field of vision, I saw Gray use a Return Scroll, and he disappeared along with his collapsed allies. Thomas tried to run as well, but perhaps he was outside of the range of the Return Scroll, and he failed to make his escape.

"—Diiiieeeeee!" Roland left a white trail behind him like an airplane as he cut through the blue sky and attempted to pierce his saber into the giant crab's head. It didn't seem like the crab could do anything about attacks from directly above, but...

The top half of the crab showed above the water, its movements restricted by the crashing white waves. Without a single sign of warning, though, it suddenly turned transparent, like a ghost.

"Roland!"

◆Current Status◆
> ★Merciless Guillotine activated Phantom Drift ⟶
  Resistance Change: Immune to physical attacks
  Speed increased
> ★Merciless Guillotine nullified Vapor Dive

As if to make light of all our hopes, Roland's attack struck nothing but air. A pillar of water erupted from the sea's surface as he plummeted into it. It took a long time for me to finally feel the racing of my heart, to hear Elitia, Igarashi, and I screaming wordless screams. Roland swung his saber at the crab, which had gone behind him. But before his blade landed, not the left pincers but the right sickle-shaped appendage flashed across and struck him.

◆Current Status◆
> ★MERCILESS GUILLOTINE activated SOUL-STEALING SCYTHE
→ Hit ROLAND

The scythe the giant crab wielded didn't strike Roland with a physical attack. It passed through, stealing something from Roland. I looked at my license, and my heart dropped. If that display was true, then Roland...

◆Current Status◆
> ROLAND'S soul was stolen

"...What the...? Why did it have to...?"

"Atobe, pull it together! If we don't do something, we'll also be—"

"Kyouka, Theresia, get out of here! This monster is too dangerous!" Elitia didn't pull back; she faced the monster to challenge it. No, she was aware of the danger and was being cautious. But that wasn't the only reason. Elitia couldn't run because she couldn't abandon another party even if they were our rivals.

The logical part of me said that we couldn't save Roland, and therefore it was obvious that we should run. But what if he could be saved? The possibility lingered in my mind, and reinforcing that was the bluish-white light now hovering near the crab after being extracted from Roland's body. But then—

◆Current Status◆
> ★MERCILESS GUILLOTINE activated SOUL TENTACLE →
Captured ROLAND'S soul

—a sea anemone–like tentacle extended from the crab's back and grabbed the light. It was a monster that cut down and bound the souls of Seekers. It was almost like revenge for continued hunting of its kind.

But the fact that his soul was captured indicted there was a chance to me—a chance that Roland's soul wasn't yet lost.

"Elitia, its resistance just changed—now it's immune to physical attacks! I know only my support attacks will get through, but can you lure it somehow?!"

"For a few minutes maybe… I'm not gonna let a stupid crab treat us like we're nothing!" said Elitia bravely, then activated Sonic Raid. The crab's giant pincers swung down but missed, kicking up sand as it crashed. Then—

"Mr. Atobe, please flee now! You can't beat that monster with your current abilities!" said Seraphina.

"Arihito, tell me if there's something I can do!" called Misaki.

"Arihito, you can't get too close… That monster is dangerous!" said Suzuna.

"Woooof!"

Seraphina and the others came running over, perhaps able to finally reason with the Alliance now that they were panicked.

"It has a long-range attack! If it looks like it's going to use it, run sideways! It's fast then, too, so you need to keep a good distance!" I ordered.

""""Understood!"""" they all replied.

Seraphina went in front of me and took a defensive stance. This battle formation meant I was at lower risk of being targeted by the giant crab, and I could still support the vanguards.

"Leader, say something! Roland! ...Dammiiiit!" The man named Thomas wasn't running and leaving Roland behind—he was trying to rescue him. Even if Roland's soul had been captured, as long as his body was safe, then... I hoped I was right, but there was no guarantee we could save him. Even so, if I ran now without doing anything, I was certain I'd regret it. Even if the Alliance brought this on themselves, it was wrong to say that they had to die because of it.

"Let's save those two from the Alliance and then get out of here... Seraphina, that's what we need to focus on."

"...Mr. Atobe... How far will someone like you go...?"

"I know what I'm saying is stupid, but even so, I..."

"You're not stupid, Arihito," said Misaki.

"Misaki's right. I feel the same way as you, Arihito. If we all work together, surely when can get back safely!" said Suzuna.

The two of them should have been scared, but they didn't run.

Seraphina didn't say anything else—she simply readied her shield facing forward. "I will protect you all... No attack will get behind me!"

The crab raised its gigantic pincers again. When Elitia drew the attack, then dodged, Theresia and Igarashi moved in. I focused on one thing: supporting their attacks.

## Part IV: Facing Death on the Shoreline

There appeared to be another hole to a crabs' nest on the beach, but the Alliance members near it had seen Roland's party destroyed and were completely unable to move.

"All of you, run! You don't have to try and support us!" Seraphina called to them, and the party in the left rear finally started to react. They used a scroll to teleport out. All who remained on the beach now were Seraphina, my party, Roland collapsed in the shallows, and Thomas.

The massive crab's eyes kept moving even while Elitia evaded its attack. It turned its attention to another target. Thomas looked like a close-range fighter, but based on his armor, there was no way he could take a hit from the giant crab.

"Kyouka, Theresia, stay far enough back that you don't get pulled in!" shouted Elitia.

"We're fine... Ah, with how big one of its attacks is...if we could just hit back...urgh," said Igarashi.

"......!!"

The massive crab's pincers swung down, cleaving the beach apart. The attack hit a terrifyingly large area. Elitia moved so close to evade I could hardly believe my eyes, and Igarashi and Theresia both barely managed to dodge. They were using Mirage Step or Accel Dash where necessary to evade, but they would never be able to avoid those attacks without those skills.

I didn't know what to do. I couldn't get too close, but I needed to move in to make it easier for the vanguards to disengage.

"Misaki, Suzuna, stick to the back like Seraphina says. You absolutely cannot let yourself get hit with the Soul-Stealing Scythe attack. Cion, don't let yourself get too far ahead, either!" I ordered.

"I'll activate Auto-Hit while I have the chance, to make sure I'll hit no matter what...," said Suzuna.

"Woof... Grrrrr!"

Suzuna prayed over her arrow. It was still too far for Misaki to use Lucky Seven, but she pulled out her dice and gripped them tight as we ran forward. Cion responded loyally to my order but then growled when she saw the vanguards evading an attack.

*And to make things worse, it's easy to trip in this sand. There's no way you can get close unless you have a speed-enhancing or evasion skill... This is an incredibly dangerous monster!*

"Eyes on me!" Elitia shouted to the crab. I watched what she was doing and tried to decide what support would be best. If she was trying to attack it to draw its attention, it would be pointless if it did no damage.

"Elitia, I'll support you!"

◆Current Status◆
> Arihito activated Attack Support 1
> ★Merciless Guillotine attacked ⟶ Elitia evaded
> Elitia activated Counter Slice 1 ⟶ Hit ★Merciless
                                                          Guillotine

No damage

```
12 support damage
> ELITIA activated additional attack ─→ Hit
  ★MERCILESS GUILLOTINE
No damage
12 support damage
```

She dodged the crab's attack, then used Counter Slice 1 to immediately strike back. The attack hit the pincers, and I could see the blade of her sword slip across the surface, not getting through, but the invisible blade that Attack Support 1 created left a slash on the surface.

"It went through... I was right; as long as Arihito's here, we can do this!"

Provided the attacks were getting through, we could defeat it. As long as we could continue whittling it down. But that was if we could keep enduring and avoiding its attacks like we'd been doing.

"Theresia, get away from that!"

"......!!"

"—Theresia!"

```
◆Current Status◆
> ARIHITO activated DEFENSIVE SUPPORT 1 ─→ Target:
                                        THERESIA,
                                        KYOUKA

> ★MERCILESS GUILLOTINE activated NECROBURST
> GHOST SCISSORS F exploded ─→ Hit THERESIA, KYOUKA
★MERCILESS GUILLOTINE absorbed vitality
```

"Agh!"

"……!"

My heart skipped a beat. It wasn't often that an attack's damage exceeded what Defense Support 1 reduced it by. But even though Theresia brought up her shield, she went flying backward. And even though Igarashi fell into a defensive stance, she couldn't defend against the explosion from one of the Ghost Scissors' bodies.

"Be careful, you three! Don't go near any of the other Ghost Scissors remains!" I shouted.

"I don't plan on it, but there's too many!" replied Igarashi.

Who knew that what the Alliance did would end like this? This Named Monster truly was the embodiment of the defeated crabs' grudge.

The corpse's explosion didn't just do damage—it recovered the large crab's vitality. Elitia saw the wound on its pincer disappear and shouted as she shook with anger.

"How dare you hurt my friends!"

She didn't hesitate to move forward to make a counterattack, but Igarashi stopped her. She was injured but didn't fall back a single step.

"You've done well…but it's our turn now!"

◆Current Status◆
> Kyouka activated Thunderbolt ⟶ Hit ★Merciless
                                        Guillotine

Weak point attack
Electrocuted

Lightning leaped from Igarashi's spear as she jabbed out with it, racing between her and the enemy in a flash, hitting the translucent giant crab. Physical attacks were insignificant against it, but the magic attack definitely got through its defenses. It was left Electrocuted, sparks flying here and there from it as it seemed unable to move for a moment.

We rearguards could now contribute to the battle. If we could hit the monster with a combination magic attack, we should be able to get in a decent enough attack.

Elitia seemed to have the same idea. "Arihito, let's do a combo…!"

But we couldn't let our guard down. The crab was supposedly Electrocuted, but its eyes were still moving. It wasn't looking at the three vanguards—it was looking at us rearguards.

"Everyone, spread out! Seraphina, you get out of here, too!" I shouted.

"Mr. Atobe?!"

I was sure the giant crab was going to use Bubble Laser until I saw its legs push forcefully into the sand and realized my assumption was wrong.

*What the hell…? Something's glowing…*

Right when I realized what was emitting light, the giant crab sparkled and transformed. At the same time, it moved in a way I couldn't believe a body that huge was capable of.

◆Current Status◆
> ★MERCILESS GUILLOTINE materialized ⟶ Nullified magic

```
Status ailments removed
> ★MERCILESS GUILLOTINE used ROLAND'S skills
> ★MERCILESS GUILLOTINE activated SKY HIGH
```

"What...the hell...? That—that's my leeeeeader's!"

Why did it cut out and capture Roland's soul? The reason was that this giant crab could use the skills of the Seekers whose souls it captured.

I heard Thomas scream. The crab didn't jump as high as Roland, but it still flew higher than I could expect something that large to. No matter who it targeted, they couldn't do anything against that much weight. If it used Vapor Dive, we were—

"—I won't let you hurt any more people!"

```
◆Current Status◆
> SERAPHINA activated PROVOKE ⟶ ★MERCILESS GUILLOTINE'S
  hostility toward SERAPHINA increased
> SERAPHINA activated DEFENSIVE STANCE
> SERAPHINA activated AURA SHIELD
```

I should have known that she would choose that route. But after it easily got past my Defense Support 1, I didn't believe she would get out of this unharmed, even with my support on top of her defense. In that case, I had one choice. I could think of only one option that made sure no one got attacked.

```
◆Current Status◆
> ARIHITO activated REAR STANCE ⟶ Target: ★MERCILESS
                                          GUILLOTINE
```

There was a momentary break in my consciousness, and the next moment, I was behind the giant crab where it jumped high into the air. I felt the blood rush from my head at the falling sensation but pulled my black slingshot back as far as I could, then released the bullet. I had no idea if it would have any effect, but I had to try.

"—Eat this!"

◆Current Status◆
> Arihito activated Hypnosis Shot ⟶ Hit ★Merciless
                                             Guillotine
Inflicted Confusion

*It worked... If this keeps going, we can get Roland's soul back, too!*

◆Current Status◆
> ★Merciless Guillotine activated Vapor Dive ⟶
  Target: Unknown

Since the crab used its skill while Confused, its target wasn't limited to someone on the land. Instead, it aimed for the water's edge and dropped suddenly. I wasn't able to steal Roland's soul back because it put such a distance between us so quickly.

I was left there in the sky. As things were, I was going to slam right into the beach.

*I can't use Rear Stance here... Come on, think! What do I do...?*

"—Awooooo!"

"Cion!"

Cion rushed forward and jumped, catching me before I hit the ground—but I wasn't sure Cion would be able support both of our weight when we crash-landed.

Yet, the impact I expected never came.

"Waaaah?!"

The ground gave with far more elasticity than I would have expected from a beach and bounced us back up. I tumbled to the ground, and Cion gracefully flipped in the air before landing nicely on her feet.

"A-are you okay?!" Thomas had used his skill that made the ground elastic, like when Roland had leaped into the air.

The giant crab had accelerated from Vapor Dive, its pincer outstretched, and slammed into the shoreline. Unlike Roland, it didn't escape the maneuver unharmed due to its weight, and it was still Confused. But—

*It's translucent again... Its resistances are changing!*

◆Current Status◆
> ★MERCILESS GUILLOTINE took damage from falling
> ★MERCILESS GUILLOTINE activated PHANTOM DRIFT ⟶
   Resistance Change: Immune to physical attacks
Speed increased
CONFUSED status removed

It switched its resistances at dizzying speed and removed status abnormalities at the same time. We couldn't find an opportunity to get in a solid round of hits on it at this rate.

"Behind me, you two!" Seraphina called as she was trying to protect Suzuna and Misaki. As its name would imply, the giant crab didn't hesitate to target the party members with low defense. It brandished its scythe. With how fast it was now, there was no way any party member it targeted would be able to dodge.

I had Cion carry Roland's body on her back. If I could buy some time, she could run for the single path out of here. But I knew we couldn't take even a single hit. That scythe that stole Roland's soul really did pass through his body. It didn't leave any sort of wound. It would probably pass right through a shield meant for defending against physical attacks. Seraphina probably had skills to deal with that, but if not, we'd just lose more people.

*Think... Before it moved...there must have been something— there had to be!*

The giant crab started to move again. It was trying to repeat the nightmare from before.

"Ack!"

It didn't aim for Seraphina. It didn't move to their flank. It was using its faster-than-the-eye-can-see speed to circle around behind them. It was trying to do what it did to Roland—but to my friends. I could never let that happen; I couldn't accept it. I had to do something, anything. As long as it saved them...

As if in response to my thoughts, a familiar presence welled up inside of me.

*Wait... We're not done just yet!*

"—hito...Arihito. My devotee, do you require my power?"

"Ariadne!"

◆Current Status◆
> Ariadne activated Guard Arm
> ★Merciless Guillotine activated Soul-Stealing Scythe

"Aaaaah!"

"Misaki!"

Ariadne called to me, having sensed the party was in danger.
That let her activate Guard Arm, which changed the path of the
giant crab's scythe as it fell. It swung over Misaki's and Suzuna's
heads, giving us a very small but definite moment to work with.

"—Misaki, use that one skill!" I shouted.

"Ah… Sure, whatever you say!"

I was talking about one of the skills we'd kept on hold, that
Misaki had called her "true power." I put my trust in it, because it
was the only way we had of getting through this nightmare.


## Part V: A Strategic Withdrawal


Misaki pulled out her Jester's Wildcards +3. Akin to normal playing
cards, they had a face and a back, with numbers written on the faces.

"I bet our victory on this card!"

◆Current Status◆
> Misaki activated Fake Hand
> ★Merciless Guillotine's action was canceled

*    *    *

You might call it a gambler's bluff. It worked as long as you could convince the enemy that *something* was going to happen.

"It stopped!" Suzuna said in surprise. The crab had brandished its giant pincers, but it definitely paused so it could closely observe Misaki's actions.

◆Current Status◆
> MISAKI acquired SURRENDER skill ⟶ Immediate
                                              activation
> ★MERCILESS GUILLOTINE's hostility dropped

Misaki listened to my orders and went even further. I remembered what we talked about when we'd considered what skills she should take.

*"This skill could save the party if we find ourselves in a pinch. But it needs two skill points, and I'm not sure I want you to spend that."*

*"So I'll just make sure I'm ready to take it on the spot. If I use it perfectly when you want me to, will you praise me, Arihito?"*

This was exactly the kind of situation we'd talked about, and she pulled it off wonderfully. But even though the giant crab's movements were slowed, it still swung down its huge pincers. Its force was cut by more than half immediately following Surrender's activation.

"...Now I should be able to take it!"

"Seraphina, I'll support you!"

◆Current Status◆
> Seraphina activated Defensive Stance
> Seraphina's defensive range increased
> Arihito activated Outside Assist
> Arihito activated Defense Support 1 ⟶ Target:
                                        Seraphina
> ★Merciless Guillotine's area attack hit Seraphina
No damage


The crashing pincers had far more mass than Seraphina did, but she endured the strike with her large shield. Her extended defensive range completely stopped the aftershock that ran through the beach.

"Agh... And here I'll...push back!"

"Me too!"


◆Current Status◆
> Arihito activated Attack Support 2 ⟶ Support Type:
                                        Force Shot
                                        (Hypnosis)
> Seraphina activated Shield Slam ⟶ Hit ★Merciless
                                        Guillotine
> Suzuna activated Storm Arrow ⟶ Hit ★Merciless
                                        Guillotine
Weak spot attack
Speed reduced
> Attack Support 2 activated 2 times ⟶ ★Merciless
Guillotine was Confused

"...GUWAAARARAAAA!"

Seraphina took her shield and tackled the crab, throwing back its pincers and creating an opening, which Suzuna used to fire off an arrow. The creature let out a screech unlike anything we'd heard thus far.

"I-it really worked... Suzu, you're incredible!" said Misaki.

Seraphina's defense and counter followed by Suzuna's arrow hitting the crab made me realize there was a way of defeating this creature.

"Fall back, you two! I'll draw it now!" ordered Seraphina.

"Wait... Those things are still here!" cried Suzuna.

I dashed across the beach, kicking up sand, and felt a strange presence coming from the giant crab.

◆Current Status◆
> ★Merciless Guillotine materialized ⟶
  Resistance Change: Immune to magical attacks
Status ailments nullified
> ★Merciless Guillotine deployed special action Create
  Golem
> 8 Sand Scissors were summoned

*This thing can even make crabs out of sand...?!*

Countless of the giant crab's kin—the Ghost Scissors—had been killed on this beach. Now, their souls rose from their bodies, gathered sand around them, and formed into their original crab shape again.

"This is nothing!" cried Elitia as she ran ahead and bravely slashed one of the sand crabs that was several times her size. A glance at my license showed me this:

```
◆Monster Encountered◆
Sand Scissors
Level 6
On Guard
Immune to physical attacks
Dropped Loot: ???
```

This was an opponent that couldn't be hurt with a normal attack, but Elitia didn't plan on holding back. We didn't have the luxury of changing our tactics when a single hesitation could mean life or death. So in that case...

*Elitia, I'll support you!*

"Return to the sand you came from! Blossom Blade!"

```
◆Current Status◆
> Arihito activated Attack Support 1
> Elitia activated Blossom Blade
> 12 stages hit Sand Scissors A
No damage
144 support damage
> Elitia activated additional attacks ⟶ 8 stages
  hit Sand Scissors A
No damage
96 support damage
> 1 Sand Scissors defeated
```

The crab exploded in a shower of sand after taking the attacks so fast the eye couldn't see them. Elitia's overwhelming number of attacks meant Attack Support 1 was still effective.

"I didn't feel my sword actually connecting, but I still cut it..."

"Everyone, normal attacks won't work against those sand crabs! Avoid their attacks and get out of here!" I shouted.

"B-but they're blocking the way...urgh, I feel dizzy from trying to use Surrender..."

"Misaki, hold it together... Just a little longer!" said Suzuna.

At this rate, even Cion, who was running away with Roland's body, would find her path blocked. Thomas was also pinned in.

*The giant crab isn't Confused anymore, but it should still be less hostile... I just hope it doesn't shoot a Bubble Laser!*

"—Come forth once more, Demi-Harpies!"


◆Current Status◆
> Arihito summoned Asuka, Himiko, and Yayoi


"Himiko, Asuka, you take Thomas and Igarashi! Yayoi, sing Lullaby!"

"Atobe!"

"Don't worry about me, Igarashi! I'll definitely make it out of here! You go on ahead!"

"Wh-whaaaat—?! A-are you a Monster Tamer...?" stammered Thomas. "Don't you go dying on me, suit guy! It'll all be for nothing if you die!"

I had absolutely no intention of dying. Igarashi did as I ordered, but I bet she'd give me an earful when we got back and ask me why I was the last to flee. The reason was because I wasn't the only person remaining. Theresia would never run and leave me. I knew that no matter what happened, she would always be there.

◆Current Status◆
> Yayoi activated Lullaby ⟶ Sand Scissors E and Sand Scissors F were put to Sleep

*It worked! I guess the targets don't need to have ears since these things are made of sand...*

"Aaah... Wh-what the heck?! The crabs are still moving?!" cried Misaki.

"Arihito, Theresia...hurry while you still can!" shouted Suzuna.

"We're fine! Everyone else just needs to focus on running over there!"

"Um, y-you don't look fine...," said Misaki. "Arihito...!"

I needed to run as far from the giant crab as possible, but the Sand Scissors had completely blocked off any available escape route. A crab that formed from the sand in front of me came at me, swinging its pincers. But she really was there. I didn't need to even give her orders; she just knew to move where I needed her.

"Theresia!"

"......!!"

◆Current Status◆
> Sᴀɴᴅ Sᴄɪssᴏʀs D activated Cʀᴀʙ Hᴀᴍᴍᴇʀ
> Tʜᴇʀᴇsɪᴀ is in Aᴄᴛɪᴠᴇ Sᴛᴇᴀʟᴛʜ
> Tʜᴇʀᴇsɪᴀ activated Sɴᴇᴀᴋ Aᴛᴛᴀᴄᴋ ⟶ Attack power
  against Sᴀɴᴅ Sᴄɪssᴏʀs D doubled
> Tʜᴇʀᴇsɪᴀ activated Aᴢᴜʀᴇ Sʟᴀsʜ ⟶ Slight knockback
Aᴄᴛɪᴠᴇ Sᴛᴇᴀʟᴛʜ terminated
> Partial destruction of Sᴀɴᴅ Sᴄɪssᴏʀs D ⟶
Sᴀɴᴅ Sᴄɪssᴏʀs D dropped loot
> Aʀɪʜɪᴛᴏ activated Fᴏʀᴄᴇ Sʜᴏᴛ (Sᴛᴜɴ) ⟶ Sᴀɴᴅ Sᴄɪssᴏʀs
  D was Sᴛᴜɴɴᴇᴅ
Action canceled


*The two of us can't take one down with a single round of attacks… In which case…!*

Theresia was able to hit the sand crab because the magic stone on her sword gave her a nonphysical attack. We weren't going to miss the opportunity gained from the Stun and went in for another round.


◆Current Status◆
> Aʀɪʜɪᴛᴏ activated Aᴛᴛᴀᴄᴋ Sᴜᴘᴘᴏʀᴛ 1
> Tʜᴇʀᴇsɪᴀ activated Dᴏᴜʙʟᴇ Tʜʀᴏᴡ ⟶ 2 stages hit
  Sᴀɴᴅ Sᴄɪssᴏʀs D
No damage
24 support damage
> Tʜᴇʀᴇsɪᴀ activated Aᴢᴜʀᴇ Sʟᴀsʜ ⟶ Hit Sᴀɴᴅ Sᴄɪssᴏʀs D
> 1 Sᴀɴᴅ Sᴄɪssᴏʀs defeated

*We finished it off... But we're screwed if we keep whittling down our magic at this rate!*

"......"

"Theresia, hang in there!"

"......!!"

The blue flame stone was very powerful, but in exchange, it drained a lot of magic. She was tripping over herself as she tried to run, so I supported her and used Charge Assist.

"......"

"Don't worry about me—I'm just fine!"

One of our obstacles for escape was the giant crab that was building up hostility after it had been reduced by Misaki's Surrender. Theresia now had enough magic back to use Accel Dash, but she'd have problems dodging if it swung with its oversized pincers. I could use Rear Stance on one of the party members that had already escaped, but I wasn't going to leave her until we'd both made it out.

"Yayoi, take Theresia!"

"......!!"

"I can go last! I wouldn't be a rearguard if I didn't!"

I didn't know if she agreed. I called on Yayoi to stop singing and carry Theresia away. Theresia stretched her hand out to me, but I chose to run on my own.

"Mr. Atobe...I refuse to let someone like you die!"

"—Seraphina!"

```
◆Current Status◆
> ★MERCILESS GUILLOTINE recovered hostility
> SERAPHINA activated DEFENSIVE STANCE
> SERAPHINA activated AURA SHIELD
> ★MERCILESS GUILLOTINE attacked → Hit SERAPHINA
```

"Agh...haah... Haaaaaah!!" Seraphina took the Merciless Guillotine's attack with her shield and pushed it back. The giant pincers many times larger than her were like chunks of rock crashing into her shield. She couldn't get out of an impact like that without injury, but she just looked at me with fire burning in her eyes.

"Mr. Atobe, I'll buy you time! You must survive at all costs...!"

I guess she intended to keep enduring the attacks and drawing the enemy's attention. But if she did that, there was a chance the remaining sand crabs would target her. I would be safe if I used Rear Stance on one of my allies who'd already fled, but...I had to do something to save her. Seraphina was trying to lure the enemy to her so that I could live.

"I won't let anyone else...go down in front of me!" Elitia had already escaped to safety, but she was about to rush out and step in front of the Merciless Guillotine, but before she could—

## Part VI: The Alliance's Collapse

The giant crab stumbled when Seraphina braced against its huge pincer, the mass of which pulled the creature back. The pincer was so oversized that the giant crab had a hard time controlling it, but it wasn't going to destroy itself from the weight of the thing. Its shoulder creaked from the strain, but it dug its feet into the sand and stood its ground, then readied a counterattack.

◆Current Status◆
> ★MERCILESS GUILLOTINE began charging GUILLOTINE
> SERAPHINA activated IMMOVABLE BREATH ⟶
  Increased chance of counter
> SERAPHINA activated WIDE STANCE ⟶
  Knockback effects against SERAPHINA nullified

The pincers slowly rose. Unlike its first attack, this one was meant solely to kill. And yet, Seraphina still did not waver.

"Come at me! I will not move from this spot!" Seraphina was three levels higher than the giant crab, but one attack from its pincers surpassed her defensive abilities.

A black magic-like aura emanated from the giant crab's body. Just before it had completely coated the crab's pincer, I heard a whisper right next to me. That voice belonged to the katana on my back. Murakumo was calling to me.

*"The blade of hatred cannot harm me. Master, call my name."*

*"And I will add my support. My arm has recovered; it is your most valuable tool."*

I completely believed the promising words. I unsheathed the katana and activated my skills.

"Here goes! ...Ariadne, Murakumo!"

```
◆Current Status◆
> ARIHITO activated REAR STANCE ─→ Target: SERAPHINA
```

"Seraphina, I'll back you up!"

"Ah... Understood!!"

She had more important things to do than be surprised. I was grateful that she decided without spending the time to consider her actions. I saw two mechanical arms appear in front of Seraphina.

```
◆Current Status◆
> ARIHITO activated DEFENSE SUPPORT 1 ─→ Target:
                                          SERAPHINA
> ARIHITO requested temporary support from ARIADNE
   ─→ Target: SERAPHINA
> ARIADNE activated TWIN GUARD ARMS
> SERAPHINA activated AURA SHIELD
> ★MERCILESS GUILLOTINE activated GUILLOTINE ─→ Power
   decreased by TWIN GUARD ARMS
```

The magic-cloaked pincer didn't seem to encounter any air resistance as it fell faster than my eyes could follow. The two Guard Arms reached out to grab it, doing so with perfect accuracy, and managed to reduce the attack's power.

"I can...take this...! Haaaaah!!"

```
◆Current Status◆
> SERAPHINA activated SHIELD PARRY ─→ Nullified GUILLOTINE
> ★MERCILESS GUILLOTINE's actions temporarily halted
```

Seraphina used her skills to force the crab into a defenseless position. But if we tried to run now, it might come after us to attack.

*My Guard Arm is broken. I advise you retreat with your party,"* said Ariadne.

"Sorry… Just one more attack…!"

◆Current Status◆
```
> ARIHITO activated REARGUARD GENERAL ──→ Abilities
  improved based on current number of party
  members
> ARIHITO activated METEOR THRUST
```

The moment I activated the skill, I felt like Murakumo was guiding my hands from behind. My body wasn't my own; I had become one with the Stellar Sword…

◆Current Status◆
```
> Partial destruction of ★MERCILESS GUILLOTINE ──→
  Attack power, defense reduced
```

The moment the magic covering the falling pincer disappeared, I thrust out my blade, and Murakumo's sword left my hands, cloaked in a purple light as it flew out to pierce into the pincers, creating a massive crack.

"…GWOORAARAAAAA!!"

The giant crab let out a horrific screech just like when Suzuna's arrow had struck it in the corner of its mouth—that must have been one of its weak spots.

"What on earth…? You put a crack in such a tough shell…"

"Seraphina, we need to go now!" She stood there dumbfounded until I called out to her, and the two of us started to retreat.

"Arihito, behind you!"

*Urgh… This thing is determined!*

The giant crab had raised its pincer and was recklessly pursuing us. The remaining Sand Scissors responded to its movements by raising their pincers, too. But before it could catch us, we dived into the narrow path leading through the stone cliffs. The giant crab finally gave up its pursuit. It stared at us but didn't try to follow again.

There was Roland's soul, captured with Soul Tentacle. It was still glowing; I didn't know how Roland's body would fare without his soul.

"Roland…! Roland, please, say something!"

"Daniella, please stop! It's bad for the baby if you get so upset…"

"…Noooooo…!!"

Cion had escaped first. The moment Daniella saw Roland, she broke free from one of her female allies and clutched Roland's body to her. I looked around and saw Gray a little way off. He must have come back to see what was going on after using the Return Scroll, but he didn't try to talk to his allies, not even Daniella. He noticed I was staring at him, and the corners of his mouth twitched up into a smile, then he left. I didn't have any energy to chase after him and question him right then. I guess I was the only one who noticed him, as no one else seemed to be paying him any attention.

Everyone was silent. Even the Alliance members who had escaped safely were staring blankly. I approached Cion and looked at Roland. He seemed like he was sleeping. His breathing was irregular, and his skin was deathly pale even though he was alive. It didn't seem like he was going to wake from his slumber.

"...We'll take him to the Healer clinic. Mr. Atobe, I greatly appreciate your cooperation. Adeline will have made arrangements to transport the Arachnomage you captured to the Monster Ranch. I will tell her to report to you on that later."

"Seraphina...that monster..."

The giant crab had turned its back to us like the beach was its personal property. It walked away, eventually disappearing from sight. Named Monsters continued to pursue the first opponent they encountered. If they weren't a member of Roland's party, it wouldn't attack them again. Except that we had fought it once. It might remember us as an enemy.

"That monster likely appeared because certain conditions were met. It has incredibly dangerous abilities, even compared to your average level-eight Named Monster. It only used the skill once, but it is possible it could use Create Golem to make as many crabs as had been killed there before... If that's the case, even my unit of Guild Saviors will have a hard time defeating it."

But if we didn't defeat the monster—if we left it there—there was a chance it would eventually cause a stampede. Seraphina was aware of that and continued to speak with displeasure.

"I'll request support from the Guild Savior headquarters. We can't just leave that monster as it is."

"...How long will it take that support to get here?"

"The fastest would be three days... If they're slow, it could take up to a week. Generally, they recommend that the party who first encountered the Named Monster defeat it. The Seekers of a given district are entrusted with maintaining the safety of their district... That's why support isn't considered urgent even when there is a stampede."

Which meant that if the Seekers ran into a Named Monster they had no way of defeating, their only choice was to run. Then if a stampede happened, lots of people would get dragged into it. The Guild Saviors weren't focused on protecting Seekers. They maintained a reasonable distance from them at all times, monitored them, and maintained order. But Seraphina tried to save us, even if that meant she ended up in the battle herself.

"The leader of the Alliance...Roland Vorn made decisions that caused a Named Monster to appear, then chose to fight it, and lost. It's not a tragedy; it's something that's happening all across the Labyrinth Country. I hope you can understand that, Mr. Atobe."

Seraphina's squad had come into the labyrinth and were taking Roland and Daniella out. Most likely, they were heading to the Healer clinic. The remaining Alliance members finally started to move. They seemed to be discussing something, probably about what was going to happen now that Roland was gone.

"Could I have a word with you...?" Seraphina asked them.

"...Sorry, no one's really in shape for talking right now. Thank you for saving us...and sorry for taking over the hunting ground."

Their spirits seemed crushed. It was understandable for them to feel that way, particularly if they accepted that it was their own actions that brought this on.

"Arihito... Let's leave," suggested Elitia.

"...Sorry. My decision was...," I said.

"...That baby is going to be born soon, but their dad...had that happen...," said Igarashi. I never wanted this to happen, but I couldn't say it. Igarashi took a shaky breath and turned away from me.

I'd been against what the Alliance was doing, and I didn't have it in me to feel sympathetic about what their actions brought. Most importantly, I needed to place my party's safety above all else. If Suzuna and Misaki hadn't joined the fight, we wouldn't have had the time we needed to escape, but they wouldn't have been fine if they'd taken a hit from that giant crab. It wasn't the right decision as their leader to put them in that situation, and a simple apology wasn't enough... I was thinking that when someone pinched my cheek.

"Ah...I-Igarashi...?"

"...I do understand how you feel, but I have been telling you that you need to put yourself first more. I did sort of want to try out Evasion Step, though."

"N-no... It'd be too dangerous to keep trying to dodge the attacks of something as powerful as that monster. If we can, you should try it on a safer monster..."

"There's no such thing as a safe monster. But as long as you're behind us, we can be all *kapow, kapow!*—you know?" said Misaki.

"Your decision wasn't one most people would make...but

I don't think it was wrong. I want to keep as many people alive as I can, whether I have connections with them or not." Suzuna was right, not many people made that decision. Actually, they shouldn't make that decision. The most important thing was to keep moving safely forward with your companions.

"...I thought it was a stupid move, too, but I couldn't just abandon them... So I agree with Arihito. I'll apologize if I have to," said Elitia.

"Woof."

"......"

Cion barked quietly, wagging her tail a little. Theresia touched my arm, patting it to try and comfort me.

"Right... Atobe, you don't think it's over yet, do you?" said Igarashi as if she could tell from looking at my face.

"...Roland's soul has been captured. If that state continues, I think he'll actually die, but..."

"It's easy enough to say we have no obligation to save him... But we were starting to fight back in the end there. I think we can beat that thing if we prepare properly. It wouldn't be reckless." Elitia's eyes burned with intensity.

Additionally, if we defeated the Merciless Guillotine, it would count toward the requirement of defeating three Named Monsters we needed to advance to District Six. If you've fought an enemy once, you can start to build strategies against it. Perfecting those strategies was paramount if we wanted to take on this monster again.

"We'll feel nothing but regret that it beat us. We didn't even try all our attacks out on it...," continued Elitia.

"I really, really feel like I can do something, too... Like, I'm scared, but I also kinda want to show everyone what I'm capable of..."

"Misaki, did you have an idea?"

Everyone started coming up with ways to beat an enemy that powerful. It was arrogant of me to think I'd protect everyone; the realization was the push I needed to self-reflect.

"What are your thoughts, Arihito? I think a strategy you come up with will be our best chance at success," said Elitia.

"...All right. I think we should..."

I accepted that Elitia might be right and considered everyone's equipment and skills to think up a few different strategies—strategies that would let us uphold our beliefs as we continued to move forward.

# CHAPTER 4

# Those Who Survive, Those Who Rescue

## Part I: The Seeker in White

We left the Beach of the Setting Sun and came out into the square in front of the labyrinth where we heard other parties who had seen Roland and Daniella carried out talking in sad voices.

"That guy there—isn't he the leader of Beyond Liberty?"

"Yeah, the one who came to the Labyrinth Country with his whole unit, but was the only one stuck here in District Seven…"

"Some people just don't have any luck. And they've left us a nice going-away present to cause problems for us."

By *unit*, it sounded like Roland had been in the military or something before getting reincarnated here, hence his Air Trooper job.

It wasn't surprising that there were a lot of Seekers who disliked the Alliance. Apparently, you couldn't even get to the second floor of that labyrinth if you didn't cross the beach, meaning no one could go into the Beach of the Setting Sun until that Named Monster was defeated.

The remaining Alliance members came out of the labyrinth a little later, but none of them appeared to have the energy for talking. Thomas faced us and lowered his head in thanks, but he didn't come talk to us. Instead he quickly headed to the Upper Guild. He was probably heading to the Healer clinic nearby.

......*Hmm?*

Someone was looking in our direction. They didn't appear to be with any other party nor with the Guild Saviors. They were wearing sunglasses, which weren't common in the Labyrinth Country, and had white hair. They wore a white coat as well, and Elitia stopped dead in her tracks when she saw them. I was about to ask her what was wrong, since she was standing frozen in shock, but she suddenly backed up and spoke in a low voice.

"...The White Night Brigade... Why is she here...?"

"Is that who that is?"

"Uuurgh... They're coming this way... Suzu, can I hide behind you?"

"Wh-what? I'm not up to any of this, either...!"

It was hard to see their build from the large white coat they were wearing, but I could see that the person was a woman when she got closer. She had on leather armor beneath her coat, but it was of a quality completely different from anything we'd found so far. She walked up in front of Elitia and jokingly raised her hand.

"Hey, long time no see, Ellie. Glad to see you're doing well."

The woman's appearance implied she wasn't any normal person, but she greeted Elitia with surprising friendliness.

"What are you doing here? Why are you in a place like this...?" asked Elitia.

"The captain needed someone to run down to the lower districts for an errand. I was on my way and heard something interesting had happened."

"...This isn't *something interesting*. A person just—"

"Monsters that steal souls are pretty rare in this district. Bit cruel to assume they could prepare for it... They should have just run when it appeared." She seemed to know what had happened. Either she was watching from somewhere or guessed when she saw Roland carried out.

"...Is that all you wanted to say?"

"Yeah, for now. Well, that and don't you think you should gather some better companions? You've got a girl whose job makes her seem more fit for a variety show. She'll just drag you down. Then you've got a Shrine Maiden, which isn't particularly great. Then you've got this guy in a suit. What, did he write *Salaryman* when he reincarnated? I don't see what good any of them can be in the long haul..."

"You can say whatever you like about me, but don't talk about my friends that way. I won't let it slide a second time," ordered Elitia, and the woman shut her mouth. Then she bowed, surprisingly cooperative of her.

"I'm sorry—I went too far. But I think you misunderstand, Elitia. It's not like we abandoned that girl. She should have been ready and understood that if she ever became a burden, then—"

"You don't even remember her name. I can't forget it... I'll never forget it!"

Was the white-haired woman that coldhearted about someone who had been her ally? She really didn't seem to remember the name of Elitia's good friend she'd asked us to help save. But she didn't seem sorry about it. Instead she started clapping slowly, seemingly in sheer amusement.

"Ah-ha-ha...haaa. You know, Ellie, I really do respect that about you. Such a low level, but so brave when it comes to battle. You advance further than anyone else and don't complain when you get hurt. I could never be like you. I could never remember the names of every single useless person."

"Rury is not useless!"

"Right, that was her name. Rury. She might've lived longer if she'd found some equipment better suited to her."

"Grr..."

Elitia believed that her friend Rury was still alive, but she didn't have a good argument ready when the woman challenged that. There isn't always hope. The longer you seek, the more you have to look at things rationally. But even so...

"Can I have you stop things there? You're trying to hurt my companion... I can't just stand by and watch while you do," I said.

"...Arihito..."

I stepped in front to face the woman and felt overwhelmed by her presence. Was Elitia really in the same organization as someone like her, and was I really standing against her now?

"...Seems I went too far again. And you don't exactly seem

like a normal salaryman, either... Those aren't the eyes of a beaten-down dog; they're the eyes of a hawk..."

"Ah... Don't you dare do anything to Arihito, Shirone!"

That must've been her name. Shirone stepped closer to me and looked up into my face, then stepped back again.

"If you stay alive, and we meet again, can I test you?" she said.

"...No. I'll pass on whatever this test is."

"I see. But you seem so interesting... If we end up wanting you, we will—"

Two people stepped in from the sides before she could finish her sentence. They were Igarashi and Theresia.

"Is that how you get allies? Headhunt other parties' leaders? Unfortunately for you, Atobe is an integral member of our party. You'll have to go after someone else."

"......"

Igarashi spoke curtly, and Theresia stood with her arms spread. I was glad they felt that way, but something about being protected by women made me really uncomfortable...but this wasn't the time to get hung up on that.

"A good Seeker moves to a party that better suits them. Even if it's not us, scouts will come running if you get famous... That's normal, don't you think? We're not playing a game," said Shirone.

"We're going to keep moving forward as we are. We have no intentions of playing games," I said.

"I see. All right, I'll just say good-bye here, then." She didn't hang around more after that. She turned and walked away, only turning back to wave once, but Elitia didn't respond.

"Ellie, you were in such an extreme party, weren't you? I'd be suuuper nervous whenever that woman was around—don't think I'd ever be able to relax," said Misaki.

"I...need to try harder. I can't let her say things like that...," said Suzuna.

"Suzuna, don't let what she said get to you. Shrine Maiden is a great job. She just thinks her own party is the best there is... She almost never compliments people outside her party," said Elitia.

"She seemed pretty strong, but with enough time, we can catch up and be the same level. When we do that, she won't be able to say anything bad about us," I said.

You can't expect someone to not feel anything when someone comes and says whatever they want to you like that. It was normal to be angry about it, but we should put that energy into something more productive.

"Ellie, what level was that person?" asked Suzuna.

"When I left the White Night Brigade, she was level twelve. She's probably a bit higher now, though."

"Wow... I get the impression that around there, it'll be harder and harder to gain levels. That would probably be the case if they're still in District Five," I said.

"If you can defeat enemies more powerful than you, it's possible to keep up your leveling pace. It's not really that simple, though... Even at the Brigade's level, people end up with serious injuries, and then they need to work around it to maintain their level."

Your level went down if you took a break from seeking. I wanted to avoid anyone getting injured to the point where they had to take a long break, but I thought it was unlikely to happen anyway since I could close most wounds with Recovery Support.

After finishing that part of the conversation, we decided to head to the Upper Guild. We needed to report what happened in the Beach of the Setting Sun and calculate our contribution points.

"Oh...Mr. Atobe! I'm so glad you're still here!" Adeline found us and came running over. She came to report that she'd left the Arachnomage with the Monster Ranch we had a contract with.

## Part II: A Promise

Adeline told us she'd entered a provisional contract for us at the Monster Ranch and gave me a summoning stone for the Arachnomage.

"I left it with William at the Seventeenth Monster Ranch. Guild Saviors are allowed to request information on Seekers, so I was able to find out you have a contract with him already... Oh, s-sorry. It was wrong of me to just go and look that up, wasn't it?"

"No, it's not a problem. You needed the information to process it. I'm the one who should be apologizing for making you do the work for us," I said and bowed my head, but Adeline brought her hand to her chest and let out a sigh. Seeing her up close again like this, I couldn't see any variation in her skin tone from suntanning, which mean that she was naturally brown-skinned. She said her job was Hunter, so perhaps she was from a hunting society.

"Anyway…I'm so glad you are all safe even though we were the ones to ask for your assistance. I ran into Seraphina earlier, and she told me you were all fine, but I was so relieved to actually see you were okay," she said.

"We're fine, but the Alliance has taken a huge hit. It's not exactly something we can celebrate…"

"It's not uncommon for even Guild Saviors to find themselves in a tough situation when trying to help a Seeker in need. She wouldn't have been punished if she'd just run, but I know Seraphina had every intention of going in to save them, even if she had to go alone. That's who she is." Adeline had likely seen Seraphina up close for a long time now and knew her personality very well. That's how she knew she wouldn't have been able to stop her.

"Thank you again, everyone. I won't forget what you did for us by saving our commander." Adeline bowed deeply and froze there. It had been a long time since I'd seen such a respectful bow.

"Seraphina has helped us more than once. And we've fought against powerful monsters before."

"…Most people can't say that. That's why the Alliance was competing against everyone else."

"If they could win against an undefeatable enemy, they'd easily be able to move up to District Six. That must have been part of the plan… They might have ended up getting stuck here if they waited for another Named Monster."

We ran into Named Monsters almost every time we went

seeking… It didn't matter if we took a roundabout way to finding them. Even so, we couldn't spend a moment longer than we had to. Rury was still alive. If we held on to that belief, we needed to end the time she spent captured in a labyrinth as quickly as possible. Elitia probably still cried over it and hid that side of herself from us.

"…I think Seraphina…can trust you to have her back because you're that kind of Seeker. That's what I think. I'm a little jealous about it, to be honest."

"Y-you don't have to be… I'm a rearguard; I'm only useful when I'm in the back."

"No, when I say she trusts you to have her back, I don't just mean in the way the battle formation is set up. It's…about a certain degree of trust."

Seraphina's Trust Levels toward me had surely gone up because I'd supported her, but I think it was only a small change compared to my party members. Apparently, Adeline didn't think so, though.

"Oh, don't let Seraphina know I said that. She's always telling me off for prattling too much."

"Don't worry, I'm pretty tight-lipped. Give Seraphina my regards."

"She's…reporting to the Guild Savior headquarters, so I doubt I'll see her for another hour or two. I think Commander Seraphina may want to speak with you afterward. Would it be all right if I make it so that I can contact you via your license?"

Since I didn't think the Savior Ticket I had could be used to contact her, it'd be helpful for us, too, if we readied a different way to get in touch with her. Adeline set it up so we could use my license for communication, then she saw us off as we headed to the Upper Guild. On the way, Elitia fell back to walk next to me.

"Arihito, you got a summoning stone, right? There's a limit to the number you can put on your pendant, but you can put on that one."

"Oh, really? Then I should add it right away."

◆Summoning Pendant: Three Monsters◆
> Can summon DEMI-HARPY I
> Can summon DEMI-HARPY II
> Can summon DEMI-HARPY III
> Can summon ARACHNOMAGE
> Slightly increases evasion.
> Adds WIND RESISTANCE 1.
> Additional effects available as Trust Levels increase with contracted monsters.

I looked at the information for the summoning pendant and saw there was one new additional effect. It seemed like monsters' Trust Levels increased just by summoning them. What kind of effects would I get once the Arachnomage's trust went up? If I got more effects the more monsters I had and the more they trusted me, I should try to take advantage of the option of capturing monsters in the future.

We arrived at Green Hall, and I was led into the back of the first floor. I entered one of the same rooms as before—the one with the nine stones inlaid in a constellation on the door—waited a little bit, and Louisa came in. Her chest heaved, as if she had run here.

"*Huff, huff...* M-Mr. Atobe, you're safe..."

Louisa already knew what happened in the Beach of the Setting Sun, or so I presumed, and I stood up to go over and meet her.

"My party and I are just fine. Sorry to worry you."

"...I'm so glad... I heard Beyond Liberty suffered heavy casualties... And the Guild Saviors reported that you supported them when they went to assist..."

So she probably already knew what had happened to Roland. Tears welled up in her eyes. It showed how deeply relieved she was that we had returned safely.

"...I am so sorry. I've completely lost my composure. How unbecoming of a Guild employee."

"No, it's my fault for making you worry. I came because I wanted to report on our expedition, but...there's something else I wanted to ask you before that."

Louisa seemed to guess what I wanted to ask just by that. It must have been hard to say, because she pressed her hand to her chest and took a deep breath to calm down before continuing with a more controlled expression on her face.

"Five members of the Alliance's central party have suffered serious injuries... Their leader, Roland, is in a fatal coma..."

"By fatal...do you mean...?"

"...He could be declared dead before long. The kind of state he's in could last for a long time, but after half a day...the Guild determines it to be a fatal coma."

Roland wouldn't recover, not even at the Healer clinic. He really couldn't live long without his soul... Now that I knew that, I found it hard to speak.

"It's possible the remaining Alliance members might be allowed back into the labyrinth to recover Roland's soul. Regardless...it's up to the survivors to make that call." Louisa was straightforward as she explained the regulations. She was such a kind person, though, that even that seemed to pain her.

"...I'm sorry I made you talk about such painful things."

"It's all right... I respect you for making the decision to try to save them as well, Mr. Atobe. What happens in the labyrinth is the responsibility of each party. No matter what happens, no other party is obligated to provide assistance."

No obligation— It was accepted that the best possible course of action for another party was to not try to save them, to run and try to keep their own party members alive.

"...But there are Seekers who try to save people, like you and your party, Mr. Atobe... The Guild does award such actions as something that should be commended." Louisa suddenly smiled after her expression had been pensive for so long. It wasn't like I wanted commendation, but the fact that Louisa would say that made me truly happy.

"I think I'll have another communique from the other Guilds again regarding this incident. The Guild's higher-ups are really quite interested in your work, considering your help in suppressing the stampede and your efforts to save Polaris. I'm sure this notification will be a good one, too..."

"R-right... When you say Guild higher-ups, I can't help but feel they'd be far too important to take notice of a novice like me. It's a bit overwhelming..."

"That's exactly how incredible your work has been. Every time I submit a report, I feel as proud as if it were my own accomplishments." Louisa put her hand to her chest and puffed up with pride as she spoke. It really accented her bountiful bosom, and my face went bright red as I was faced with my own desires.

"Now, then... Shall we move on to your report? Please let me see your license," Louisa said, and we sat down on opposite sides of the table. I passed her my license, and she swiped her finger across it to display our results.

◆Expedition Results◆
> Raided Beach of the Setting Sun 1F: 20 points
> Captured 1 Arachnomage: 120 points
> Rescued Beyond Liberty: 480 points
> Retreated from ★Merciless Guillotine: −20 points
> Battled ★Merciless Guillotine: 40 points
> Party members' Trust Levels increased: 35 points
> Seraphina's Trust Level increased: 30 points
> Roland's Trust Level increased: 10 points
> Conducted a combined seeking expedition with a total of 9 people: 45 points
Seeker Contribution: 760 points
District Seven Contribution Ranking: 45

I got more contribution points than I'd expected. The largest contribution was saving Beyond Liberty.

"You captured a monster and then saved Beyond Liberty... Is that correct?"

"Yes. Looks like you get a lot of contribution points for rescuing someone... How is that calculated?"

"In these situations, they award twenty points per person in the group you rescued. The Alliance has a total of twenty-four people, bringing the total to four hundred and eighty points."

The larger the organization was that you were saving, the more contribution points you got. I also didn't get a lot of contribution points because we didn't defeat a Named Monster. I got less from just fighting it for the short time we did than I would if we'd defeated one Grand Mole.

"There are other ways to calculate contribution points when you rescue someone. There's also another system that could apply here... Please allow me to explain. It is Guild regulation, after all."

"What system would that be...?"

"We have the proxy compensation system where one party formally accepts a request from another party or organization to defeat a monster they could not." Louisa took out her own license and opened the free-draw page. She started drawing a diagram while she explained.

"For example, say a monster has defeated a party of Seekers... That party would be penalized in the form of a large deduction from their contribution points. The Guild evaluates that sort of situation very severely because monsters become more powerful the longer they live."

A monster became stronger with every Seeker it defeated... It sort of made sense. It was probably one of the reasons that Named Monsters had far more vitality than was normal for a monster of their level.

"A party can ask other Seekers to defeat the monster they couldn't. When they do that, if the other Seekers are successful in defeating it, the contribution points that the first party lost from the penalty are added in when calculating the second party's contribution points when they defeat the monster."

I didn't know how big this penalty was, but I wouldn't have been surprised if it was more than if you defeated the Named Monster. That's what this system was for.

"There's more to the proxy contribution system. You can also receive personal or monetary compensation as well. There are very few instances in which this system is applicable, though, so it's not utilized very much."

"I see. I'll have to remember that."

This proxy contribution did give me one idea: to formally accept a request from the Alliance to defeat the Merciless Guillotine. Then we'd fulfill the requirements for going up to District Six in no time. The problem was that I'd need to meet with Daniella to do that. Would she even want to talk to us? We were practically enemies... Nothing I could do if she refused to meet with us.

"...Mr. Atobe. I...want to closely observe you and your party as you advance through the Labyrinth Country. If just for a bit longer... Rather, if at all possible..."

"I also want you to always be there watching me, Louisa. It might be out of line to say it, but that is how I feel."

"Ah...M-Mr. Atobe..."

"You came all the way from District Eight to District Seven for us. I just feel like it'd be sad if we were separated partway through or if our caseworker changed... Uh, Louisa?"

Louisa's strapless top had slipped, and she tugged it back in place. Did I say something to shock her that much?

"...Have you forgotten that I'm your exclusive caseworker? That isn't something I say lightly." Louisa removed her monocle, and she looked angry, so I panicked, thinking I needed to apologize. I thought she still seemed angry even after seeing my reaction...but I was wrong.

"...What I have told you so far was spoken with the knowledge of what decision you would make," she said.

"I'm sorry, Louisa... Thank you for still telling me..."

"It's all right... But to be honest, I am very worried. Please make sure you proceed in such a way that we can have dinner together again tonight."

That was her way of saying she hoped we'd be safe. She held out her pinky, and I blushed a little but wrapped my pinky around hers to promise I would be. I swore to keep that promise.

# Part III: Trust

After finishing the report, I went back out to the lobby where I was supposed to meet back up with the others. What I saw there made me feel like I was having déjà vu and gave me a bit of a headache.

"What are you saying? That you have the right to find replacements for the members you lost?" Elitia's sharp words were directed to a gray-haired black-clothes-wearing man. It was Gray from Beyond Liberty.

"Elitia Centrale. Whenever you see a talented dropout Seeker such as yourself, they normally get every party out there begging them to join. The thought did cross my mind the first time I saw you."

"...I'm not listening to this. If you have the time to waste on recruitment, why don't you put it toward trying to save your leader instead?" Elitia looked quite hostile when she heard the word *dropout*, but she realized it was just an attempt to provoke her and didn't ask what he meant by that. Gray was basically saying that the fact Elitia was working with my party made her a dropout. This man was really completely incompatible with our party.

"That leader you speak of is me, girlie. The former leader—Roland—saw how much I did for the party. He asked me to take his place in the Alliance if anything happened to him."

Theresia looked over at me when she heard him say that. He was lying. We were certain of that, but some way or another, Gray apparently did end up as the Alliance's leader. I could see the remaining members of the Alliance in the entrance to the Green Hall.

"…But Roland's wife is in the Alliance, too, right? What reason could there possibly be for her to not become the leader?" Igarashi's voice was colder than I'd heard in a long time. She had a habit of speaking so icily you could see your breath from the temperature drop whenever one of our company's partners failed to live up to her expectations or if someone made a joke that bordered on sexual harassment. She was seriously angry. Gray half smiled, half grimaced in the face of her anger and straightened his crooked tie. Must be a nervous habit of his.

"Something very unfortunate happened to Ms. Daniella, but she was planning on retiring soon anyway. She was taken to the Healer clinic with our former leader and…well, you know her condition, right? That kind of thing can happen to a married couple at any time. You couldn't do much to help Roland, but we never blamed those two for their carelessness. It's unfortunate that it came to this, but it was a long time coming, you know?"

Something seemed off. Daniella was always working alongside Roland even though she was pregnant, and they were so close to moving up to District Six. But now that this happened, Gray was stealing her position as the new leader without her fighting back at all.

"Anyway, that suit guy you've got in your party, he didn't even look like he did anything. He just followed around behind you. Our party has a way better collection of jobs than that, and I could even make sure you end up the star of our main party. And if we do that…we could accomplish your goal even more quickly, right, Death Sword?"

Elitia and the others stared at him as if they were implying he'd put on a good performance. Misaki had a fake smile plastered on her face, but she was gripping her dice. She was angry enough to punch him, but she just about managed to hold herself back.

I felt the same. I had gone so far past anger that I actually felt nothing. I don't mind letting someone say something if they wanted to—I had no right to deny someone that anyway.

"Right, shall I ask again? We at Beyond Liberty have had a slight setback, but we choose to make it to District Six no matter what, and even farther. I would like to ask you six to join as new members… So won't all of you here join us?" Gray seemed to gain confidence as he spoke, seemingly fine even if his closing argument wasn't perfect.

*Is something making Gray this confident…? He does seem used to negotiating, but I wouldn't say he's such a smooth talker that it amazes me…*

You could kind of guess from a person's manner and speech if they were particularly good at sweet-talking women, but Gray looked like he believed he could succeed in persuading them to join after one interaction. I couldn't help feeling something was off about that.

*"Arihito, my devotee—a word of caution from your Hidden God."*

*Ariadne? A word of caution…?*

Just as I asked her what she meant, I felt like my license in my pocket was trying to say something. I turned the display so Gray couldn't see and realized my hunch about him was right.

```
◆Warning from Hidden God◆
> GRAY activated TRICKSTER ⟶ Activation of GRAY's
  skills is hidden
```

No one actually activated their skills in town unless absolutely necessary. But if someone did have a skill that could hide the fact that they were using skills, there was the risk that you'd never know if the person right in front of you was using a skill as long as they acted innocent. Ariadne had seen through Gray's attempt to hide his skills, though, and warned me. No one else in the party noticed... The warning only reached the party's leader, a devotee to a Hidden God.

```
◆Current Status◆
> GRAY activated GENTLE PERFORMANCE ⟶ Impression of
  self from members of opposite sex boosted
> GRAY activated NEGOTIATION ⟶ Negotiation success
  rate increased
```

His job was "Suit," like the kind of people who worked in clubs and restaurants and they'd need to be good at persuading the establishment's cast sometimes. Apparently, that translated into a skill for Gray when he came to the Labyrinth Country. Even so, I never expected for one moment that something unexpected could happen.

Gray extended his right hand to Elitia. He thought he'd just about succeeded as he smiled like a kind man, but—

"Sorry, but I can't pretend to work together like the Alliance does. Maybe you should ask someone else."

"Ah… H-hey! W-wait, is not even one of you…?"

Elitia turned back to me and smiled. Everyone else realized I was there. Gray's skills hadn't worked on a single one of them. Elitia was the first to walk past Gray, then eyed the remaining Alliance members sideways as she left the Green Hall. The rest of the members followed behind her, one by one.

"I'll warn you once: Stop ogling Four Seasons. Nobody likes someone that pushy."

"Wha…? H-how could you…?"

"Don't be saaad—you've still got plenty of members in the Alliance!"

"We're going to be rivals now, as Seekers. Good luck."

Igarashi put a nail in his coffin, Misaki brushed off his invitation with a joking comment, and Suzuna finished it off with a polite bow. None of them turned back to look at Gray again as he scrambled after them.

When I tried to pass by Gray, the last one in the group, he blocked my way and tried to pick a fight. I'd seen this coming.

"I don't have to tell you twice, do I? The Death Sword is going to waste in your party. You'll tell them, right? Tell them they should switch to the Alliance." He seemed to think he could say whatever he wanted without even knowing what was going on. But it did let me know that he really wanted my party members to join him.

"What? I'm not going to do anything bad. And even if you end up alone, I'll give you enough money that you can live in this district comfortably. You should be fine with a thousand gold, don't you think?" he continued.

"Isn't that money you worked hard to get? It doesn't matter; I don't want it anyway."

"...Huh? Do you not get what I'm saying, old man?" He seemed pretty annoyed that he wasn't able to steal away my companions, but it was stupid to be angry at me about it.

"You know, the guys in Triceratops are way better men than you are. I have a hard time believing it was Roland who upset all the women in District Seven."

"That's... Listen here—!" Gray raised his voice threateningly, but I was relieved that *she* managed to hold herself back.

"......"

Theresia was standing behind Gray. He finally noticed and broke into a nervous sweat, then raised his hands.

"Y-you gonna do me in? If you do, you'll all end up in jail..."

"We have no intentions of doing that. The fact that you teleported your injured allies out of there means there's room to try and be reasonable with you... But I've got my own plan if you intend to keep on with your absurd actions."

"...Oh, you saw that? You act like a moron, but maybe you're sort of clever... You cling to the Death Sword and those girls the same as me. You want them to take care of you, right? Don't preach like you're better than me."

"Preach... Yeah, maybe I am. I've never done something that worthless in my entire life, even before I was reincarnated." I wasn't really suited to preaching at people, and I didn't really want to talk in a way that could be taken that way. I didn't see any point in speaking with him further, so I walked past him.

"I'm not done talking to— Agh?!"

I didn't even say I was the one who'd be deciding if the conversation was over. Gray just turned around to follow me and was so surprised by Theresia that he slipped and fell. That's what people would remember when they thought about the new leader of the organization that was running to the top of District Seven.

I took Theresia along with me and walked away. She was slightly behind me at first but quickened her steps to walk beside me.

"You're not going to get away with this! I'm going to be there laughing when you fail!"

What did the Alliance members think of Gray's disgraceful behavior? All I could tell now was that their expressions were not happy.

Thomas was among the members lined up. He must have known that Gray was lying to become the leader but was keeping the truth to himself for some reason. I wanted to ask him, but this didn't seem like the right situation. That's what I decided, but Thomas ran out to meet me alone. He must have been prepared for whatever Gray would say to him for doing that, so it wouldn't be right of me to refuse to listen to him.

"...I know it's not my responsibility to say this, but I apologize for Gray's behavior...and I have a favor to ask you," he said.

"A favor?"

"Would you mind meeting with Daniella? She was the second-in-command in the Alliance, meaning she had the right to become leader in Roland's stead. Gray is only our temporary leader, but if he can make Daniella give that right to him, he'll soon become our real leader...but..."

Roland was still alive. Thomas hadn't given up, but he couldn't get the Alliance to act and go back into the Beach of the Setting Sun.

No one else seemed to object, so I asked Thomas what room Daniella was in at the Healer clinic, and we headed off that way.

## Part IV: A Request

I requested visitation at reception in the Healer clinic, and it was approved since Daniella was conscious.

"It's still very important that she remain calm, so we must limit the number of visitors to two at any given time. Please try not to discuss anything to upset her. Now, then..." A female Healer showed us to Daniella's room, explaining what we needed to be careful of.

Since we could only go in with two people, we decided that it be me and Igarashi. The rest of the party stayed in a waiting room, and we entered Daniella's room. She was lying on the bed, but the Healer helped her sit up when we entered. The Healer left the room, and Daniella looked at us, then smiled weakly. She was so fragile now that I had a hard time believing she was the same person who'd stood up to Seraphina.

"Please sit, if you like. Not that I'm in a position to greet you properly…," said Daniella.

"No, it's okay… Thank you for your consideration," said Igarashi, who then went to bring over some small stools meant for visitors. Daniella's hair was pulled back in a ponytail, and she wore the simple clothes provided by the Healer clinic.

"Please keep warm. We wouldn't want the baby to get cold," I said.

"I appreciate your concern. I did panic earlier, but the baby is fine… I'm sorry you had to see me like that. You must think something awful of me…," said Daniella.

"…I've wondered why you would go that far, sure. A large organization like yourselves must have had other options available."

Daniella seemed uncomfortable sitting up in bed, so Igarashi helped her turn so she was sitting on the edge.

"…You mean, why did we choose the method we did? Is that what you came to ask?"

"Yes. And after you answer our question, we would like to make a proposal. We need to respect your wishes, though, and have no intention of forcing you to answer, but I feel we need to talk so we can understand each other better." I was hesitant to open fresh wounds, considering Roland was in a coma, but we couldn't take too long to do what we needed.

"…Atobe, may I say something?" said Igarashi. I realized I was gripping the knees of my pants tightly. Igarashi had noticed and continued to speak in my place.

"We want to defeat that monster."

"Ah...what...?"

"We do believe that what the Alliance was doing was unfair. I'm sure you're wondering why we would want to do that, if that's how we felt. The thing is, we have reasons why we need to move up quickly."

Without knowing much about us, she might wonder if that really was reason enough for us to take on the risk of fighting the Merciless Guillotine.

Daniella sat looking down, but the silence didn't last long.

"...Roland... My husband originally came to the Labyrinth Country with his friends. Before they reincarnated, they were in the military for some country. They were in the air force. He said six of them reincarnated together, used their military experience, and made it to District Seven."

It made sense that if they were in an environment in their past life that tested their physical and mental fitness, they'd be quicker to adapt when they reincarnated. However, Roland suffered a setback in District Seven. Daniella continued the story to tell us that as well.

"Roland's party became rank one in District Seven two years ago. However, Roland covered for one of his companions, and he was injured, and it resulted in him coming down with an illness. The disease was inflicted by an unidentified Named Monster, which even now there is no effective treatment method for... He was very lucky, I think. A Healer was dispatched from the cathedral in District Four who treated him, and he narrowly escaped death."

At the time, Daniella was working as a Doctor in the Healer clinic. She had gone into support instead of seeking early on and ended up overseeing Roland's treatment. That's where they first met.

"...Roland was still bedridden and unable to walk for about six months after he regained consciousness. During that time, his companions advanced to District Six, but they left him a message: *Sergeant Roland Vorn, we'll see you again sometime in the higher districts.*"

"I guess that was them...hoping he'd get better..."

"I'm sure that was part of it, but Roland did so much for them, and they didn't even wait a month for him. He always said that they should leave him if he ever slowed them down, and that's exactly what they did... Roland fell to level one while he was in treatment, making it so hard for him to do anything on his own."

"...So you helped him, as a friend. That's what happened, isn't it?"

Daniella nodded. Her level had fallen to 2 when she'd retired for a bit, but she went back to seeking when she accompanied Roland to District Eight, where the two tried to find their footing again.

"In the beginning...it bothered me that he could only think about chasing after his friends even though he'd almost died. I wanted to yell at him, and part of the reason I went with him was out of nosiness... But slowly we found more companions, and eventually we were able to seek in District Seven again. That's when I remembered how it felt when I was a Seeker. My friends and I wanted to unravel the mysteries of the Labyrinth Country."

The Guild never told me to solve those mysteries, but I have always felt like I wanted to. This country had some massive secrets. I'd always had that feeling, ever since I met Ariadne in the hidden floor of the Field of Dawn.

"But... It was around when we made it back to the Upper Guild in District Seven. Roland started to remember the past. He had horrific nightmares every night, like he was being thrown into a deep black pit. He started to get weaker and weaker. But he still endeavored to follow his former companions. He wouldn't give up, no matter what."

Then the Alliance found the Beach of the Setting Sun and discovered they could use it to farm contribution points safely.

"Roland felt bad about it, to a degree, but he hoped people would forgive him. He knew he'd be criticized and alienated, but he didn't care... He knew it was disgraceful, which made him act really terribly, even to the Guild Saviors who tried to reason with him. He thought they couldn't blame him... It's obvious that twisted logic wasn't working on anyone, though."

But their overreliance on contribution points from the crabs brought around something they never expected. She couldn't say she regretted it now that things had turned out this way, but she knew it was normal for people to blame her.

The Alliance had had twenty-four members at its largest, but they'd lost a lot of those now. There was something about that that bothered me.

"Why were the five injured members removed from the Alliance? It feels strange to me that you would agree with that considering you're Roland's wife," I asked.

"...I am unable to fulfill my duties as second-in-command in my current condition. I think it's best to leave policy decisions to those who will keep the Alliance alive."

I decided I really did need to tell her Gray plotted this, to act as the person with authority in the Alliance. He probably used underhanded tactics to get it, too.

"...Gray came to you and asked that you let him be leader in your place, didn't he?"

"N-no. Roland trusted him, with this last strategy, too... And he's accomplished so much, and the other members recognize that..."

"That's not true. I heard him and Roland talking. Roland said his stance was to consider the contributions of members who had been in the Alliance longer—instead of Gray, who had joined fairly late. Didn't he tell you about that?" I was mostly speaking from conjecture, but Daniella did seem aware, which meant I wasn't that far off the mark.

"...B-but...he achieved a lot by getting the summoning charms we needed for this strategy..."

"It is true that those summoning charms were one way to achieve the Alliance's goals. However, it was him using those summoning charms and forcing monsters to appear that caused this situation. On top of that, Thomas was the one who stayed behind and fought with Roland until the very end... He can't have accepted this situation, where Gray has become the new leader."

"If that's the case, you may need to speak with him again... Also, why is Gray acting like he's already the official leader?" asked

Igarashi. Daniella was flustered, and I was hesitant to say more that would confuse the situation even further, but I could only tell the truth as I knew it. If she needed proof, I had it. Before coming here, I'd been warned so that I wouldn't miss that particular display on my license. I pulled out my license and showed her that section.

"...Trickster...activations of skills...is hidden...," she muttered.

"This is how Gray improved his position in the Alliance. He activated skills that gave him an advantage in all negotiations so that no one would notice. This is the record of the skills he used when he tried to pull my party members into the Alliance."

"What is this...? Me, Roland, the other members...every person who has ever helped the Alliance...has had these skills used on them..."

Things had gone exactly how Gray wanted them to. Daniella held her head in her hands—no greater sign than that could have showed how true it was that Gray had gotten his way.

"Atobe was able to notice what Gray was doing. I can't forgive Gray for using such dirty tricks!" said Igarashi.

"I was surprised that a skill like this even exists. I always thought Seeker skills were for fighting or for helping your allies. Gray uses his with the intention of trapping others... And he set up what feels like a conspiracy inside Seekers' competitions with each other," I said.

There's no way he could move forward using only those methods. Even with the job he had, he should be able to use his skills in a positive way. But Gray chose his path.

"Please try not to speak with Gray alone from now on. There's a chance he used his skills to be allowed to come in last time he came to the Healer clinic, but it should be more difficult for him to get in if you refuse to see him. That alone won't be enough to stop him, so I'll try to think of some other strategy."

"...If you can, please. It seems like I won't be able to turn him down if he asks me to make him the official leader again. If he does that with skills but I don't notice, there's nothing I can do about it."

"We could call him out in front of the Alliance members... Atobe, what do you think we should do?" asked Igarashi.

Even if we did destroy his reputation within the Alliance, there was a chance he'd take in other Seekers in the future. It was risky to leave Gray to his own devices right now, but we could also consider using whatever he was planning right now against him.

"Right now, I want to prioritize defeating that Named Monster. Daniella, as it is currently, even if we defeated the Named Monster, the contribution points that the Alliance lost would just disappear. But if you have authority to do so as second-in-command of the Alliance, would you please formally request that we defeat it?" I asked.

"...But...Roland is already... Even if you defeat that monster, he won't..." Tears streamed down Daniella's face. The flow become constant, no break in the stream as she covered her face and started to sob. Igarashi took her hands and pulled her into a hug.

"We can save him. Atobe saw that giant crab steal Roland's soul. If we can get it back..."

"I know it must be difficult to trust me—you hardly know

me—but we don't have much time if we want to save Roland. Only we, who fought with it once, and the remaining Alliance members can fight that monster again. We are the only ones who have a realistic chance of defeating it," I said.

Elitia's level was high, but the next highest level in the party was 6. Could we really defeat a level-8 Named Monster with our current stats? But I knew very well that level wasn't the only deciding factor. You could get through a difficult situation if you used every single tool at your disposal instead of being too choosy.

Daniella looked at me, her cheeks stained with tears, as if she was trying to cling to hope. About all I could do was not to act like it was a troubling decision—but to smile.

"I want that child to meet both their parents. I can't be sure… but I think people were happy I was born, and I want that child to have that."

Igarashi parted from Daniella. Daniella lowered her head deeply and, with heavy sobs, said, "…Please beat that monster. Save him…somehow…please save him…"

"Yes… We will. We accept your request. We will defeat that monster. Anything that happens in the process will simply be part of defeating it," I said.

"What my leader means is that us getting back Roland's soul will just be part of the job. In other words, we fight for a reason, like I said before. We won't put ourselves in unnecessary danger to save others." It seemed like Igarashi was trying to lessen the worry in Daniella's heart. I didn't want her to be anxious, either; I hoped she could be relaxed as she waited for us. There was no point if she didn't.

Daniella knew how to make the formal request. She took her license that had been on the bedside table and did something. I expressed that we would accept the request, and that formed the formal request agreement.

"...You have to all be safe... Don't do anything to put yourselves in danger...," she said. To be honest, that was a hard promise to make, but Igarashi shook hands with Daniella.

I already had a few ideas for beating that giant crab. We would definitely be back here before half a day had passed, with all of our party safe.

◆Active Requests◆
> Request from BEYOND LIBERTY: Defeat ★MERCILESS
  GUILLOTINE


## Part V: The Pavis


When we went down to the first floor of the clinic and passed through the lobby, I got a message from Adeline on my license. As commander, Seraphina had finished her report to the Guild Savior headquarters and would like to speak with us.

"You know, when you and Kyouka were walking together, I

really sort of felt like you two were partners. It looked sooo nice that Suzu and I were super jealous," said Misaki.

"I wasn't j-jealous… I was just saying that you two were probably like that when you worked together. Right, Misaki?"

"U-um… I mean, back when we were coworkers, I sort of dragged him all over the place… But now I feel like it's nicer to do what Theresia does and follow directly behind him, that's all."

"……"

A bewildered expression came over Theresia, as if she'd never imagined Igarashi would use her as someone to model her behavior on. I hadn't really seen it coming, either.

"I bet it'd be fun to work with Arihito… You know, it's just a thought. But he looked so tired when I first met him that it probably was actually quite difficult," said Elitia.

"People did say that about me right after I'd reincarnated. I have a lot more energy now, so I feel kind of strangely lively."

"It's the feeling of working as hard as you possibly can every day. Though, if you'd asked me if I wanted to live my life like this when I worked in the company, I'm sure I wouldn't have said yes," said Igarashi. Cion seemed to understand because she came up to Igarashi, who then smiled and stroked Cion's head.

"And it's not all labyrinths and being so scared you can't breathe. Sometimes it feels a bit like you're traveling… But I think you might get angry at me for not taking it seriously," continued Igarashi as she looked at me. As far as I was concerned, there was no way I could consider her not serious enough since she never hesitated to make serious decisions when the time came in combat.

"Kyouka, you're trying to cheer up Arihito, aren't you? And us, too," said Elitia.

"Everyone agreed to fight that monster again. I'm grateful for that, too…," I said.

"I'd go to the end of the earth if you told me to… Uh, is it inappropriate to say that in a time like this?"

"Misaki, I feel like you're getting more and more attached to Arihito… Are you two really that close?" asked Igarashi.

"Uh, w-well, now that you mention it… I feel like Suzu has, don't you think?"

"Th-that's not true… Arihito and I just did what was necessary… I mean, y-you don't understand; we didn't do anything weird…" Suzuna was probably flustered because she remembered when we worked together to raise Ariadne's devotion level. I also knew there wasn't anything strange that happened but could only smile awkwardly. Even so, I had a feeling the other members would see it as a problem due to our keeping it a secret from them.

"……"

It was Theresia who followed up on the situation. She stretched her hand out and patted me gently on the shoulder, looked at everyone, then shook her head slowly.

"…Theresia, are you saying it's okay because there's nothing going on? I believe you if you say that."

"We're also starting to understand Theresia from her mannerisms alone. We're nowhere as good as you, though, Arihito," said Misaki.

Everyone looked in our direction with smiles on their faces.

Theresia's lizard mask turned slightly pink, perhaps because she was so close to me.

"Theresia, are you blushing just 'cause you patted his shoulder? Awwww, it's such a lie when people say demi-humans don't have hearts," said Misaki.

"......"

Theresia didn't shake her head. She quickly stepped away from me and pressed her hands to her mask. The red slowly faded as she did. Maybe doing that let her disperse heat a little.

"We have more than one reason to quickly move ahead, which is why we need to work hard," said Elitia.

We needed to make it so that we could break the demi-human curse as quickly as possible. There was no way we'd lose sight of our goals; we had a reason that meant we could never stop moving.

Seraphina and Adeline were waiting for us in front of Green Hall.

"Mr. Atobe, I do apologize for calling you out here when you must be tired... I hope you weren't resting," said Seraphina.

"No, we're fine. We were about to get ready to go back into the Beach of the Setting Sun."

Seraphina appeared momentarily astonished, but she quickly calmed down and looked at me with a quiet fire burning in her eyes.

"...Mr. Atobe. If it is possible, could you please use your Savior Ticket?"

"S-Seraphina... It's against regulation for a Guild Savior to ask someone to use a Savior Ticket. If you do that, you may be punished...," said Adeline.

"I am aware. But our only option at the moment is for me to go into the labyrinth with Mr. Atobe and his party... Guild Saviors are currently forbidden from entering the Beach of the Setting Sun. In fact, we are required to prevent others from entering. The only exception to that would be if a party who has the right to enter the labyrinth requested that I fight with them."

As a Guild Savior, Seraphina was required to control who could enter the dangerous Beach of the Setting Sun, but at the same time she was restricted by the same rule. That's what it came down to.

"When I face that monster, I will try to be conscious of its threat. The more people I have who have experience fighting it, the better... It may be pushy of me to want that, but still, I..."

"...Seraphina, you helped us even when we didn't use the ticket. If you say you want to fight with us, I have no reason to refuse," I said.

"Ah...Mr. Atobe, that's..."

"If it's true that it's against regulations, then I suppose I can't ask for your help. But if possible, I would like you to help us... I meant that."

Seraphina turned to Adeline. At first, Adeline seemed like she wanted to stop Seraphina, but she looked away when Seraphina stared at her, unable to handle it.

"Oh, well... You wouldn't listen to me even if I said something. And I assume you're going to leave me behind and ask me to look after things?" said Adeline.

"...Adeline, you know me so well, just because we've worked together for so long."

"Y-you have to say that in a time like this... Haaah. I want to come along, you know. But someone has to handle everyone else, too. I know that, I do... Because we're partners."

I could tell Adeline truly respected Seraphina, and that she was very worried for her. But whether or not we had Seraphina with us greatly changed how we could fight. It was the same when we fought against Murakumo. Her defense created opportunities for a number of counterattacks.

"Adeline," I started. "We—"

"I know. Your party has a lot of promise, and I've seen your strength in action. I trust you."

I had a feeling there was way more Adeline wanted to say than what she actually put into words, but it seemed like she was trying not to take too much of our time.

"Commander Seraphina, I will use my own initiative to act alone as I see fit," said Adeline.

"I owe you. We'll be in touch once we return from the labyrinth."

"Understood. Commander, everyone, may luck be with you." Adeline saluted and bowed her head to us before walking away. We watched her go, then Seraphina explained how I could use the Savior Ticket.

"This ticket uses a special metal and functions as a magic item. Could you please hold it in your hands and mentally express your request for assistance to it?"

I took out the ticket made from the aqua metal and did as Seraphina instructed. When I did, this happened:

◆Current Status◆
> Arihito used Savior Ticket ⟶ Requested battle assistance from Seraphina
> Seraphina joined Arihito's party

That brought our party to eight members in total. We were already at the maximum number, but there was still another person I wanted to join in on the battle. Even if we split into two parties, I could still support the other one. However, since our enemy had skills like Phantom Drift and Sky High, that gave it high mobility; it was too dangerous to have Madoka join the battle just so she could use Item Effects. Better to have her wait somewhere safe.

"Mr. Atobe, everyone, I look forward to fighting with you a second time against this monster," said Seraphina. There was something I wanted to check with her, which was what kind of attacks her shield could defend against. After her repeated greeting, she turned to head toward the labyrinth entrance, but I stopped her.

"Seraphina, I hate to make you waste time, but could we have a strategy meeting first?"

"Ah… F-forgive me. I asked to be included, and you allowed me to fight with you, but then I go and act on my own…"

"Arihito, let's go back home for a moment. We should be fine; there's still time."

We went with Elitia's suggestion and headed home. We had to tell Madoka that we were headed out on another seeking expedition and get Melissa to help us strategize.

We called Madoka and Melissa and headed off to our rental storage unit. Madoka had refitted the unit for us, even bringing in a table and chairs to use for meetings. Granted, I'd asked her to do that because I thought we could talk and consider what equipment to take into the labyrinth with us. She'd already been in close contact with the District Seven Merchants Guild, which let her finish the job incredibly quickly.

"So you're going into the labyrinth again... Is there anything I can do for you, Arihito?" asked Madoka.

"The battle's gonna be really tough this time. I'm always looking for opportunities to increase your level, but I'd like you to sit this one out. Don't worry—I promise we'll come back safe."

"O-okay...I understand. Ceres and Steiner are still here, too, so I'll wait with them." Madoka couldn't hide her concern. I felt bad, but at the same time, I was happy that Ceres and Steiner had come to District Seven. If Madoka would have had to wait alone, I might have asked her to wait in the Guild with Louisa.

Everyone except me took a seat. Madoka had brought out a chalkboard and chalk, which I used as I explained things.

"Right, I think we'll start the strategy meeting now. This monster—we'll call it the giant crab for convenience's sake—is quite large, and there aren't many opportunities for us to get in close for attacks. Additionally, one of its major traits is that if we attack it with physical attacks, it makes it so they won't hit, and then magical attacks become effective. And when we attack with magical attacks, it returns to its original state. That's the first thing I want everyone to understand."

"Th-that's what was happening? I did notice that it turned almost invisible…," said Suzuna.

"And when you shot it with your Storm Arrow, it definitely materialized… So that's how it works," said Misaki.

As the rearguard, I was the farthest away from the monster and could therefore observe any changes. That was part of my role in the party, and I wanted to keep working to understand what was happening in a battle.

"I'm mainly a physical attacker, so I'll have to wait until it's materialized to make sure my attacks are effective…," said Elitia.

"That's right… Also, I'd like to get in combo attacks as much as possible. Two things need to happen in order to do that: The giant crab needs to be materialized, and it can't be able to counterattack. Our vanguard could get instantly wiped out if we push too hard and the monster counters with its large pincers," I said.

"…Physical attacks need to work, and we need to make an opening. One way to create that situation would be if, when the monster is materialized, I take an attack and push it back," suggested Seraphina, but I had one concern.

"That could work, I agree. However, the giant crab has other moves at its disposal. Bubble Laser and Soul-Stealing Scythe are two particularly dangerous ones. Seraphina, I believe those two attacks are magic-based—can you defend against them with your shield?"

"...My Aura Shield skill reduces damage regardless of whether the attack is physical or magical. However, the shield's abilities itself are heavily weighted toward defending against physical attacks. I think I could only halve the damage from magic-type attacks."

It was exactly because I expected that to be the case that I wanted to avoid Seraphina having to defend against the Soul-Stealing Scythe. That didn't mean Seraphina couldn't fulfill her role as our front line's tank, however. We actually had a shield that might have higher defense against magic attacks than the shield she currently used.

"Madoka, which rack has the shield made from the Paradox Beetle's shell?" I asked.

"I've placed it on the armor rack. It's so big that I need a cart to move it..."

"May I see it? I'm constantly training so that I can use heavy shields." Seraphina stood from her seat, and Madoka led her to where the shield was. She lifted the shield that was almost as big as she was and let out a small gasp of surprise. Thankfully, the Mirrored Shell Pavis seemed to have as good abilities as I expected it might.


## Part VI: The Pavis and the Scythe


It was so finely finished that it was hard to believe it was originally a giant bug's carapace. Instead, it looked like it was forged from metal.

"I can't believe you could get a shield like this in District Seven... Does this use materials from a Named Monster?" asked Seraphina.

"Yes. It uses materials from a Named Monster we ran into in Silvanus's Bedchamber, and the people at Mistral Forge worked it for us," I replied.

Seraphina paused to set her current shield against the wall and tried lifting the Mirrored Shell Pavis in both hands.

```
◆★Mirrored Shell Pavis◆
> Reduces damage from physical attacks.
> Reduces damage from magical attacks.
> Magical defense greatly increases when skills
  using the shield are activated.
> Can reflect magical attacks. Attack power is
  reduced when reflected.
> Can reflect breath attacks. Attack power is
  reduced when reflected.
> Grants wielder SURGING WAVE ADVANCE skill.
```

Its defensive capabilities were significant enough, but it provided a movement-type skill for chasing after the enemy, which must have been a specialty of the Paradox Beetle. What was important, though, was whether Seraphina would use it or not. I imagined most people would think the shield they'd been using was better, but I was wrong.

"There aren't many people with jobs that can use a pavis, and they take so much material to make that you can't get one very often... I imagine the shield you're using is very valuable as well," said Elitia.

"In District Eight, they sold wooden pavises for beginners. I wasn't even able to change my shield until I got to District Six; it made battling very difficult. I barely avoided getting stuck, thanks to the help from my companions." Seraphina also worked as a Seeker before becoming a Guild Savior. I was kind of curious what happened to her previous party, but since we were so short on time, I decided not to ask.

"Seraphina, do you think you can use that shield?" I asked.

"Yes. Its physical defense is lower my current shield's, but I should be able to cover the difference with my skills. I take essentially no damage if my Shield Parry is successful... But are you sure I can use it? It's a very valuable shield to lend out..."

"It's part of our strategy. If we can increase the types of attacks you can handle, that results in less damage to the party. Not that it's acceptable to let our tank take damage, either."

"...Thank you. I will use this shield to fulfill the role you have assigned me." Seraphina switched her equipment and left the Shuddering Tower Shield +3 she had been using in the storage unit. It had an effect for improving the wielder's muscular strength to make using it easier, but it was so heavy that it ended up being no different than the Mirrored Shell Pavis.

"The power of my Shield Slam and similar attacks will be reduced, but since I'm the one taking attacks and creating openings, I don't think that will be much of an issue," she said. What she said was so close to what I'd been thinking that I didn't need to add anything. I already knew from fighting with her before that she would be able to join the party and take an active role immediately, and that was reassuring.

"Atobe, we'll be observing the enemy to see whether physical or magical attacks will be effective, then making the appropriate strike, correct? We need to make sure we can execute them properly…," said Igarashi.

"You're right…," said Elitia. "And we need to think of a countermeasure against Create Golem. I hope it hasn't been summoning things the entire time since we last fought it."

"Some Named Monsters don't become hostile unless a target is present. The giant crab stopped pursuing us when we retreated and actually disappeared. It probably won't appear again unless its target comes close," said Seraphina. I shuddered to think of the entire beach swallowed by Sand Scissors, but we wouldn't have to worry about that if she was right.

However, monsters like the Shining Simian Lord that had captured Elitia's friend were still active and taking down other Seekers. Highly intelligent and powerful monsters moved in to attack parties who had already retreated, meaning it was possible that they were capable of strategizing like a human.

"The giant crab will probably make more allies using Create Golem sometime after we start fighting. There're also the remains of the crabs that the Alliance hunted today… The ones they hunted up until yesterday have probably been taken away for their materials, but the ones from today are still there. We need to be cautious of Necroburst," I said.

"They must have hunted more than a hundred Ghost Scissors there... Create Golem requires their souls, but we can basically think of it as unlimited. We need to finish the fight before their numbers get too high," said Elitia.

"Ideally, we don't want it to use Create Golem even once. Probably won't go that way, though... If it does, and it uses Phantom Drift, the risk of us rearguards getting attacked will be quite high," I said.

The giant crab's normal movements weren't all that fast, and it required some preparation time before attacking. But once it activated Phantom Drift, its long legs became faster, and it skidded when turning, like a drifting racecar, kicking up sand and barely losing any speed. Complaining that its movements were all over the place wouldn't get us anywhere in battle, though. Elitia, Igarashi, and Theresia had ways to evade, but Misaki, Suzuna, Melissa, and I didn't. I could think of one way to deal with that.

"The Demi-Harpies... Right, Arihito?" said Melissa.

"Yeah. That, and Cion is another member we have who can move quickly over the sand. She's fast to begin with, but her armor has a speed-increasing effect, which seems to negate any effects from poor footing."

"Woof!"

We'd strengthened her Hound's Leather Vest, which would be effective if things came down to the wire. Our other equipment probably had effects that we weren't aware of.

"...Leader, if it's my job to destroy parts of the enemy, I'll need to move fast. I should ride Cion," said Melissa.

"Ooh, Melissa, you called Arihito *leader*. Hey, Leader, can I go to the ladies' room before we put our plans into action?" said Misaki.

"Yeah, in a bit… I know that's important, but try not to veer off topic too much, okay?"

The issue never came up when we were in the labyrinth, but I just imagined no one ever mentioned it. And maybe it was something I needed to be aware of.

By riding on Cion, Melissa would be using her Wolf Rider skill. The teamwork between them wasn't a problem. Thinking of the role I was giving her, it was better to pair her with Cion than the Demi-Harpies because Cion could move quickly at the drop of a hat.

"We'll get the Demi-Harpies to help, and we'll go somewhere the enemy's attacks can't reach us. But for attacks that can reach the sky…," I started.

"I can use Provoke to increase the enemy's hostility toward me if it uses Bubble Laser, making it focus the attack on the ground. I should be able to control its use."

"…Sorry I'm asking you to take the riskiest role, Seraphina."

"It's fine; that's the entire reason my job exists… You don't have to worry about using my abilities like that. If the vanguard works together, we can scatter the attacks and reduce the risk any one person faces."

"Yeah, I'll help with that… I'll draw it as much as I can. But, Arihito… If we are able to make multiple openings for attacks and get in combos but aren't able to finish it off…," said Elitia.

"It's so big that our attacks aren't very effective unless we hit its weak spots," said Igarashi.

"I was considering learning a new skill to help with that. Then I think we should be able to focus our attacks on a location I target... One of its weak spots is its mouth, but there's a chance there are some others spots, like the crack I made in its pincer when I used Murakumo. I'd like to think that spot is weaker now..."

It was getting harder to get enough strength to defeat enemies if only the set damage from Attack Support 1 got through. We needed to maximize the power of individual attacks that weren't displayed in numbers like Attack Support 1. But at least this time, that didn't mean we had to focus on landing attacks to beat the enemy.

"It is important to aim for the weak spots as much as possible. Then there's one other strategy I'd like to try, which is possible because we have a chance to prepare," I said.

"...Ah, Arihito, are you thinking of using *that*...?"

"Uh... Ellie, do you know what Arihito's thinking?" asked Igarashi.

Elitia had probably been thinking about *that* since we got it. There was no rule saying only our enemy could use an instant-kill attack. It's something we should also try, if we could. There was a high risk that we'd destroy a valuable weapon, but it could bring us a definitive win.

"The Forbidden Scythe... There are quite a few monsters with instant-kill skills, but it's not a strategy one can constantly use. It would probably work on the Merciless Guillotine when physical attacks can hit it. I don't think the scythe's ability to automatically kill the target on a critical hit has a high probability of working... but we have Misaki."

"Whoaaa... Are we finally getting to my big debut?! Arihito, if I pull this off, let's take a vacation and hang out together!"

"Don't get too worked up or you'll get confused... But I agree with your suggestion. I'm sure Madoka's bored of being left behind and working, too," said Igarashi.

"I—I...I'm just happy if everyone comes home safe. But maybe I am a little...," said Madoka.

"...Elitia, would a short break be all right?" I asked.

"Yeah...I don't have any way to move forward but to work with everyone. It would be sad if no one ever enjoyed themselves."

Misaki must have been joking when she said it; she was flustered that people actually seemed supportive of her suggestion, but she also seemed happy. Madoka was the same. She really must be lonely when she was left behind.

"I equip the Forbidden Scythe...then what? Tell me," prompted Melissa.

Misaki's Fortune Roll guaranteed the next action in battle would succeed. Once that was activated, Melissa would make her first move. She would get a critical with her normal attack. If we combined the auto-kill on critical effect with Fortune Roll's effects, we should theoretically be able to defeat an enemy in one hit, even if it was that leaping tank of a monster.

"So you've found that kind of weapon as well... And all party members are agreed on the course of action. It's because you're this kind of party that you're being called the new star," said Seraphina. Everyone looked at one another and smiled awkwardly at her compliments. I also truly believed it was a good thing I was able to build a party with these members.

We went ahead with the strategy we had decided on. We changed our equipment, and then all of us, including Madoka, left the storage unit and headed toward the labyrinth's entrance.

"......"

"...Oh...I-I'm fine. Thank you, though, Theresia."

Theresia seemed to sense Madoka's nervousness because she patted both of Madoka's arms. Watching the exchange, I had one thought on my mind: We would make it through this trial.

## Part VII: Rain and the Setting Sun

We went to the Beach of the Setting Sun for the second time. Other Seekers were forbidden from entering, but they couldn't stop us from going in since we were going to be fighting the monster they were on guard for.

"Please be careful, everyone—don't even let your guard down!" said Madoka.

"We won't. Thanks for seeing us off, Madoka. And be careful on your way back home, too," I said.

"I'll be fine. I won't get lost just because I'm alone or anything... Uh, th-this isn't what you think... I'm not crying..."

Everyone gathered around her as her eyes filled with tears a little. They all tried to cheer her up and promised again that we would make it back safely.

"Commander Seraphina, you will be going into the labyrinth yourself, won't you…? If so, we could help, too…," said one of Seraphina's squad members.

"No… You could be punished for assisting the party in an unofficial capacity because of the entrance restrictions in place. Don't worry about me. I want you to stay here and carry out your duty."

"…Understood. Please do us proud and come back safely. We respect you as our captain, even if you do get penalized for this. I pray for a good fight."

"Thank you. Give Adeline my regards… This isn't the last time we'll see each other, but I've caused her a lot of worry. I was thinking it would be nice if we had the opportunity to throw a thank-you party, but I wasn't able to arrange it… I am sorry for that."

It was clear from their conversation that Seraphina was really admired by her unit.

"Atobe, were you thinking…if only Seraphina had been your manager?" Igarashi was watching me. She must have thought I was looking at Seraphina with admiration. "If I had showed the people in my department I appreciated them like that…"

"No, it's not… You already did plenty to encourage the people in the department. I was just wondering if it was really okay to take her away to participate in the strategy meeting and now this."

"It seems like the Guild Saviors really want Seraphina around, too... But she's helping our party out right now. We have to thank her for that."

"You're right. And normally Savior Tickets are taken right when you use them, but she said she'd only take it once the job was done."

How could we pay her back for what she'd done for us? Well, we'd have to think about that once we got home safely. Then I realized something. One of Seraphina's squad members who hadn't spoken up yet seemed to want to say something.

"Um, excuse me, is everything all right?" I asked.

"Ah... Umm, there's something I'd like to report to the commander..."

"What's this...?" Seraphina heard us and came over. The woman straightened up and spoke not just to Seraphina but to me as well.

"We received a communication a short while ago... The Guild Savior headquarters has determined this situation to be an emergency and will be dispatching the third-class dragon captain. They will arrive once they've completed their duties in District Six, but it does appear that it will take a few days."

"The third-class dragon captain... I see. The fact that they'd send someone like that must mean they really do take the stagnation issue in District Seven seriously."

"I had heard it was becoming an issue before. Perhaps they see this as an opportunity to step in."

A problem with District Seven... When Seraphina said

*stagnation*, it made me think they were talking about all the Seekers who gave up on advancing to District Six. There were only a few more hours in our limited time... We couldn't choose to wait around until the last minute in the hope that this third-class dragon captain would arrive much sooner than expected.

"I see... Thank you for the report. Have you heard anything else?" said Seraphina.

"Y-yes... Actually...someone went into the labyrinth before we'd completely implemented our entrance restriction. I am incredibly sorry."

"...Understood. I will advise them to leave if we happen across them in the labyrinth. I assume you didn't see what this person looked like?"

*...It's probably Gray... And if it is, he'll try to pull some trick on us. Did he come right back to the labyrinth after we talked to him at Green Hall? Is he trying to get revenge on us?*

"And it wasn't a group of people that went into the labyrinth?" asked Elitia.

"N-no... It was only one person. They entered from the opposite side, where we hadn't set up a guard yet. When one of the squad members noticed, they were already disappearing into the labyrinth entrance."

Somehow this person had thrown off the pursuit of the higher level Guild Saviors and gotten into the labyrinth... I couldn't think of anyone else who would go that far.

"We probably won't find them easily if we search... We need to be on our guard," said Elitia.

"Yes. If they try to do something after we've won, we won't be able to let our guard down even after we've beaten the giant crab," I said.

"Would they really try something reckless in a situation like this...? Actually, if it is who I think it is, he definitely will," said Igarashi.

"Since there are Guild Saviors outside, he couldn't even run away if he did do something bad, right? And we have Seraphina in our party," said Misaki. I agreed with her. It was possible he'd use a method that meant his karma wouldn't go up, like Bergen and his group did, but we couldn't focus solely on preparing for that possibility.

"...Mr. Atobe, do you know the person who entered the labyrinth?" asked Seraphina.

"I can't say for sure, but it is possible. One of the members of the Alliance doesn't see us in a very favorable light."

"I see... I have some words I'd like to give them as well. I just hope they don't do something careless."

Gray had completely lost any desire to fight when he'd been face-to-face with the Merciless Guillotine. It was hard to imagine he'd go all the way to the beach and try to hinder our battle.

"...I'm sure he wouldn't take the path through the cliffs. He must be aware that he's the one hated most by the monsters' ghosts that were hunted on the beach," said Suzuna. Her opinion was reliable since she could sense spirits. If Gray had any intelligence at all, he'd realize he was one of the reasons that the Merciless Guillotine appeared in the first place.

"Anyway, we just need to focus on doing what we can. Let's all be careful, you guys," I said.

""""Okay!"""""

We started walking, and everyone naturally fell into battle formation. In the front was Seraphina, and when she was about to enter the labyrinth, I was suddenly conscious of what was behind us. I turned back and saw her guard unit all standing at attention and saluting.

"Seriously…I told them not to do that kind of thing when I'm off duty," said Seraphina, but she was smiling. Everyone seemed tense but put on a smile. We were all able to move forward without fear.

The time inside the labyrinth didn't match with the time outside. In front of us we saw skies and fields stained red with the evening sun.

First, we checked the area to ensure we were safe, and I started preparing so we could use our Morale Discharges. It normally took about forty minutes, but we'd already gone seeking once that day, meaning pretty much everyone's morale was up. After thirty minutes, everyone but Melissa had one hundred morale.

"Good… Now Melissa's morale is one hundred as well. Everyone ready?" I said.

◆Current Status◆
> Arihito activated Morale Support 1 ⟶ Party's
  morale increased by 10

"…Whenever you speak, Mr. Atobe, my morale increases… I have heard specialized jobs can have skills that encourage others, but this…," said Seraphina.

"Whenever Arihito cheers us on, I get strangely full of energy, like, I've got a hundred and ten percent motivation now!"

"But, Misaki, then your morale probably wouldn't really go up at all…," said Suzuna. There were a lot of benefits from having high morale. We couldn't keep morale at one hundred at all times, and it appeared that using Morale Support at the same place before battle reduced the amount that the party's morale went up with each use. The boost from my equipment should have brought it up by twelve each time, but right now it was only going up by ten each time.

Anyway, with that, our preparations were complete. I summoned the Demi-Harpies and asked them to carry me, Misaki, and Suzuna. They used their feet to grab us. Their legs looked rather slender, but they were strong, perhaps like an eagle's claws, so they held us firmly.

"Who would have thought you could team up with Demi-Harpies and use this kind of strategy… I wish other parties would take note of the diversity of the strategies your party has available to them," said Seraphina.

"Except that only parties with expendable funds can afford to train human-type monsters since they level up slowly and it takes money to care for them," said Igarashi.

"It's also really difficult to capture them without killing them.

I've heard of instances where people would use a skill to force the monster unconscious, but they'd take a hit at the same time and it would kill them," said Elitia.

I remembered the time I fell with the Demi-Harpy and Cion caught us, as well as Astarte, Cion's mom. If it weren't for her intimidation, we probably wouldn't have been able to capture the first Demi-Harpy.

"Actually...Atobe, the way that Demi-Harpy is carrying you makes it look like you're about to be hit with a scissors takedown by a winged lady...," said Igarashi.

"Oooh, don't say that! It makes me think of what's gonna happen to us with the scissors monsters... Call this an eagle grab instead," said Misaki.

"Oh, right... The Sand Scissors... Haaah. Misaki, you always help by making me feel relaxed," said Elitia. She had become more and more tense as her morale increased, but now a good amount of tension drained from her shoulders.

Melissa was riding Cion with the Forbidden Scythe across her back and did a final check of the plan with us. "There is a chance we could have a Bubble Laser shot at us right when we go in."

"If that happens, I can use Mirage Step...," said Igarashi.

"There's a chance that Mirage Step won't work to avoid straight magic attacks. I can at least react if I'm shot at...," said Elitia.

"No, leave it to me. I'd like to try out this new shield." Seraphina looked like her entire body radiated fighting spirit. If she said it would be fine, I could trust her to handle it.

The path through the cliffs led directly into the sun,

momentarily blinding us. If Seraphina could definitely take the enemy's attacks, then we could at least avoid getting shot down right when we exited the pass while our eyes were still adjusting.

"I'm gonna use a skill to prevent any Fear effects. Mist of Bravery!"

"Thank you, Ms. Kyouka... Now, here we go!"

```
◆Current Status◆
> ARIHITO activated DEFENSE SUPPORT 1 ⟶ Target:
                                         SERAPHINA
> KYOUKA activated MIST OF BRAVERY
> SERAPHINA activated DEFENSIVE STANCE
> SERAPHINA activated SURGING WAVE ADVANCE ⟶
  Movement speed increases while defending
```

"Haaaaaah!" Seraphina lifted the shield bigger than her and rushed so fast I could hardly believe it. A massive ghost-like form suddenly appeared in the direction she was moving.

```
◆Monster Encountered◆
★MERCILESS GUILLOTINE
Level 8
Variable Resistances
Area Effect: FEAR
Dropped Loot: ???
```

"You won't get past...this shield!"

```
◆Current Status◆
> SERAPHINA activated PROVOKE ──→ ★MERCILESS GUILLOTINE'S
  hostility toward SERAPHINA increased
```

Seraphina was wrapped in dense light. She used every skill she had at her disposal, and the moment she left the narrow passage, the giant crab unleashed a jet of water so powerful, it carved a gouge into the rock.

"...GUWAARARAAAAA!"

```
◆Current Status◆
> SERAPHINA activated AURA SHIELD
> ★MIRRORED SHELL PAVIS'S special effect activated
  ──→ SERAPHINA'S magic defense rose sharply
> SERAPHINA activated DEFENSE FORCE
> ★MERCILESS GUILLOTINE activated BUBBLE LASER ──→ Hit
                                                SERAPHINA
No damage
```

For a moment, Seraphina's shield looked like it'd grown larger. The attack, which I believed was the one that devastated Roland's party, was deflected with her shield, the scattered water falling down like rain again.

"Let's go, everyone!"

"Yeah!"

"......!"

Elitia, Igarashi, and Theresia dashed forward. Seraphina continued to advance using Surging Wave Advance, maintaining her position in the front of the formation.

"We're in this, too! Let's go, Himiko!" I shouted.

"Thank you, Asuka!"

"Here we gooo, Yayoi!"

"Us too...!"

"Woof!"

The Demi-Harpies flapped their wings powerfully and flew over the beach in the rain as Cion rushed over the sand.

For a moment, I was stunned at the beauty of the scene. If we hadn't come here for a battle, I would probably have just stood, silently staring at it. An expansive white sand beach was cut out from abundant fields by a towering rock cliff. The sun started to slip behind the ocean's horizon, and the Merciless Guillotine raised its massive pincer.

# CHAPTER 5

# The Reaper and the Scarlet Swordswoman

## Part I: A Golden Opportunity

Just like our first battle, the crab started off materialized, making physical attacks effective. Unfortunately, it wouldn't let us get close easily. In exchange for her increased magic defense, Seraphina could no longer defend completely against those gigantic pincers. Elitia accelerated and went in front for a moment, and the Merciless Guillotine had two targets: her and Seraphina with her Provoke.

"Kyouka, Theresia, let's spread out!"

"Got it!"

◆Current Status◆
> Elitia activated Sonic Raid
> ★Merciless Guillotine attacked ⟶ Elitia evaded

Elitia drew the crab's attention and evaded the huge pincer as it crashed diagonally down into the ground. Sand was kicked up from the impact, and Theresia and Igarashi moved in to where they could get in a counterattack.

*If I can Stun or Confuse it now, then maybe Melissa can get in there with her auto-kill... Crap!*

◆Current Status◆
> ★MERCILESS GUILLOTINE deployed special action GHOST BODY
Resistance Change: Immune to physical attacks

*It can change its immunities with skills other than Phantom Drift...!*

That ruined any chance we had of getting an auto-kill hit in right away, or even of starting a combination attack with Elitia. But that didn't change the fact we had an opening. I didn't know if this would be effective now that it wasn't materialized, but I used the new skill I took before we arrived.

*Command Support!*

◆Current Status◆
> ARIHITO used HAWK EYES to perceive ★MERCILESS GUILLOTINE's weak spot
> ARIHITO activated COMMAND SUPPORT 1 ⟶
Now capable of guiding party members' target

*I knew it... The wound I made with Murakumo is a weak spot now!*

"Theresia, Igarashi! Do a combo with magic attacks!" I shouted.

""......!""

I was going to try and get a status effect in there, specifically, Confusion. Stun had worked on the Sand Scissors, but either would work as long as it slowed down the crab.

"Cooperation Support...long-range attacks!"

◆Current Status◆
> ARIHITO activated COOPERATION SUPPORT 1
> ARIHITO activated ATTACK SUPPORT 2 —→ Support
  Type: FORCE SHOT (HYPNOSIS)
> THERESIA activated ACTIVE STEALTH
> ARIHITO activated FORCE SHOT (HYPNOSIS) —→ Hit
  ★MERCILESS GUILLOTINE
Weak spot attack
Flinch
Combined attack stage 1
> THERESIA activated AZURE SLASH —→ Hit ★MERCILESS
                                          GUILLOTINE
ACTIVE STEALTH terminated
Combined attack stage 2
> KYOUKA activated SPIRAL LIGHTNING —→ Hit ★MERCILESS
                                           GUILLOTINE
Caused ELECTROCUTION
Combined attack stage 3
> ATTACK SUPPORT 2 activated 2 times —→ ★MERCILESS
  GUILLOTINE resisted CONFUSION

```
> Combined Attack: FORCE, AZURE, SPIRAL ⟶ ★MERCILESS
  GUILLOTINE was CONFUSED
Continued ELECTROCUTED state
```

While in the sky, I pulled back my slingshot and fired off a magical bullet, with a single spot in my sights. It'd become difficult to make out all of the giant crab, but it wasn't enough to hinder my aim since I'd found the weak spot with Hawk Eyes.

The bullet struck as it tried to raise its pincer, and it stopped moving for a brief moment.

"......!"

"Hyaaa!"

Theresia used that moment to slash at it with a blue fire–covered blade, and Igarashi jabbed it with a lightning-coated spear.

```
◆Current Status◆
> ★MERCILESS GUILLOTINE's shell broke ⟶ Defense fell
Status ailments nullified
```

"GWAAARARAAA!!"

"...Its pincer broke!" cried Elitia. The crack in its pincer widened until it was no longer able to support its weight and almost half the pincer broke off. The part that fell to the ground materialized, its tip piercing the sand.

*We were able to get in a huge hit when only magical attacks were effective... Last time, this is the kind of situation where it materialized. But there's a chance this thing won't follow the same pattern all the time!*

"Leader!" called Melissa.

"Arihito, I think now's the time!" said Misaki.

"No, not yet!"

◆Current Status◆
> ★Merciless Guillotine activated Phantom Drift ⟶
Speed increased

*I was right... It knows that we've come with a weapon that can kill it immediately!*

"Melissa, wait until you're sure you can hit it!" I ordered.

"Ah... Okay!"

The giant crab's two eyes moved strangely. One eye looked up to the sky while the other stayed on the ground.

"Chirp!"

Right after, the Demi-Harpies let out a noise that sounded like a quiet scream. I felt an indescribable shudder run up my spine and decided to trust my instincts.

"Everyone, scatter! Misaki, Suzuna, get as far away as you can!"

"Okay!"

"R-right!"

◆Current Status◆
> ★Merciless Guillotine activated Sky High
> ★Merciless Guillotine activated Typhoon ⟶ Wind-
inflicted area attack

"—Aaaaaah!!"

The giant crab noticed us in the sky and deemed us a threat. The moment it leaped into the air, its body released a violent torrent of wind.

""Eeeek…!!""

*God…dammit… How many skills does this thing have?!*

The Demi-Harpies managed to hold on to us, but the lashing winds the giant crab produced left cuts on their skin. My suit was torn, and I saw small lines of blood running down. It was clear that my friends had been injured as well.

A light shone on the crab's back. This gale-creating skill must be one of the ones it stole from Roland. I regretted not learning about all of Roland's skills before coming here. But even if I had known, it would have been nearly impossible to evade that attack, beyond trying to fly higher in the sky.

"Ch-cheep…"

"Himiko, can you still fly?!"

"…Chirp!" Himiko mustered up some strength and replied.

It didn't seem like the giant crab could continue to use two skills while in the sky, because it fell to the ground again. It wasn't materialized, though, so it didn't take any damage from the impact.

"Misaki, Suzuna, are you okay?!"

"Y-yes… I somehow managed to make it, thanks to your warning," said Suzuna.

"Urgh… My eyes are spinning from being swooshed around…," said Misaki.

I should have made sure I was behind them even though we

were in the sky. Now I moved around to their backs and activated Recovery Support.

"Ah… It's fast… But that's not enough to hit me!"

◆Current Status◆
> Elitia activated Sonic Raid
> ★Merciless Guillotine activated Soul—Stealing Scythe
  ⟶ Elitia evaded
> ★Merciless Guillotine activated Soul—Stealing Scythe
  ⟶ Elitia evaded

The giant crab targeted Elitia with wide-swinging violent attacks, but Elitia continued to evade. If she could at least activate Counter Slice 1, then I could use Attack Support 1 to get in a small hit, but she didn't have the time to move in right now.

*If only we could make it so that physical attacks are effective… What do we do?!*

I couldn't decide which path to go down… Any choice here couldn't be changed, and it would have an impact on our future strategy. But I couldn't sit around confused. The Merciless Guillotine was already starting to target Theresia and Igarashi.

"Agh!"

"—!"

◆Current Status◆
> Theresia activated Mirage and Shadow Step

```
> KYOUKA activated EVASION STEP
> ★MERCILESS GUILLOTINE activated SOUL-STEALING SCYTHE
  ──→ THERESIA evaded
> ★MERCILESS GUILLOTINE activated SOUL-STEALING SCYTHE
  ──→ KYOUKA evaded
> KYOUKA's evasion rate increased
```

"Ms. Theresia, Ms. Kyouka!" cried Seraphina.

The three of them were using everything they had to draw the enemy's attention and make sure it didn't focus all its attacks on Seraphina, our tank. The problem was, it took everything they had to keep up with the crab's speed, and they weren't able to take a single opportunity for a counterattack. Even if I tried to support them from the sky, the giant crab kept moving so that it was keeping someone in the vanguard engaged.

"It's fast...but I can still dodge!" Igarashi's speed increased even more. I could tell she was getting more confident.

It was right then that I started to think they could keep dodging forever.

"Kyouka, look out!"

"Igarashi!!"

```
◆Current Status◆
> ARIHITO activated DEFENSE SUPPORT 1 ──→ Target: KYOUKA
> ★MERCILESS GUILLOTINE activated NECROBURST
> GHOST SCISSORS exploded ──→ Hit KYOUKA
★MERCILESS GUILLOTINE absorbed vitality
```

＊　　＊　　＊

"Eeeek!"

"......!!"

◆Current Status◆

> Kʏᴏᴜᴋᴀ'ѕ Vᴀʀɪᴀʙʟᴇ Aʀᴍᴏʀ +4 broke

Unfortunately, Igarashi had come close to the remains of a Ghost Scissors, and it exploded with a flash of magical light. Despite the fact that her Protection Necklace guarded against equipment breaking, it wasn't able to prevent it. About half of Igarashi's armor was blown off, injuring her in the process.

"How dare you—!"

"Ellie, wait!"

◆Current Status◆

> ★Mᴇʀᴄɪʟᴇss Gᴜɪʟʟᴏᴛɪɴᴇ activated Sᴏᴜʟ–Sᴛᴇᴀʟɪɴɢ Sᴄʏᴛʜᴇ

　→ Eʟɪᴛɪᴀ evaded

Elitia was enraged, but Igarashi got her under control. At the last minute, instead of stepping forward to charge in, she leaped backward and avoided the scythe.

"Ow... This is nothing...!"

"—!!"

"Kyouka!"

Both Theresia and Elitia moved in to help Igarashi. Before the giant crab could lash out at her, Seraphina moved in to block the attack.

"GUWARARAAAA!!"

"Mr. Atobe, some support please!"

◆Current Status◆
> Arihito activated Defense Support 1 ⟶ Target:
  Seraphina
> Seraphina activated Immovable Breath ⟶ Increased
  chance of counter
> Seraphina activated Wide Stance ⟶ Knockback
  effects against Seraphina nullified
> Seraphina activated Aura Shield
> ★Mirrored Shell Pavis's special effect activated
  ⟶ Seraphina's magic defense rose sharply
> ★Merciless Guillotine activated Soul-Stealing Scythe

I felt like my heart stopped. I'd guessed that attack had been magical because it had slipped right through Roland's defense, but it wasn't impossible that I was wrong. The scythe swung down toward Seraphina's shield. There was no going back.

The moment the scythe touched the shield, there was an impact totally unlike when two physical objects collide, and the giant crab's scythe was repelled with a loud noise.

"Haaaaaah!"

◆Current Status◆
> Seraphina activated Shield Parry ⟶ Nullified Soul-
  Stealing Scythe
> ★Merciless Guillotine's actions temporarily halted

"She did it!"

"Amazing… Seraphina blocked the scythe!"

That defense brought us back from the brink of destruction and set us up for a counterattack. Both Igarashi, who had taken damage, and Theresia fell into offensive stances. Melissa was also likely coming in for an attack. This was a once in a lifetime golden opportunity to get through this.

## Part II: Crimson Petals

I was going to give the order to start a combo attack using the opportunity Seraphina made for us, but I saw Igarashi touch a hand to her broken armor.

*What on earth is she…? Oh, right!*

"Theresia, back me up!" said Igarashi, and Theresia readied her sword to make the second stage of the combo, followed by Seraphina.

"Suzuna, take Sacred Words!" I ordered.

"Okay!" She didn't hesitate. Her license glowed, responding to her will to take a new skill.

"Holy symbols that repel the wicked, grant me your power!"

◆Current Status◆
> Suzuna activated Sacred Words ⟶ Holy attribute
  added to Arihito's weapon

A white character appeared on my black slingshot. I had a suspicion that the Holy attribute would be effective against the giant crab while it was immaterialized like this since it was a Named version of the Ghost Scissors and had a skill with "phantom" in the name.

Would it end up for better or for worse? If I was wrong and it wasn't going to materialize even if we hit it with a massive attack while only magical attacks were effective, we'd have no choice but to keep fighting without our instant-kill attack.

*Our magic attacks haven't been our main strength up until now. Can they be powerful enough to become a threat...? It's now or never!*

"Cooperation Support...defensive line!"

"...!!"

◆Current Status◆
> ARIHITO activated COOPERATION SUPPORT 1
> ARIHITO activated ATTACK SUPPORT 2
  ⟶ Support Type: FORCE SHOT (STUN)
> ARIHITO activated FORCE SHOT (HYPNOSIS)
  ⟶ Hit ★MERCILESS GUILLOTINE
Combination attack stage 1
> THERESIA activated AZURE SLASH ⟶ Hit ★MERCILESS
                                              GUILLOTINE

Weak spot attack
Slight knockback
Magic power combustion
Combination attack stage 2

Theresia targeted the weak spot even without an order from me. That meant each person understood what area was effective to attack after I'd used Command Support once. The giant crab was engulfed in blue flames as it burned. It had been temporarily stopped, and now it flinched, followed by a knockback effect that pushed it back.

Igarashi was already spacing herself to get in the third stage of the combo. That was when my guess as to what she was doing turned into a certainty.

"Ethereal Form!"

◆Current Status◆
> Kyouka activated Ethereal Form
> Kyouka switched weapon to ★Ambivalenz
> Kyouka's armor changed to Ethereal state
  ⟶ Abilities restored
Increased speed, magic defense

"Sh-she transformed… Arihito, she transformed!" cried Misaki.

I doubt Igarashi herself even anticipated this. Her magic filled in the sections of her broken armor, and winglike shapes sprouted from her back. Then she switched to her double-headed spear, whose power increased by the amount of damage the user had taken. After switching, she lashed out with a magic attack that she could use with any spear she used.

"Come forth…*Lightning Rage!*"

◆Current Status◆
> Kyouka activated Lightning Rage ⟶ Hit ★Merciless
                                        Guillotine
Weak spot attack
Caused Electrocution
Combination attack stage 3
> Additional attacks from Lightning Rage
    ⟶ 3 stages hit ★Merciless Guillotine
Weak spot attack
> Attack Support 2 activated 5 times
    ⟶ ★Merciless Guillotine was Stunned
Weak spot attack
Continued Stunned state
> Combination attack: Force, Azure, Rage
    ⟶ ★Merciless Guillotine's Stun state was lengthened
Weak spot attack
Continued Electrocuted state


Blue flames licked at the crab's shell. Igarashi closed in on it
and thrust her spear at its mouth. Lightning exploded from her
spear, and since there were no other potential targets in the area,
all the lightning that would have struck the surrounding area
arced toward the giant crab, increasing the power of the attack.

*Will this do it...? Maybe Elitia can get in there, too!*

If Igarashi had her mirage warrior, we'd get even more attacks
in there with one volley, but Cooperation Support 1 only worked
for up to three people. Instead of aiming for simply increasing our
number of fighters, I was hoping to get in a huge combo hit.

Everyone watched what happened after that volley. The crab had been translucent, but suddenly we were no longer able to see through it to the other side…

```
◆Current Status◆
> ★Merciless Guillotine materialized ⟶ Nullified
                                              magic
Status ailments removed
```

The Stunned, blue flame-engulfed giant crab suddenly materialized.

"GUWAAARARAAAAA!!"

It still had plenty of vitality. The giant crab raised its broken pincer and scythe as if to testify to that, but—

"Now! Misaki, Melissa!"

"Take it out, Melissa! Morale Discharge, Fortune Roll!"

```
◆Current Status◆
> Misaki activated Fortune Roll ⟶ Next action will
  succeed automatically
```

I didn't know where Melissa had gone—at the very least, she wasn't in front of the giant crab. Seraphina's gaze alerted me to Melissa's location: She'd been waiting this whole time and was about to use the Ambush skill she'd just learned.

"I'll bring you down!!"

```
◆Current Status◆
> MELISSA attacked ⟶ AMBUSH effects activated
Hit ★MERCILESS GUILLOTINE
Critical hit
```

I just barely caught sight of Melissa circling behind the giant crab in midair and raising the sinister-looking Forbidden Scythe.

Time seemed to stop. Would the auto-kill effect actually work? All I could do in that moment was pray.

```
◆Current Status◆
> ★FORBIDDEN SCYTHE's special effect was activated
> ★MERCILESS GUILLOTINE was hit with auto-kill
  effect
> 1 ★MERCILESS GUILLOTINE defeated
```

"—GUWA...RAARAAA...RAA..."

The fierce giant crab fell. Rumbles echoed across the beach as the ground trembled from the crash when its long legs lost their strength and its body plummeted to the ground.

"We did it... Wow, we really did it, Arihito!"

I heard Misaki crying in joy. Igarashi and Theresia turned back to look up in my direction. But I, along with several others, noticed something. I didn't want it to be true; I didn't want to think that the battle would continue even though our strategy had succeeded.

```
◆Current Status◆
> ★Merciless Guillotine activated Reincarnate
> ★Merciless Guillotine summoned ★Merciless Mourner
```

All of a sudden, a figure clad in a crab shell appeared in front of the immobilized Merciless Guillotine. It looked like the humanoid version of the giant crab and was vastly smaller, but I could sense that it was even more powerful.

```
◆Monster Encountered◆
★Merciless Mourner
Level 9
Dropped Loot: ???
```

"A-Arihito... It's..."

"It's coming!"

It started moving without a moment's delay. The blades on the outside of its shell-clad arms flashed as it went for the closest person: Theresia.

"—!!"

"No you don't!"

"Elitia!"

```
◆Current Status◆
> Arihito activated Defense Support 1 —→ Target: Elitia
> ★Merciless Mourner attacked —→ Elitia defended
```

∗   ∗   ∗

Elitia covered Theresia, who didn't have time to react, and defended against the attack with her sword. They weren't that different in size, but the Mourner's attack pushed Elitia backward. Just before I thought she might try to get in a Counter Slash 1, the monster lashed out with its other arm.

◆Current Status◆
> ★MERCILESS MOURNER activated PHANTOM BLADE ⟶ Hit
ELITIA

"—Aagh?!"

Its second attack landed before Elitia's. If this thing was faster than her, then no one in the party would be able to keep up with it.

◆Current Status◆
> ★MERCILESS MOURNER activated EXECUTION ⟶ KYOUKA
evaded

"Ah… It's so fast!"

A slash of its arm meant it could reach even an opponent it wasn't engaged with. It looked like it cut nothing more than air, but its range was longer than it appeared. Igarashi managed to evade thanks to the effects of her Evasion Step. Even so, if she had used it a split second later, she would have been hit.

Theresia knew it would target her next, but she didn't fall back, instead readying her sword and shield. But I knew she wouldn't be able to handle this monster; it was faster than Elitia.

*"O devotee, my Guard Arm has recovered. It is now available for your use."* I heard Ariadne's voice in my mind. She'd deemed that this was a time when it was necessary.

"All right... Go, Ariadne!"

"......!!"

◆Current Status◆
> ARIHITO requested temporary support from ARIADNE
  ⟶ Target: THERESIA
> ARIADNE activated GUARD ARM
> ★MERCILESS MOURNER activated PHANTOM BLADE ⟶ Hit
                                                    THERESIA
No damage

Ariadne answered my request, but even though the Guard Arm halted the attack, it didn't stop the monster.

◆Current Status◆
> ARIHITO activated DEFENSE SUPPORT 1 ⟶ Target:
                                          THERESIA
> ★MERCILESS MOURNER attacked ⟶ Hit THERESIA

"......!!"

Theresia wasn't able to completely brace herself against the horizontal slash with her shield. She was launched into the air and went crashing into the sand. I couldn't cry out or even go down to save her. I knew that if I lost my composure, people would die.

"—No more…!"

◆Current Status◆
> ARIHITO activated DEFENSE SUPPORT 1 ⟶ Target:
                                          SERAPHINA
> SERAPHINA activated PROVOKE ⟶ ★MERCILESS MOURNER'S
  hostility toward SERAPHINA increased
> SERAPHINA activated IMMOVABLE BREATH ⟶ Increased
  chance of counter
> ★MIRRORED SHELL PAVIS's special effect was
  activated ⟶ SERAPHINA's magic defense rose
  sharply
> ★MERCILESS MOURNER activated PHANTOM BLADE ⟶ Hit
                                          SERAPHINA
> ★MERCILESS MOURNER activated PHANTOM BLADE ⟶ Hit
                                          SERAPHINA

The intervals between its attacks were so quick that I couldn't respond with another Guard Arm request. Seraphina couldn't even bring the damage from one attack down to zero, but she didn't fall a single step backward thanks to her Immovable Breath skill.

"—Seraphina, it's no good!" shouted Suzuna. She, along with the rest of us, knew that Seraphina was risking her life to buy us time.

"I will not retreat a single step… You cannot push me back!"

"Suzuna, use Auto-Hit! That should be able to land!" I ordered.

"Okay!"

◆Current Status◆
> Suzuna activated Auto-Hit ⟶ Next two shots will
  automatically hit
> Arihito activated Attack Support 2 ⟶ Support
                                          Type: Force
                                          Shot (Stun)
> Suzuna activated Storm Arrow ⟶ Hit ★Merciless
                                       Mourner

*It wasn't Stunned or slowed down...but still!*

The monster was wary of Suzuna's arrows and stopped its series of attacks against Seraphina to fall back. But it was still within range to use its long-range Execution attack. Even our lowest-level member, Melissa, was in range.

◆Current Status◆
> ★Merciless Mourner activated Execution

It didn't turn around; it just whipped its right crab shell–covered arm behind it. Neither Melissa nor Cion had any way of dodging it. I should have ordered her to get out of there the moment her auto-kill attack was successful...before she was targeted.

All sound faded. I couldn't do anything to intercept. This creature was faster than Elitia—there was nothing the rest of us could do to beat that speed.

She'd always been that fast. She had always saved us from destruction with that sword of hers.

"—Hyaaaaaa!"

```
◆Current Status◆
> Elitia activated Berserk and Red Eye ⟶ Attack
  power and movement capabilities increased
Magic drain begins
> Elitia activated Slash Ripper ⟶ Hit ★Merciless
                                         Mourner
Action canceled
```

A red blur streaked across the beach and blew the enemy away. Based on what happened, I guessed she had slashed at it horizontally.

"Ellie!"

Her eyes were dyed crimson, and a red aura surrounded her body. This was completely different from when she'd just used Berserk.

"I will not let my friends get taken from me again... I will scatter you across this beach like crimson petals!"

The monster's shell was gouged, but it stood against Elitia with no less hostility than before.

"*Master, Elitia cannot maintain this state for very long,*" came Murakumo's voice. She was right; we needed to end this as soon as possible.

```
◆Current Status◆
> ★Merciless Mourner activated Create Golem
> 16 Sand Scissors summoned
```

*    *    *

The creature spread its arms, and I saw Sand Scissors sprout up here and there, and I knew. I knew that it was thinking the exact same thing as us—that it absolutely wasn't going to lose this fight.

## Part III: All-Out War

Each of the Sand Scissors was still level 6, the same level as the Arachnophilia. I didn't waver even though I saw an absurd sixteen of them appear. We still had ways to handle this; we hadn't exhausted the attacks available to us.

"Melissa, Cion, you did a great job! Get out of there before they surround you!" I ordered.

"...But I can still..."

"Woof!"

Melissa was still trying to get in an auto-kill hit. But it wasn't like Elitia could stop the monster every time it targeted Melissa. Cion seemed to understand that well.

While the Merciless Mourner was glaring threateningly at Elitia, it seemed to radiate hostility in every direction. In the sky, the Demi-Harpies were terrified and didn't seem like they could move in any closer, but they were prepared to do what was needed if it came down to it.

Then, before Elitia and the Merciless Mourner could cross blades again...

"Morale Discharge, Soul Mirage!"

"......!"

◆Current Status◆
> KYOUKA activated SOUL MIRAGE ⟶ All party members
  gained a MIRAGE WARRIOR
> THERESIA activated TRIPLE STEAL ⟶ All party
  members received TRIPLE STEAL effects

The Demi-Harpies didn't get a mirage warrior, but everyone
in the party other than Cion, who was in the secondary party, was
strengthened by the effects of Igarashi's and Theresia's Morale
Discharges. That meant there were two Elitias' worth of attack
power, both of their abilities skyrocketing thanks to Red Eye.

"Hyaaaaaa!"

Elitia started the fight. Two blurs of the golden-haired swordswoman closed in on the monster.

"We're going in, too... Suzuna, your flute! Misaki, can you still
keep going?!" I said.

"I—I think I can just about do it somehow... I won't hold you
back!" said Misaki as Suzuna pulled out her flute. It was made
from a massive horn but looked like a normal sideways flute. The
two Shrine Maidens readied their flutes.

◆Current Status◆
> ARIHITO activated ATTACK SUPPORT 2
  ⟶ Support Type: DARKNESS BULLET

> Elitia and her Mirage Warrior activated Blossom Blade
> ★Merciless Mourner activated Blocking


Elitia used her strongest skill as her first move. It reached sixteen stages because she was in Berserk, and then went past sixteen. As hard as it was to believe, however, the monster raised its arms and took Elitia's vicious attack straight on.

"—I'll cut you down!"

While she was violently slashing away, a light emerged from Suzuna's flute. The Sand Scissors had just started to move, but they froze the moment her music started. And I had already pulled the trigger of my magic gun to support Suzuna's sound attack with another bullet.


◆Current Status◆
> Suzuna activated Sacred Words ⟶ Holy attribute
  added to Suzuna's weapon
> Suzuna and her Mirage Warrior inflicted area attack
  with ★Silvanus's Flute ⟶ Hit 10 Sand Scissors
Ineffective against ★Merciless Mourner
> Attack Support 2 activated ⟶ Hit 10 Sand Scissors
> Attack Support 2 activated for Mirage Warrior's
  additional attack ⟶ Hit 10 Sand Scissors
> 10 Sand Scissors defeated
> Suzuna recovered vitality and magic
Successfully stole loot from 8 targets


The Holy-attribute sound wave crashed into the Sand Scissors, stopping them in their tracks where they were shot by black lightning from the Darkness Bullet. Having a mirage warrior didn't double Attack Support 2, but since my support applied to Suzuna's mirage warrior, the black lightning struck the Sand Scissors twice.

"W-wow... That combo was, like, insane!!" said Misaki.

I hadn't expected it to go that well, either. The Merciless Mourner seemed to have an immunity to sound because the attack didn't affect it. On the other hand, ten Sand Scissors turned back to sand, and a number of them left behind what looked like magic stones. On the ground, Igarashi and Theresia attacked the Sand Scissors coming at them. They, along with their mirage warriors, used Lightning Rage and Double Throw, and that, with my support, meant we'd wiped out all the summoned crabs in the blink of an eye.

But Elitia and the Merciless Mourner continued to exchange ferocious blows. The Mourner was being hit with a rain of slashes from a second round of Elitia and her mirage warrior's Blossom Blade. I started to feel concerned when Elitia went to use it for the third time.

"Urgh... Ah..."

The strength suddenly went out of her body. Being in Red Eye state drained too much of her magic. It was already depleted.

"Ellie!"

◆Current Status◆
> ★MERCILESS MOURNER activated REVENGE BLADE ⟶ Attack
  power increased by number of times defended

*   *   *

*I have to make it!*

"AAAAAaaaaah!!"

◆Current Status◆
> Arihito activated Charge Assist ⟶ Elitia recovered
                                       magic
> Elitia and her Mirage Warrior activated Rising Bolt
  ⟶ ★Merciless Mourner defended
Nullified attack
Critical hit
> Elitia's Unicorn Ribbon's special effect was
  activated ⟶ A portion of the attack ignores
  the enemy's defense on critical
> Elitia and her Mirage Warrior activated additional
  attacks ⟶ Hit ★Merciless Mourner
> Attack Support 2 activated 4 times ⟶ Hit
  ★Merciless Mourner
> Elitia recovered vitality and magic
Failed to steal loot

"—!!!"

The Merciless Mourner screamed in wordless rage and stumbled back as it was hit with Elitia's strikes and my black lightning. Elitia and her mirage warrior had used Rising Bolt, a skill with few attacks, but she was able to use it with the magic I'd given her with Charge Assist. It managed to completely destroy the Merciless Mourner's defense, despite how perfect it had seemed.

Smoke wafted from the Merciless Mourner, but it didn't fall. Elitia recovered a lot from the effects of Triple Steal and moved in to strike again, but—

◆Current Status◆
> ★Merciless Mourner activated Jet Slaughter
　→ Targets: Kyouka, Theresia

*What?!*

Instead of attacking Elitia, who was directly in front of it, the Merciless Mourner pointed one arm at Theresia and one at Igarashi, then launched its bladed shell covering at them. It was trying to take down at least one person with it. A single attack from a level-9 Named Monster like this could be fatal to anyone in the party.

But *she* was there with her large shield ready, as if she'd read the attack.

*"O devotee, now is the time to give strength to your ally. Call on the armor of your Stellar Mechanical God,"* came Ariadne's voice. That's right, she'd said something before. She'd said that when our party's combined level reached 20, I would be able to use a Guard Variant.

"Ariadne, I request your support!"

◆Current Status◆
> Arihito requested temporary support from Ariadne

```
> Ariadne activated Guard Variant → Targets:
  Seraphina, Seraphina's Mirage Warrior
```

This wasn't the Guard Arm—it was a different protection from Ariadne. It worked by strengthening a member of the party who carried a shield. Thankfully, Seraphina accepted the change that happened to the shield in front of her eyes and continued with her action.

```
◆Current Status◆
> Seraphina activated Aura Shield
> Seraphina's Mirage Warrior activated halved Aura
  Shield
> ★Mirrored Shell Pavis's special effect activated
  → Seraphina's magic defense rose sharply
> Seraphina activated Bodyguard → Target: Theresia
> Seraphina's Mirage Warrior activated Bodyguard
  → Target: Kyouka
> Jet Slaughter hit Seraphina and her Mirage Warrior
  → Guard Variant's special effect was activated
Physical attacks reflected
> ★Merciless Mourner hit with 2 stages of reflected
  attacks
> Seraphina recovered vitality, magic
Failed to steal loot
```

"—Gah...ah!!"

The two shell pieces the Merciless Mourner shot bounced off

the huge shield and were repelled. Actually, they were launched back with the same force.

"This shield...does more than protect!" exclaimed Seraphina. The shield returned the enemy's physical attacks as they were. You could tell from looking at the damage of the impact left on the Merciless Mourner's shell that it was a threatening attack, even to itself.

The mirage warriors hadn't yet disappeared. All the monsters it had summoned had been defeated. Its shell was no longer in one piece. But the Merciless Mourner still faced down Elitia.

"...I'm ending this!"

◆Current Status◆
> Elitia and her Mirage Warrior activated Blossom Blade
> ★Merciless Mourner activated Desperate Measures →
  Attack, defense, and speed increased
> ★Merciless Mourner activated Blocking

The red blurs that Elitia and her mirage warrior left in the wake of their swords looked like bountifully blooming flowers. The monster took those attacks head-on and continued to hold its own. It didn't have only incredible offense; its defense was probably head and shoulders above that of other Named Monsters that appeared in the labyrinths in this district.

But we were a group, and the enemy was alone. Even if it maintained its impenetrable defense from its front, its response to attacks from behind was slow. That moment of delay could mean its death.

"I've been waiting...for this!"

◆Current Status◆
> MELISSA and her MIRAGE WARRIOR attacked

Melissa and her mirage warrior had been waiting for a chance. There's no way she wasn't afraid, but she still waited for that brief opening.

"Melissa!" cried Elitia. She knew I would have been looking for that opening, too, and supported Melissa's decision.

◆Current Status◆
> 2 stages hit ★MERCILESS MOURNER
Critical hit
> ★FORBIDDEN SCYTHE broke
> MELISSA recovered vitality and magic
Successfully stole loot

"Ah?!"

The auto-kill effect didn't always succeed. That's why we'd planned our strategy around using it after having used Fortune Roll.

*But we can't let it get us down. That spot's behind it!*

"Come forth, Murakumo!"

◆Current Status◆
> ARIHITO activated REAR STANCE ⟶ Target: MELISSA

```
> Arihito and his Mirage Warrior activated Meteor
  Thrust ──→ 2 stages hit ★Merciless Mourner
> Arihito recovered vitality and magic
Target no longer has loot
```

I wasn't directly behind the enemy—I was at a distance, which I could close immediately with Meteor Strike. It was thanks to Melissa being there that I could even use Rear Stance to reach it.

The monster couldn't handle the attacks from behind and both sides. Even so, how little its shell was destroyed on the front really spoke to its horrific strength. But Elitia wasn't going to miss the opening I made for her. She moved in to use her strongest skill, and I would fulfill my duty as a rearguard. I used the last remaining drops of magic to activate my skills and support her in the end.

"Scatter, my crimson blooms! *Blossom Blade!*"

```
◆Current Status◆
> Arihito activated Rear Stance ──→ Target: Elitia
> Arihito activated Attack Support 2 ──→ Support
  Type: Blade of Heaven and Earth
> Elitia and her Mirage Warrior activated Blossom Blade
> Scarlet Dance increased offense and decreased
  defense
> 24 stages hit ★Merciless Mourner
Additional attacks from Mirage Warrior
> Elitia and her Mirage Warrior activated additional
  attacks ──→ Hit ★Merciless Mourner
```

> Attack Support 2 reached its limit
> Blade of Heaven and Earth activated 16 times

"Aaaaah...aaah!!"

Red slashes formed crimson flowers. Elitia abandoned defense to focus everything into the might of her sword as each strike she made looked like a move in an elegant dance. Each of her strikes was accompanied by one from Murakumo, bringing the total number of attacks close to one hundred. The first few dozen strikes continued to rain down on the monster in the air where it had been flung. Its shell suddenly shattered; it fell to the sand without bouncing—and didn't stand again.

◆Current Status◆
> 1 ★Merciless Mourner defeated
> 1 Soul Prison Stone recovered

*"Huff, huff..."*

"You did it, Ellie! ...Uh, wh-what's wrong...?"

"Igarashi, wait! Right now, Elitia's..."

Even though the battle was over, Red Eye hadn't ended. That meant Berserk was still in effect, which made her attack anything. But...

"Ellie, it's okay now... We've won." Suzuna dropped to the beach and pulled Elitia into a hug, not a single shred of fear in her. At first, Elitia seemed to be having a hard time, but the red magic surrounding her body faded as Suzuna stroked her back.

◆Current Status◆
> Elitia's Berserk and Red Eye have terminated with
  the end of battle
> Elitia's abilities temporarily decreased


"Ah...S-Suzuna...?"

"Oh, Ellie... Thank goodness..."

"...I'm sorry; I don't have much strength left... Could I lean on you?"

"I'm here for that kind of thing, toooo! I didn't even have time to use my exploding cards, so I'm pumped full of leftover energy!"

Misaki and Suzuna both helped support Elitia. I asked the Demi-Harpies to retrieve the stone that was stuck onto the giant crab's shell. If we had that stone, which I thought housed Roland's soul, we should be able to bring him back.

Melissa sent the materials from the giant crab and the Merciless Mourner to her storage. I went closer to the Merciless Mourner to check and discovered there wasn't a humanoid monster inside the shell. I decided it was safe to assume that it was simply a set of armor housing the giant crab's soul, which was what made it move.

*"I cannot say I was able to completely use my abilities as my master's sword. I have to make it to the limit of your abilities...,"* said Murakumo sadly from my back where I'd returned her to her sheath. She was half-right.

*My skills and sword-wielding abilities... They both have room to grow. We're only in District Seven—we can't stop improving just yet.*

Murakumo didn't respond for a little while. She seemed to be thinking about something. Either that, or perhaps she was discussing it with Ariadne.

"*Arihito... Your growth has been incredible. However, I do not expect you to gain a level even having fought an enemy like this one. This will be because of the usefulness of the skills you can get at each level, as well as the fact that Elitia was the primary attacker,*" said Ariadne.

*You were listening, too, huh, Ariadne? ...You're right, my level didn't go up. But I wouldn't say it was nothing since I was able to get about eighty percent of the experience needed for the next level with just a few fights.*

It was harder to get experience because of the difference in levels between me and Elitia. The reason I hadn't really noticed until now was because we'd gotten so much experience before the adjustment was applied. But there was no way we could have had Elitia back off just before the enemy was defeated. I thought we were making good progress as we were, but I didn't want to have an extended face-off against an opponent who could kill us if we made one wrong move. I'd love to be incredibly cautious, if only we didn't have any time restrictions.

"*...I am not sure if this is what you wish for, but I... From the day you came to me, I have felt the hands of fate at play,*" said Ariadne.

I'd had a similar thought. We encountered far too many Named Monsters and unique circumstances for it to be coincidence—for instance, the chest left behind by the Merciless Mourner. I'd never seen this kind of chest before. It wasn't a Black Box; engraved on the front of this chest were the words *White Box*. Theresia brought it over to me. We knew how big of a threat the traps on Black Boxes were, so there was no way we could try opening this one. We'd managed to find something I wasn't sure even Falma could open.

"Atobe, that chest...," started Igarashi.

"I thought Black Boxes were the most valuable, so I don't even know how to react to this one... But there's a risk of traps. We can't open it now. I want to try talking to Falma about it later."

"Y-yeah... I've heard how bad it can be for Black Boxes if you try to force it open, fail, and end up activating a trap..." Igarashi must've remembered what Falma had told us because she hugged her body tight with worry. Her magic armor made from the trans rune was still doing fine, but I didn't know what would happen once her magic ran out... I decided to worry about that when I couldn't help her out with Charge Assist anymore. I couldn't use it too much during battle, but if I ran out of magic even after having recovered some from Triple Steal, I could just drink a mana potion.

Seraphina approached while we were talking. Her shield had returned to its normal form, no longer strengthened with Guard Variant.

## Part IV: The Joint Battle

"Mr. Atobe...that was incredible. Every single one of you possesses not only strength but also courage and compassion. You have my utmost respect."

"Seraphina, you're the one who helped us in the most crucial moments."

"Only because of this shield. Without it, I would surely have been killed without being able to fulfill my duties as your defense… I will provide the funds necessary for its maintenance after this."

"Oh, no, that's fine. Actually, if you like it, you can keep it. We still don't have anyone in the party who could equip it, and I have a feeling we'll want to ask for your help again sometime."

"Arihito, going in for the direct invite… I like it. I wanna get invited like thaaat," said Misaki.

"I would feel better having Seraphina in our party, but her Guild Savior duties are still important. I would be honored to just fight by her side like this once in a while," said Igarashi.

I wasn't really planning on recruiting her, but it wasn't as though I never wanted to work with her again. Having her in our party gave us access to a much wider array of strategic options. But I couldn't force her. She had already helped us so much.

"We need to get stronger so that we don't rely too heavily on Seraphina. With that, I just hope we can fight together again, at another time, on a different day," I said.

"What are you saying…? Your party is exemplary. Level is not the only factor when considering a party's actual strength."

If Seraphina said it, then I could believe it. Everyone smiled at me as I thought that.

"Arihito's the one who contributes more than you'd expect for his level. Compared to him, even I need to work harder."

"Ellie…that's far too humble of you—look at the incredible attacks you made," said Suzuna.

"…It was cool. I can't be like you, but I admire you," said Melissa.

"Wh-what's this all of a sudden…? I'm not cool or anything…" Elitia's face flushed red as even Melissa started to compliment her. I doubted there was anyone who wouldn't be happy if they got complimented for the way they fought.

"Mr. Atobe, please feel free to drop in whenever I am stationed nearby. You have no need to hesitate; I myself would like to assist you when possible."

"Thank you, Seraphina." I shook her hand on behalf of my party. She removed her gauntlets for it, and while her hand was large for a woman, it felt smaller than I expected it to.

"While we might have some time left, I don't want Roland to spend a long time like this. Let's go, Atobe," said Igarashi.

"Right… Except, there's something bothering me."

I was still thinking about that person who'd entered the labyrinth before we did. If it was Gray, he must be waiting for his chance to make his move. I hoped he wouldn't do something stupid. Even though a part of me expected he would, I couldn't help hanging my head in disappointment when we made it out of the narrow path through the cliffs.

"So you finally finished, huh? …Hey, ladies, and you, asshole in the suit. Bet you're pretty worn out after fighting that monster!"

Ahead of us was the cave that led out of the labyrinth. On the path leading to it stood Gray, with a number of giant monsters following behind him.

"...So that's how far you were willing to go. You intend to let them destroy us?"

"Aaaah... Th-there's three of those giant mantises!"

"He even has Arachnophilias... How'd he pull that off?!"

◆Monsters Encountered◆
3 Ocean Mantises
Dropped Loot: ???
3 Arachnophilias
Dropped Loot: Black Web

"...Did you use summoning charms to gather them and then bring them all the way here? If that's the case, you probably have a skill that lets you push the target's hostility onto someone else," I said.

"Ha-ha-ha, I'll let you know before I send you off to the Healers! I have a skill that eliminates hostility toward me. Look at these guys; they won't target me even though I'm closest to them."

Well, that explained it. If he was willing to talk that much, there was one other thing I wanted to ask him.

"What are you trying to do here?"

"I can't tell you my whole plan. I just happen to be here, you know? And you just happen to get attacked by a bunch of monsters. That's nothing but some really bad luck... Haaa-ha-ha!"

I had an idea of what he was going to do—I figured I'd ask

first is all. I imagined he'd go pick up something as proof that he defeated the Merciless Guillotine and use it for his own benefit.

"...It seems you have some misconceptions about us, but we're not kind enough to tell you what those are," said Elitia.

"Misconceptions? Are you saying that you, the Death Sword, could easily kill all these monsters? You can't even walk without someone helping you right now!"

Elitia huffed but didn't seem to have any desire to respond to him. I agreed with that move. All we had left to do was to show this guy what was going to happen.

"All right, I'm simply going to stand by and watch what happens. I can add more monsters if there aren't enough... Though these summon charms don't come cheap. You fellas better work hard enough to justify the cost!"

The three mantises looked at us with hostility and jumped forward in unison. Seraphina stepped up to take the front vanguard position; we put Elitia down to rest in a safe place, and we got ready to battle.

But what happened next was something that not I, not even Gray, could have ever imagined. The three mantises were all hit at the time—from behind.

"SCREE!"

"GRAAAAAH!"

A glowing symbol appeared at the feet of one monster before it was engulfed in flames. A glowing mass struck another one forcefully, and the last one recoiled when it was hit by two bullets.

"I see you and your party are doing perfectly fine!"

"Arihito... Everyone...!"

```
◆Current Status◆
> CERES activated FIRE TEXT ──➤ Hit OCEAN MANTIS A
> TAKUMA activated AIR SHELL SHOT ──➤ Hit OCEAN MANTIS B
> LUCA activated DOUBLE ACTION ──➤ 2 stages hit OCEAN
                                              MANTIS C
```

Entrance to the labyrinth was supposed to be restricted, but these entirely unexpected people appeared. There was Ceres riding on Steiner's shoulders, Takuma, Shiori, and then Luca, with a small magic pistol in each hand.

"Madoka... Did you bring everyone here?!"

"I didn't. I was in the workshop with Ceres, but they all just kept coming... They all said they wanted to help you..."

"I don't think I can do much but watch my brother fight...but it's been so long since I've seen him make a move to do anything on his own. I'm sorry; I'm babbling," said Shiori.

"I'd be a mess if you didn't come in to pick up the suit I'm making for you for some reason. I'll show you that even a support person like me can still have it, as long as they practice," said Luca.

"*Mr. Atobe, we came to fight alongside you as well! It appears it will take a little longer to defeat these monsters, but please just wait and see!*"

Gray couldn't seem to understand what was happening. The mantises started to turn toward Ceres's party, and he couldn't do anything about it. Only the Arachnophilias were left.

"S-spiders… Get them! Those people are your enemy, make no mistake!"

I'd figured this might happen… But we might as well show Gray ourselves.

"Come forth, Arachnomage!"


◆Current Status◆
> ARIHITO summoned ARACHNOMAGE


I gripped my pendant with the summoning stones and called on the Arachnomage. The moment Gray saw it, he jumped and tripped backward exactly like he had when he first saw the Merciless Guillotine.

"A M-Monster Tamer… You've even got one of the spiders?!"

The Arachnomage seemed to be communicating something to the Arachnophilias. I couldn't hear anything, but the Arachnophilias must have because they turned around and headed into the field.

"…They're all making a fool of me… Goddammiiiit!" Gray didn't even try to come at us in one last desperate attempt. Instead, he scrambled to his feet and ran to the labyrinth's exit.

"Hmph… It has been far too long since my last battle… I've gotten rusty!" said Ceres.

"—!!"

"The mantises are supposed to be the strongest type of monster in District Seven… They're not going to make this easy!" said Igarashi.

Ceres and the other four with her were fighting well, but it wasn't an easily won fight. Theresia and Igarashi had already rushed out. Melissa got on Cion, and they circled around behind the enemy, looking for an opening to use the butcher's knife Melissa switched to.

"I might be losing my edge with age... In the past, two shots would have sent these guys off to heaven!" said Luca. His boots must have been reinforced with metal because he kicked up his foot to block a slash from one of the mantis's scythe-like arms. Fighting like that while wearing a suit like he did would surely have affected his reputation as a master of kick-style fighting.

◆Cooperation Request from Other Parties◆
> Ceres's party asked to join forces

"—!"

Takuma was a master of hand-to-hand fighting. He moved in quickly and attacked a mantis with a palm strike, pushing it off balance. Igarashi and Theresia used the chance to get an attack in.

"Do it, Atobe!" cried Igarashi.

".......!!"

I accepted Ceres's cooperation request, grateful that they came to reinforce us, then raised my hand and shouted, "I'll support all of you... Complete Mutual Support!"

◆Current Status◆
> Arihito activated Complete Mutual Support

```
Time limit: 120 seconds
> Widened support effect range for ARIHITO'S
  party and cooperating party
> All individual buff skills applied to entire
  party and cooperating party
> Entire party buffed by WOLF PACK
> Entire party buffed by SECRETS OF THE SWORD 2
> Entire party buffed by KNIFE ARTISTRY
> Entire party buffed by INCREASED DROP RATE
> Entire party buffed by CHILD OF LUCK
> Entire party buffed by SECRETS OF THE SHIELD 2
> Entire party buffed by SECRETS OF MAGIC 2
> Entire party buffed by BOXING MASTERY 2
> Entire party buffed by DANCING MASTERY 1
> Entire party buffed by ARMORED FIGHTING 1
> Entire party buffed by HAUTE COUTURE
> Entire party buffed by ASSASSINATION MASTERY 2
```

"Ah... Wh-what on earth...?!" stammered Ceres.

"A strengthening skill... Is this because of Mr. Atobe...?" said
Shiori.

"That's not half-bad... Arihito, if you're going to go this far
for us, we're going to have to liven things up in here... Hah!" said
Luca.

"......!!"

Everyone's buff skills were shared with everyone else—that's
what Mutual Support meant. The person who seemed to benefit
most from it this time was Takuma, since a lot of the buffs were
compatible with his fighting style.

My own party wasn't going to be outdone, though. Igarashi prepared a Lighting Rage and Theresia readied an Azure Slash.

"Here we go, Theresia!"

"……!"

"Igarashi, Theresia, I'll support you!" Without a moment's hesitation, I loaded my magic gun with a dark bullet stone and fired it. Luca was fairly far away, but he still saw me do it—and whistled when he did. Seraphina readied her shield to tackle a mantis in the second wave of attacks.

"Haaaaaah!"

"Whoa… She's very brave. Steiner, we can't let them show us up!" said Ceres.

*"B-but, I'm not very good at fighting… But I guess that doesn't cut it right now!"*

"Arihito, we're ready whenever you aaaare!"

"Just let us know when, Arihito!" cried Suzuna.

"I know… Let's go, you two! Cooperation Support…rearguards!"

Misaki's Blast Card, Suzuna's Storm Arrow, and my Darkness Bullet struck all three of the mantises. Our attacks were strengthened with Complete Mutual Support, and the three mantises' vitality had already been worn down, and they all crumpled to the ground together.

◆Current Status◆
> 3 Ocean Mantises defeated

The mantises were finished, but what happened to Gray? I could tell with my Hawk Eyes that he hadn't actually managed to flee.

"Sorry we're late…but it looks like we were able to stop this would-be runaway."

The four members of Four Seasons had blocked Gray's path just before he was about to make it out.

"K-Kaede… Hurry, out of my way… G-get out of my way!" shouted Gray.

"Aha… You really hate surrendering, huh? I knew that's the sort of person you are," said Ibuki. Kaede was blocking the path, and Gray started to shout at her, but Ibuki quickly moved around him, pinning him in so he couldn't escape.

"How about you give up? I'm sure whatever you did here was terrible," said Anna.

"She's right… You should really get yourself together and stop constantly thinking about doing terrible things," said Ryouko.

"Sh-shut up! I…I'm—!"

"Gray, stop!"

Gray wasn't responding to Anna's or Ryouko's attempts at persuasion. He pulled something out and threw it at the ground. It was a smoke bomb.

"Get outta my… Gah… Aaaah?!"

But he didn't manage to flee. When the veil of smoke cleared, there was an eyepatch-wearing armored man holding Gray up by the lapels with just his right hand.

"Whoa there, kid. You're a real prickly one, eh?"

"Khosrow, I only want him unconscious."

"Yes'm… As you wish, Captain Kozelka."

With the man was a woman wearing a kind of black armor that I hadn't seen in the Labyrinth Country yet. Her outfit made it look like she'd chosen *knight* or something for her job, but I still couldn't tell for sure.

"Kozelka…the third-class dragon captain…" Seraphina's eyes went wide. We were told it would take a few days for the help we requested from the Guild Savior headquarters to arrive, but they were already here. In other words, even this third-class dragon captain felt the situation was unusual enough to warrant a speedy response.

Kozelka had flowing silver hair. I couldn't tell how old she was, but I guessed around Seraphina's age or maybe slightly older.

"You must be Lieutenant Seraphina Edelbert. I apologize for providing you with incorrect information… The higher-ups determined this issue to be more pressing than our previous assignment. I was ordered to prioritize this mission in District Six, which is why we have arrived sooner than originally planned," said Kozelka.

"I understand the situation. This group, the party of Arihito Atobe, has defeated the Named Monster that was causing the damage," Seraphina reported. "I apologize, but our priority mission as Guild Saviors has already come to a close."

Kozelka examined us. She carried herself gracefully, but her gaze was sharp when she looked at me, making me feel like I couldn't get away.

She gave the man named Khosrow an order, and he finally lowered Gray to the ground—but Gray had already passed out.

"The Guild already received a number of reports about this man's actions. Based on eyewitness testimony, we will have to investigate the records retained in his license. He will be tried at the headquarters to determine if he has committed a crime," said Kozelka.

"'Course he has; it's written all over his face. Guys like him usually get beat into shape over at the training facility... Oops. My apologies."

Kozelka glared at Khosrow, and he shrugged. An official punishment would probably be given to Gray for his attempt to pin our deaths on monsters and his use of force to get people to join his party.

"That sounds too kind, considering what he's done... But this facility does sort of sound like imprisonment with forced labor." Igarashi must have felt that the sentence was light because she was very angry at him. I was quite happy to wash my hands of Gray altogether, so the Guild could just take care of everything.

"Hmm... That was tough. But I felt power welling up in me whenever Arihito called out to us. I wonder what kind of skill that was," said Ceres.

*"Master, you should have recovered more magic before coming. You weren't nearly as strong as usual."*

"......"

"Takuma does good work as a mercenary, which means he hasn't lost his skills. I'm glad to see it," said Shiori.

"Arihito, I can't believe you know this many support people. And here I thought I was the only one you were exclusive with. Ha, I'm just joking. It makes me as proud as if it were myself to see a fine customer like you gaining the trust of so many people," said Luca.

Even though it was the first time they'd fought together, the five of them, including Shiori, made a pretty good team. Madoka was the one who brought them along, but she used Hide just in case. Now that the fight was over, she was handing potions out to everyone.

"Oh good... Arihito, I'm so happy... I was sure you'd get injured this time..."

"Sorry to worry you, Madoka. We're all fine, though, as you can see... Elitia, are you doing better?"

"Yeah, it seems that my abilities will gradually recover over time, but it'll take a couple of hours for me to be back to normal. My vitality's completely recovered, though, thanks to Theresia's Morale Discharge."

Triple Steal was good for its ability to steal a monster's dropped loot, but the vitality and magic recovery part of it was a lifesaver. It worked well with Soul Mirage, which meant it wasn't uncommon for us to finish a battle being completely recovered.

"Make sure you bring us along next time. I can't wait until we seek together again. But you seem like you're going to move up to District Six anytime now...," said Kaede.

"...I want to show you guys the racket you helped me make," said Anna as she showed us the racket she had but hadn't used this time. Ryouko and Ibuki smiled happily as they watched the exchange.

"Anna gets that look when she's with Arihito and no one else," said Ibuki.

"You only need to consider us if you have the time, Atobe," added Ryouko. "We're going to do our best, too, to hurry up to District Six."

It was reassuring to know there was another party trying to move up as well. I was looking forward to another opportunity for us to fight together.

Four Seasons, along with Ceres and her party, teleported out of the labyrinth first. Kozelka had Khosrow go ahead, and she was the only one left with our party.

"Mr. Arihito Atobe, I'd like to speak with you briefly. Could you come with Lieutenant Seraphina to the Upper Guild later?"

What Third-Class Dragon Captain Kozelka wanted to discuss would end up becoming a major turning point for our party—something I couldn't possibly have fathomed at the time.

# A Late-Night Status Change

It was the night Arihito slept on the first floor after offering his bed to Falma, who'd had nowhere to stay that evening.

"Honestly... That was awfully bold of you. I mean, Atobe is still a man...," said Igarashi.

Falma went down to the first floor but never came back, so Kyouka and Louisa went to check up on her. What they saw terrified them. Falma had been standing in the doorway of the changing room, talking to someone inside—most likely Arihito.

"You don't have to worry. I said it before: I see Mr. Atobe like a little brother, that's all," said Falma.

"W-well... That doesn't quite make it all right for you to go watch him while he's bathing," said Louisa, trying to choose her words carefully. But no matter how hard she tried, she kept stumbling, and her face turned bright red. Falma looked at her, brought her hand to her own cheek, and smiled.

"What's this now? ...Goodness, Louisa. And you, Ms. Igarashi. Do you have a thing for...? How sweet. Seeing all of you reminds me of when I was young."

The three of them had gotten a lot closer over dinner, to the point that they were starting to feel more like friends than a strict relationship of a Chest Cracker and her clients.

"A-actually, I think you've gotten the wrong idea... I mean, I understand why you might think that, but he and I are just party members to each other," said Kyouka in a quiet voice, sticking up her pointer finger as she explained. Falma seemed to find that amusing because her eyes shone as she listened.

"I'm sorry, I should have shown more restraint. I'm sure the two of you haven't gone to take a bath with Mr. Atobe yet... Oh?"

Kyouka and Louisa glanced discreetly at each other. Louisa had been drunk when she'd gone in, but she did vaguely remember washing Arihito's back and using her massage skills on him. Kyouka had been with Elitia, but her face turned even redder as she remembered seeing Arihito in the bath.

"That's right—you're just in the same party. But you know, my husband and I hadn't even taken a bath together when we were still fellow party members, so you two are a bit further than we got."

"N-no, we're not... Theresia always seemed to want to take a bath with him, so we couldn't let her do as she pleased...," said Kyouka.

"Th-that's right... I agree. I know there's nothing suspicious about Mr. Atobe and Theresia's relationship, but if they're going to take baths together, I'm going to tell them it bothers me...," said Louisa.

"And that's how I feel as well. I think everyone does. I was actually a bit nervous when I went to check, but as I had suspected,

Mr. Atobe was being a perfect gentleman. It was very reassuring," said Falma. Obviously, Kyouka and Louisa weren't going to overlook the fact that she tried to wash the back of a man who was around the same age as her, even though she had a husband and children. She did think that Arihito understood the situation the best, though.

"Atobe will beg for your husband's forgiveness if he ever meets him... He's very serious about that kind of thing," said Kyouka.

"I know... And I definitely understand how that makes you want to tease him a little," said Falma.

"Indeed... O-oh, no, I would never tease Mr. Atobe..." Louisa realized Falma was saying something ridiculous and got flustered, but Falma just put a finger to her lips as if she was saying they should be quiet.

"...Theresia is resting downstairs as well. We could probably at least go see... How about it?" she said.

"I think that's fine as long as we don't go too far... Why do you want to do that, by the way?" asked Igarashi.

"I wonder... Maybe you two were right, and I had a little too much to drink, and it's starting to get to me."

Falma looked like she'd already sobered up, but Kyouka and Louisa didn't say anything. They were starting to think they could learn a thing or two from Falma and her assertiveness.

Before Falma went downstairs, she went to the other bedroom to check on the girls. Kyouka and Louisa finally followed behind in their pajamas. They didn't want to all go together and make a lot of sound walking or they'd wake up Arihito. Louisa knocked quietly on Misaki and the other girls' door, and they heard an almost panicked-sounding voice from inside.

"Hmm...? It sounds like they're all still awake. What are they up to?" said Igarashi.

"That's why you just open the door in situations like this."

"B-but, Falma, that's a bit..."

Falma opened the door and went in. The three of them couldn't have imagined the scene they'd walked in on.

"Aaaah... Wh-why'd you open the door? Can't you tell that now's not a good time?!" cried Misaki.

"Ah... Th-this isn't what you think—Misaki just...," said Suzuna.

"R-right, Misaki asked Madoka to find some swimsuits. We just got together to try them on... We're not doing anything weird," said Elitia.

"Even Ellie is all in...," said Kyouka.

"Wh-what's that supposed to mean? Are you saying that I'm not being serious enough even though we're going seeking tomorrow? That might be true, but Misaki said we needed to get bathing suits ready since we're going to the Beach of the Setting Sun..."

"Heeeey, you two were totally gung ho about all this a minute ago! Are you throwing me under the bus just 'cause we got caught?"

Elitia and Suzuna glanced at each other and shrank back. Kyouka and Louisa couldn't help but smile awkwardly at Misaki, who was for some reason looking quite full of herself.

"I know you didn't know we were coming, but it is a little strange for all of you to be wearing swimsuits together in your room," said Kyouka.

"...Kyouka, you didn't think you were the only one safe from this, did you? Oh-ho-ho, I don't think so!" said Misaki with a meaningful smile, then pulled out the bag she had hidden behind her. "Madoka is so amazing at what she does. You know what this is, right?"

"I—I wonder... Though I guess there's really no point in faking ignorance now..."

"It's...a swimsuit, isn't it? But I'm not a party member; I'm only a registrar who's sharing a house with you, so I'm sure that's just one for Kyouka. Right?" said Louisa.

"Not at all. Louisa, you are still a member of Arihito's—of our household."

Louisa didn't even have time to feel relieved before Misaki pulled a bathing suit out of the bag, as if to say that one was for Louisa. The only problem: It was a string bikini type, with very little fabric to speak of.

"W-wait... I am incredibly sorry that you went to the trouble of getting this kind of bathing suit ready because you thought I would wear it, but I really must insist on a different bathing suit..."

"Louisa, swimsuits are incredibly valuable and rare. It's hard just to find one! It's so annoying to go around to all the shops in District Eight and Seven to see if they happen to have any in stock. Madoka had to use every connection she had in the Merchants

Guild to get these. Don't you think she did a great job?" said Misaki.

"Ah... W-well...I do want to respect Madoka's intentions, but...," said Louisa as she glanced at Kyouka, who didn't know what that expression meant, but a moment later she was also accepting the bathing suit that Misaki was pushing on her in a fluster.

"Ohhh...!" Louisa wailed while Kyouka hugged her swimsuit to her chest as if she cherished it.

"Madoka got one for me, too. I'll have to thank her later," said Kyouka.

"Yeah, I think she's still awake, so we'll go by her room later. This is soooo cool! I can't waaait to see you try this on, Kyouka," said Misaki.

"Huh...?" Kyouka spread out the swimsuit she'd been clutching in order to get a better look. It was white—that much was okay. It was a bikini, the kind that you fastened with strings on the side of your hips, but the strings were placed quite high. Kyouka suspected it would be pretty risqué if she actually put it on. She looked at Louisa, surprised that the Labyrinth Country would have swimsuits this elaborate, but she also felt like she wouldn't be comfortable going in public wearing something like this.

"...Is the fabric used for swimsuits this rare in the Labyrinth Country?" asked Kyouka.

"No—at least, not the kinds used for these...," said Louisa.

"Misaki, you must've had quite a time finding my size. I might as well accept. I could never really find a good one myself, though I'm a bit old to be showing off that much... What's this?" asked

Falma, but then saw Misaki holding yet another bathing suit. They were supposed to be rare, but she kept pulling them out one after another. That left Kyouka and Louisa feeling a bit shocked, but it was really just that Madoka was that well connected as a Merchant and that good at negotiating.

"We got an extra one in that size in case Kyouka or Louisa couldn't wear the one we got for them," explained Misaki.

"Wait... That one is clearly a much less embarrassing design!"

"Kyouka, that's just how things happen sometimes... But yours is even better than mine. I almost want to switch with you," said Louisa.

"Ah... W-well...I'm really sorry, Louisa, but I have to draw the line somewhere."

"U-um... If you like, you can trade with me... But actually, I've already worn it once, so I guess that wouldn't work, would it?" Suzuna seemed concerned when the older group of women started bickering, but Elitia patted her gently on the shoulder.

"Do you think Kyouka and the others could even wear our swimsuits?" she said.

"Oh... S-sorry, I just..." Suzuna shrank back, and Kyouka and Louisa seemed sorry for upsetting her. Elitia adjusted the shoulder strap of her tricolor-striped bathing suit, then went back to her own bed. She looked like she had something on her mind about Kyouka and the other older girls but didn't say it.

"Misaki, can we change soon? Arihito's probably asleep by now, and I also...," she started.

None of them had noticed a certain *thing*, even now. Last night,

Arihito had slept in a separate room on the same floor as them, on his side so that his back was to them. Even if he rolled over in his sleep and ended up on his back, their location in relation to each other wouldn't be a problem. That night, however, Arihito was on the floor below. If he slept on his back, that would mean that he was "behind" them.

The day's fatigue had already been washed away by his Recovery Support 1. Even so, at a steady interval, everyone in the party felt a certain sensation. Each one experienced it slightly differently, but it was mostly the same.

"Ah... It's been a while since I've felt this... It feels like I'm being warmed...," said Misaki.

"Hmm... Is this...because Atobe is on the floor below us...?" wondered Kyouka.

"What's going on, everyone? All your faces are red..." Louisa was confused by the change in the other girls, but Falma looked at them, then at her own bathing suit.

"It seems that you and I aren't quite one of the group, Louisa... I wonder if we could join in if we all wore our bathing suits together."

"Huh...? What do you mean, Falma...?"

"Louisa, let's get changed. Everyone else seems to want to wear their bathing suits and go see Mr. Atobe... Right, Ms. Igarashi?"

Louisa assumed that there was no way Kyouka would want to do something like that, but she was shocked when she looked at her face. Kyouka didn't deny it. In fact, she seemed to be warming up to the idea of changing into her bathing suit.

"...If we make sure he doesn't wake up... W-we can't let him notice, so we'll just be quick about it..."

"Yeah... He'll at least have to let us watch him sleep," said Elitia.

"I'm a little nervous. I think Theresia is still awake...but...," said Suzuna.

Now Elitia and Suzuna also wanted to go see Arihito. Louisa looked at their blissful expressions, seemingly stemming from the warmth they felt, and had a feeling that she'd get hit with whatever it was as well.

The lights were out on the first floor, and Arihito was lying on the couch. They saw that he was in fact sleeping on his back. Kyouka breathed an excited sigh.

"Really... But I guess there's nothing we can do. I did ask him to face the other way when he slept in the beginning, though."

"...Theresia, do you mind? Just for a bit?"

"......"

Theresia seemed like she'd been half-asleep, but her eyes opened when the others came down the stairs, and she moved to Arihito's side. She did protect him while he was sleeping, but it wasn't like she wouldn't let anyone touch him at all. She checked he was breathing slow and steady and touched him softly.

"U-uh... Is it really okay for us to do that? Even though he's sleeping so peacefully...?" asked Madoka.

"I feel like I do when he's behind me, encouraging me. If this happens every night...I think I understand how things ended up like this," said Melissa. The two of them were joining in for the first time and seemed a little unsure. They saw the other girls were all wearing swimsuits, so they'd decided to change as well.

"Everyone... Oh, is something like this really okay...?" said Louisa.

"It must be quite...difficult for the party if Mr. Atobe does this every night. You won't be able to get much sleep," said Falma, seemingly so interested that Louisa couldn't say anything against it. Louisa had assumed that Falma would take some joy in participating, but she thought it was best that Arihito didn't see her and how curious she really was with the whole situation.

"...So do you just stare at him the whole time?" asked Falma. All of the swimsuit-clad members began fidgeting nervously. Kyouka and Louisa pressed their hands to their chests in anxiousness, the motion almost causing the small pieces of fabric of their bathing suits to slip out of place, but it barely managed to stay put. Even considering the situation, they weren't ready to show Arihito that much skin.

"Falma... Is there anything we can do that won't wake him up...?" asked Kyouka.

"Hmm... Should I really tell you? I think this is something that people should consider for themselves once they're adults..."

"F-Falma... Don't, they're too young for that...," said Louisa in a quiet voice as she tried to stop her, but Falma took off a bracelet she was wearing and showed it to everyone.

"This is a Quiet Bracelet... My husband gave it to me as a present so I could do chores while the kids were sleeping without waking them. I'll let you all borrow it."

All of their minds raced at what they could do if they had that bracelet. Madoka couldn't think of anything, but when she saw Melissa lick her lips, Madoka's entire face went red, all the way to the tips of her ears.

"Falma, could I borrow it first?"

"Sure. You can show everyone else what they can do, since you're the eldest in the party." Falma handed the bracelet to Kyouka, who promptly put it on. Equipping the bracelet gave the wearer a valuable skill that let them act without waking a sleeping person. Even when Kyouka moved close to Arihito and touched his arm, he showed absolutely no signs of stirring.

As usual, Arihito didn't notice what happened while he slept. He still didn't fully understand what Recovery Support 1 actually did when it activated in the middle of the night. By the time he woke up in the morning, he would no longer be able to see the records of what had happened the previous night. As for what exactly was transpiring, Arihito and the girls wouldn't find that out for some time. Even if they could see the display on his license, that wouldn't solve all of the mysteries.

◆Current Status◆
> Arihito's Recovery Support 1 activated ⟶ Overheal
> Arihito's party received Trust Level bonus
   ⟶ Party-wide status change: ※✕?△

A hello to all the new readers and a huge thank-you to those of you who continued from the previous volume. This is the author, Tôwa, speaking.

Time has really flown by; we're already on the fourth volume of this series, but Arihito hasn't even spent a month in the Labyrinth Country yet. That's how incredibly jam-packed his schedule has been. As the author, I've come to realize that Arihito, who was described as *"tired to the core of his soul"* when he got reincarnated, has done nothing but work without rest. I have thought about giving him a break, but there's been so much going on that it just wasn't in the cards.

Misaki demanded in this volume that they take a breather, and that had some serious truth to it. I don't think Arihito would change his policy of advancing as fast as possible, but I have been thinking of putting in a bit of a rest in the next volume.

They went camping in District Seven and came across a spring and even the ocean, then that all-powerful word *swimsuit* started appearing, so I'm sure there are quite a few readers who sensed a vacation coming on. And that was definitely my intention. The only reason it didn't was because of the party's tireless work. Some of you are surely begging to see Arihito and the others have some time off, but even as the author, I can't guarantee that he'll listen to you.

With a series like this, every time I start writing, I need to ask myself, *What are the characters thinking?* and *What would be the most natural action for them?*—which can lead to changes in my plans and the content of the story. On top of that, when it goes to publication, I can ask for the editor's opinion, which gives me the opportunity to look at the work more objectively.

The published version of the story has been revised quite a lot as I've taken to heart the advice from the editor or the carefully thought-out recommendations from the proofreader. They do let me write entirely new scenes or dig deeper into other ones, which I do because I have always wanted to give you my absolute best work. My editor has the same hopes and is great at determining exactly when I, as an author, am content. They'll tell me, "Well, I'll accept the extra changes you made if you think it's your best work..." Then I say, "Take your time checking it! You're the boss!" and then obviously I send the head editors (Kadokawa Books' editing department) a passionate letter (i.e., the manuscript for the volume with all the marked-up corrections). I really should get a thousand punishments whenever I'm seemingly close to settling, though. As that one person who affects the temperature of the entire Japanese archipelago always said, "Don't give up!" Or as another quote goes, "If you give up, the game's already over." That is perhaps one of the most famous quotes in manga history.

Where exactly did I write with such passion, you ask? Well, it would be obvious if you compared the web version to the new print version, but as of right now, it's a secret I am completely incapable of spilling.

The prologue of this volume was an extra piece I wrote for publication that follows from the previous volume. It acts as a tiny glimpse at the secrets of the Labyrinth Country, which are very unlikely to become completely clear anytime soon. It's fairly difficult to do something like that with the serialized web version. I want to experiment with a variety of different composition types while accepting that the print version is print and the serialized version is serialized.

Due to the nature of the series, equipment updates and new skill selection has become a section that has appeared in pretty much all of the volumes. But I've been forced to adjust how I show that as the number of party members increases, as well as the number of skills they each have. I want to make it easy to see only the necessary information, but I'm worried that readers will be like, *Wait, they had a skill like that?* if I don't show the skills they don't take immediately for a long time. I'm paying close attention so that the characters don't suddenly get skills they didn't have before.

I have five whole pages for my afterword this time, so I'd like to touch on what happened in this volume as well as the characters in it a little.

First is the three members of Triceratops. Some readers of the web version wondered if they were villains, but they're actually generally decent guys. They joined the Alliance for stability, and they're ambitious Seekers who thought they could get a chance to move up to the next district as well. District Seven had become a de facto sieve for filtering out the weak, so many Seekers ended up stalled by the monsters' strength even if they tried their hardest. That meant they were one of the few groups of Seekers who still managed to cling to their ambition and gave a well-needed vitality to District Seven.

Four Seasons didn't join in on the battle against the giant crab. The biggest reason for that was because the crab's scythe and Bubble Laser were too dangerous. There weren't very many members in Arihito's party who could handle those attacks anyway, and adding more people to the battle would spread out the attacks more. I imagined that Arihito wouldn't be willing to expose an additional party to such danger.

Falma tried to wash Arihito's back even though she's married. That was because she sees him as younger than her, but also that he seems so utterly honest about that kind of thing. Even Misaki has taken the stance that Arihito isn't someone she need be cautious about, and the fact that he takes what she says at face value is proof of that. She is a pretty carefree person, but she's actually got a lot going on in her mind. Ever since she joined the party, the bright streak of her personality that can be seen in her decisions has come to the fore the most. Depending on the situation, though, she could have become a sort of queen bee who makes men fight for her so she can earn experience and make a living. The fact that she didn't run into danger when she was doing that previously was largely due to her good luck.

I suddenly realized as the author that having Misaki participate in such a dangerous battle to use Fortune Roll, a very important role, was like a secret spotlight. This series is written almost entirely from Arihito's viewpoint, making any scenes that give the readers an insight into the other party members' thoughts all the more valuable. I think those are exactly the kinds of elements I can add in bonus content or special content. I plan to be on the lookout for opportunities to really dig into stories about the new members as more join or the members of the party who generally don't come to the fore.

Another thing I want to touch on is Kyouka's Ethereal Form, Theresia's strengthened equipment, and Elitia's new powerful skill, but first I'm going to talk about Suzuna's flute. It is part of a Shrine Maiden's job to perform the kagura, a performance of dance and music dedicated to the gods. Suzuna had experience practicing musical instruments before she reincarnated, and she would have practiced dancing and musical performances. In this volume, she used the flute that was made from the curled horns of Silvanus's Messenger as a weapon, but the flute itself is very close in shape and tone to the straight transverse flutes you'd find in an orchestra. I don't think there are any kagura performed with that type of flute, but I hope that you can accept a Shrine Maiden playing a flute like that as just another part of this fantastical other world.

In the web version of the story, I had Arihito seeing through Gray's Trickster skill himself. My explanation was that his Hawk Eyes increased his ability to discern what was happening around him. While I do imagine there are a lot of situations in which that skill could be applicable, I was concerned that would easily become overpowered. That's why I changed it so that Ariadne was helping him to see through Trickster. I want to make sure there isn't a sense of incongruity between the web version and the published version, but I hope you can all understand that there are small details that I may adjust to make the published version better.

Well, I'm starting to get to the end of the space I have, so I'd like to move on to my thanks.

A huge thank-you for all the work the head editor had to do with this volume. Your incredible patience in waiting for me to finish the volume allowed it to become what it is. I hope to improve on various fronts so that I can be your best author when it comes to keeping to the schedule.

Thank you to the illustrator, Huuka Kazabana, for drawing such vivid scenery and depictions of the Labyrinth Country, as well as incredibly lively images of the characters! The view Kazabana created into the world is, without a doubt, the reason this work has become what it is. I cannot thank you enough.

Perhaps the greatest help has been from my proofreader, who thoroughly checks the book despite all the equipment and skill names, and the special displays. Thank you.

Thank you very much to Rikizou, the artist behind the manga adaptation. You have taken this work and created something bigger, an absolutely wonderful manga, which I enjoy very much as a reader.

Finally, a million thanks to all of the readers who support this series. I couldn't do it without you.

Tôwa, on a Certain December Day